Wendy Salisbury is an author, broadcaster, linguist, social commentator, and antique dealer. Her monthly magazine columns led her to write a lifestyle guide: *Move Over, Mrs Robinson*, and when the chapter on older women/younger men provoked mass media interest, she responded with two volumes of dating memoirs: *The Toyboy Diaries* and *The Daily Male,* now adapted as a stage musical. Wendy's tempestuous travels through Spain in the 1960s researching the biography of iconic matador, El Cordobés, inspired her roman à clef *Blood on the Sand,* the true story behind the gore and the glamour. Wendy divides her time between London and Marbella and embraces the gift of five grandchildren and two granddogs.

For my cherished grandchildren
Tatiana, Normandie, Noah, Xenia, and Eden,
I have three words:
Be Less Macy.

Wendy Salisbury

TAKE TWO TABLETS

AUSTIN MACAULEY PUBLISHERS™
LONDON • CAMBRIDGE • NEW YORK • SHARJAH

Copyright © Wendy Salisbury 2023

The right of Wendy Salisbury to be identified as author of this work has been asserted by the author in accordance with sections 77 and 78 of the Copyright, Designs and Patents Act 1988.

All rights reserved. No part of this publication may be reproduced, stored in a retrieval system, or transmitted in any form or by any means, electronic, mechanical, photocopying, recording, or otherwise, without the prior permission of the publishers.

Any person who commits any unauthorised act in relation to this publication may be liable to criminal prosecution and civil claims for damages.

This is a work of fiction. Names, characters, businesses, places, events, locales, and incidents are either the products of the author's imagination or used in a fictitious manner. Any resemblance to actual persons, living or dead, or actual events is purely coincidental.

A CIP catalogue record for this title is available from the British Library.

ISBN 9781398479944 (Paperback)
ISBN 9781398479951 (ePub e-book)

www.austinmacauley.com

First Published 2023
Austin Macauley Publishers Ltd®
1 Canada Square
Canary Wharf
London
E14 5AA

To my much-loved sister, Marilyn, for your enduring patience and unconditional support; to my darling daughters, Gabrielle and Lauren, for whom my doors and ears are always open, and to my wider family and friends, especially Adrianne, Bernice and Ruth, for indulging me yet always being there when I need you. Special thanks also go to Yael (you had me covered!) and to all at AM for helping to make it happen.

Also by Wendy Salisbury:

Move Over, Mrs Robinson (co-author Maggi Russell)
The Toyboy Diaries
The Toyboy Diaries II - The Daily Male
Blood on the Sand

"We learn the rope of life by untying its knots."

Jean Toomer
Writer and Philosopher
1894 – 1967

1

It wasn't that Macy set out to break all Ten Commandments in one day – it was just the way it turned out. From dissing her mother for buying own brand KoKo Pops, to cursing the bus driver for setting off without her, to swatting a wasp so hard it spiralled dead to earth – three out of ten before school wasn't bad.

Monday mornings that began with double RS compounded Macy's conviction that she should have stayed in bed; feigned a fever, pled a period, anything to avoid facing the day. For this was *the* day. The day she had to read. Her essay. OUT LOUD IN CLASS.

Macy crushed her knuckles into her eye sockets and burrowed back beneath the duvet, whimpering.

"You up, Mace?"

That voice. Flat. Irritating. Pitiful yet not pitying, and she could hear it through ten togs of poly-fibre filling. Macy scrunched her duvet around her ears and hunkered down deeper.

"Macy? It's…"

"YESS! I KNOW!"

She balled her fists, punched off the covers, pulled on her uniform, barged into the bathroom, stomped downstairs, sneered at the cereal, grabbed her school bag and slammed out of the house *sans* "Hi" or "Bye".

Francine's expression slid off her face. What was the point? Truly. What *was* the point?

Arriving on the tardy bell, Macy fought the urge to bring up her breakfast then remembered she hadn't had any. Vomiting, fake or otherwise, would only provoke another lecture on 'Eating Disorders, Anorexia, Bingeing and Bulimia' and she didn't need that today of all days.

Dragging her feet like a convict to the gallows, she climbed the grand mahogany staircase, doubts spiralling around her brain like a Texan typhoon. She'd plumbed the very depths of her…intellect? – to write what she considered a pretty 'outré' essay. She liked that word – it sounded a bit like 'out-tray' – the wire basket her grandad's secretary kept the post in. Macy had temped at his construction company the previous summer and he'd paid her well for making tea and filing. In truth, she'd spent most of her time reading but she'd been thrilled even so to receive the little brown envelope from Accounts at the end of each week.

Pocket money was thin on the ground at home. Vodka, cigarettes, sickly white chocolate that wasn't chocolate at all, and pills – so many various pills! – but pocket money? Nah.

Macy reached the top step knowing, with unwavering certainty, that the essay she'd taken such pains to write was terrible. Truly appalling. Overworked, overwritten, and laughable but not funny. Everyone would hate it. And they'd mock her. They'd mock her more than they did already.

Or might it actually be good? Original? Innovative? A veritable *tour de force*? No. It couldn't be. She'd have to pretend she hadn't written one. Lost the homework. Left it on the bus.

A bubble of bile burst in her throat turning her face sour and contorting her mouth into an ugly moue. Some nob from the Lower Sixth standing on the landing above thought she was gurning at him. He squared his puny shoulders and was about to move in when another boy ripped his cap off and Frisbee-d it down the stair well. Macy smirked and continued on her way.

She reached her classroom and sat down stiffly at her desk. Her pulse was going for gold, but she took a deep breath and reached a decision. She *would* read it. To Hell with them. Classmates? Primates, more like.

She knew it could go either way: Proper respect or epic fail – but at least, she might impress Mr Fairclough.

She really hoped her work would impress Mr Fairclough.

2

Airey Fairclough – or Airy Fairy as he was commonly known – sat at his desk waiting for his students to settle. He called them 'students' in the loosest sense of the word – they were savages really, more interested in the contents of their noses than the content of their schoolbooks. Their comportment reminded him of a paper penned by an African explorer of the 1800s, entitled *The Chronobiology of Cohabitation:*

'The circadian system of animals is remarkable. The co-housing of pairs of golden hamsters results in a persistent change in the free running of one of the pair. Although similar breeds can live side by side in relative compatibility, rivalry is evident where animals cohabiting in the same spatial arena might synchronise their behaviours to achieve common goals or actively avoid each other to lessen competition for limited resources.'

This study could effectively be applied to the mammalians before him, who, for all their private education, might just as well be swinging from the rafters in the Refectory picking nits out of each other's fur. Where were those fresh-faced infants he'd once known, poised like peaches on the edges of their seats, thirsty for his gift of knowledge? Gone to rot, every one. Puberty had reversed their social development, turning the little darlings into wild beasts. Or maybe it was him? Sapped of his earlier commitment, he no longer felt up to the task of hatching viable adults out of squirming amoeba.

While the boys continued to perform feats from *The Anthology of Bad Behaviour, Vol 1V*, Mr Fairclough contemplated his future within the class dynamic. Promoted to Head of RS at the tender age of twenty-six, he'd promptly adopted the mien and apparel of a man decades his senior: Mustard corduroys, Viyella shirt, Fair Isle tank top, Harris Tweed jacket with suede elbow patches and an old school tie from a school he'd never been to. The ensemble, more ordure than couture, had been curated from the local Oxfam shop, referencing a character from *Wind in the Willows* without the whiskers.

The metal pince-nez – 50p at a local car boot sale – now honoured its Gallic promise to pinch his nose. Mr Fairclough removed it and placed it gently on his desk, then ducked deftly as an unidentified flying object whizzed over his head and hit the wall behind him with a soft thud.

He turned momentarily to watch a slither of slime slide down the paintwork like fresh ejaculate. Returning to face front, he towered his fingers like a steeple and wondered if the moment would ever come when he actually had to try and teach them something.

The renegades eventually got bored with drawing penises on their palms and reverted to the tried and tested technique of seeing how noxiously they could fart. The girls, drama queens in training, cried, "Euww!" and fanned the air with their exercise books.

Mr Fairclough collapsed his steeple and looked at his watch. He cleared his throat and ran his index finger down the register.

"Lord?" he intoned, knowing The Almighty would not respond. "*Macy* Lord?"

"Good Lord!" Some wag exclaimed, followed by: "Praise the Lord!" and: "Lawdy Miss Clawdy!" from elsewhere in the room.

Macy pressed her back deep into her chair hoping the wood would splinter and pierce her through the spine.

"Macy *LORD*!" Mr Fairclough repeated, knowing she was out there somewhere in the malodorous jungle. "It's your turn to read your work. Come to the front, please."

Macy wobbled up to standing and looped one foot around her chair leg. In a move worthy of an Argentine tango dancer, she flipped the chair backwards crashing it into the desk behind. The returning shove smacked her hard on the calves causing her to cry out in pain.

Mr Fairclough brushed an imaginary piece of fluff off the front of his jacket and stood up. He crossed the room, opened the door, checked the corridor left and right, and returned to the blackboard. Picking up a piece of chalk, he wrote, in oversized letters:

Shut. The. F***. Up!

Some clapped, some whooped, but for one magical moment, they all obeyed. With a sweeping gesture as if inviting her onstage at The Old Vic, Airey Fairclough proffered Macy the podium. She stepped up hesitantly and tried to insinuate herself through the wall.

"Stand up straight please," Mr Fairclough murmured, without looking around.

One of the lads eyed her up and mouthed: "I would!" Like he knew what that meant.

An impromptu boy band started miming *SUCK IT N C* by SkRoTe while two of the girls reprised their appraisal of Revlon versus Rimmel nail varnish.

Mr Fairclough was about to slam his hand down on the desk and yell: **"ORDER!"** when Macy Lord stepped forward book in hand, and, tentatively at first, then loud enough to be heard, read out her title:

"The Goddess with the Thousand and One…VAGINAS!"

The ensuing silence was broken only by a garrotted gurgling from deep in Mr Fairclough's throat.

3

Francine rubbed the fifth chair vigorously with a moist cloth and moved towards the sixth. There were four chairs at the table, and she was going round again. She sank onto the nearest seat and let the cloth slide from her hand.

Raking her fingers through her hair, she stared blankly at the hank of lank strands threading their way across her palm.

Was I that vile at her age? She wondered, twisting the loose hairs into a knot. The memory of her father's spankings clouded her mind. She'd hated him and feared him too – that time she'd fled to her room but not quite fast enough and he'd grabbed her by the wrist and slammed her against the wall.

"Have you heard of The Ten Commandments?" He'd snarled into her face. There was a 1950s movie with that title, but she doubted her dad was inviting her to join him on the sofa. She'd cowered beneath his raised fist, saved only by her mother calling from downstairs. He'd shoved her back against the wall, spat the words: "Honour thy father and thy mother!" twisted her ear hard and marched off.

This Draconian discipline had kept her and her sister in check until the older girl rebelled and ran off with a scruffy musician she'd met down the pub. Down The Pub, for God's sake! They weren't even allowed anywhere near 'the pub'! In a defiant effort to outdo her sibling, Francine got herself knocked up by a tattooed garage mechanic, who was at least prepared to 'do right by her'.

Their father was apoplectic. These low-class losers were hardly the kind of sons-in-law he'd envisioned for his girls. And of course, he had been right. Her sister's spouse was always 'on tour' performing under, over and alongside a gaggle of groupies, and it wasn't long before Francine's husband, who had a penchant for a pint or six, led him to confuse her face with the panel of a car he'd been beating.

Their father had cut them off without a penny, then promptly died of an aneurism in self-defence.

This bitter recollection forced Francine back to the work surface to scrub away the memories. Single parenthood had not been her lifestyle choice, but what choice had she had? Stay married until he killed her? – Or worse…started using their daughter as a fresher, younger punch bag.

Crushed by fear and failure, she empathised with Macy's mood swings but had no idea how to deal with them. And how could you love someone who so clearly hated you? They'd so enjoyed their cuddles when she was little but hugging and hormones now seemed a bad fit.

The painkillers and anti-depressants took the edge off, but Francine was dogged with recriminations and regrets.

When Macy arrived home from school, her mother was on her hands and knees tormenting the lino.

"How was your day?" Francine asked flatly, without looking up.

"I triumphed!" Macy crowed, omitting to explain. "And as a recompense, I need a designer handbag!"

Francine stopped what she was doing.

"Nobody *needs* a designer handbag. You may *want* one but that's a different matter…"

"*You* don't understand," Macy sneered. "Zenith's got one and it's right there in my face every day of my life! How am I supposed to *cope* with that? Plus, I'm famous now, and not having a designer handbag makes me feel like a retard!"

"Famous?" Francine queried. "For what? Anyway, you know designer handbags are out of my league, and Zenith – is that *really* a name? – is clearly out of yours."

Macy stormed out of the kitchen. She wasn't about to have her Nobel Prize for Outstanding Literary Achievement torn from her grasp by her miserable mother. Francine braced herself. She jumped when she heard the bedroom door slam then jumped again as it was yanked open and slammed once more.

Just for effect. In case, the message hadn't been received loud and clear the first time.

4

In Your Faces, losers – Macy had thought as she'd swanned back to her desk resisting the urge to high-five everyone in sight. Some of the primates were actually clapping!

Now in her room, she transported herself back to recreate her reading live as it happened:

"There's not much point having one if you can't flash it about!"
"One is normal, Yoni dear," Ling replied, *"but we're not talking about ONE, are we? We're talking about **One THOUSAND and One**! A little excessive, don't you think?"*

Out of the corner of her eye, Macy spotted someone's hand shoot up. She ignored it and carried on.

"Yoni shrugged then giggled – that girlish, churlish giggle that made the others want to sprout an extra head. Ling swished his mul-ti-tu-dinous tails. Maybe he was right, Yoni thought. Maybe she had gone a little OTT but how was she meant to grow her fan base…"

"Fanny base?" A boy exclaimed, and the class collapsed into giggles.
"It gets better." Macy challenged. "Trust me."
Mr Fairclough swept the beads of sweat up towards his hairline.

*"…but **how** was she meant to grow her **fan** base unless she offered them more than other deities? Eight arms and the proboscis of an elephant were all very well, but a true Celebrity Goddess needed that little extra je ne sais quoi. Yoni had therefore blessed herself with what she considered the ultimate*

crowd-pleaser: One Thousand and One Vaginas, one for every one of her Thousand and One Nights."

Airey Fairclough struggled to suppress a smile. During the early part of the reading, his complexion had risen to the hue of stewed rhubarb, draining swiftly to the pallor of boiled semolina. Despite himself, he now emitted a low, almost sensual, groan.

His proposal of Eastern Culture as an addendum to the usual themes of religion, theology, and ethics, had not taken into account Macy Lord's fulsome imagination nor her crude creativity. And – bless her mismatched socks – she'd got her myths mixed up: *The Arabian Nights* belonged to *The Golden Age of Islam* not *Hindu Deities*.

He scanned the room for a sign as to how to handle this. Should he put a halt to it or allow her to read on? There was certainly no precedent for the class's attention: The words 'rapt' and 'awestruck' came to mind. From past experience, Year 11 viewed Religious Studies as a load of old bollocks merely to be endured for an extra 'O' Level pass.

The introduction of *Legends from India's 330 million Divinities* had been something of a coup on Airey's part. In order to embrace the variety in society, he'd asked his pupils to create their own imaginary deity. Macy Lord had obviously discovered the obscure myth of the lusty god Indra, King-God of Heaven, who'd been caught *in flagrante* with another god's wife. Indra had subsequently been cursed with a thousand vaginas *'because he loved them so much'*, but legend had it that he'd been so contrite in his apology that the female genitalia were later replaced with eyes – although the apocrypha of this tale varied in the telling.

And of course, Airey only had himself to blame. Open their minds and you open a canning factory full of worms…yet he was loath to stop the reading because, for once, the little tykes were actually listening.

Macy turned to him and raised an eyebrow. He nodded for her to continue, unwilling at this point to arrest her (and their) mental development.

"In her desperate quest to attract followers, Yoni dreamt up ever more fanciful ways of catching her public's attention. She'd grown her hair ten miles long; perfected the art of splitting mountains with her tongue; conjured up chariots made of sunbeams which she then destroyed with bolts of lightning.

Ling had been displeased to see his protégée turning into such a little show-off and this 'thousand and one vaginas' nonsense was the last straw. He'd have to rein her in, revert her into believing in No Other God but Him.

Reclining on his gilded charpai *upholstered in chartreuse silk and trimmed with baubles of 24-carat gold, Ling deployed his powers of conception. In the same way as a tree sprouts buds, he began to sprout phalluses, dozens, and dozens of the wrinkly little things.* (Gulps, gasps, and guffaws from the class). *They manifested through his pores and out of the follicles of his epidermis until his limbs and torso flourished with them. They protruded from his ears, flowered from his nose, mushroomed from his mouth. Uncertain if he'd attained the requisite number, Ling summoned forth his underLings* (Macy looked up and winked as if to say: "See what I just did there?") *to bring forth a four-screen mirror, to count them one by one then count them again. Inspired by his font of abundance, his penile plethora, his* opus genitalis, *Ling lingered lustfully before the looking glass before exploding in a sea of semen…"*

Mr Fairclough shot to his feet, palms outstretched like a blind man who suspected he was on course to an open lift shaft. Gasps of: "What The…!" and "No Wayyy!" could be heard. She could *not* be allowed to continue. Not only was this provocative and inflammatory, but it was also bordering on pornographic. What if the Head Teacher passed by and heard?

And yet, despite thinking he must put a stop to it, the story had structure and the child was making an impressive use of alliteration. He was surprised and not a little envious at the symbolic images she was painting as well as the reaction she'd provoked. Her classmates were more entranced than he'd ever seen them. She'd overpowered them, and he admired her for it.

"May I, sir?" Macy asked disingenuously, knowing she had the upper hand. Mr Fairclough was stumped. If he refused, he'd alienate his pupils, and realistically, on what grounds could he silence the girl? She was neither blaspheming nor using words they hadn't been taught in Sex Ed – words that also featured in the Oxford English Dictionary. Plus, *d he* had introduced the topic and Hindu gods *were* a weird and wonderful lot.

As he continued to procrastinate, an eruption swept over him like a choral tsunami. "May-cee! May-cee!" They chanted, winding their fists in the air. He was outdone as well as outnumbered.

"You may continue," he said gruffly once the clamour had died down. "But please mind your language. We are in a school room not a…bar room!"

This wisecrack was greeted with cheers. Mr Fairclough stifled a smile. Macy Lord had raised *his* game as well as her own and for once, the class were with him rather than against him.

As luck would have it, the Head *was* passing, and she heard the echoes of Year 11's approval. She smiled with satisfaction. She had fought the Board for young Fairclough's appointment and *his* achievements would reflect well on *her* future at the next AGM.

Macy continued with renewed aplomb.

"Yoni, as fertile as a fresh-grown flower, revelled in the glory of her newfound fame and fortune. True to her deepest desires, they were queuing around the block and her popularity soared through the roof of Heaven, right up to Cloud Ten. Shrines and temples rose in her honour; hymns and fables were composed praising her femininity.

And out through every orifice flowed the fragrance of Nirvana – an aroma so seductive, it could only be compared to the Perfume of Paradise. She was the hostess with the moistest, the goddess with the hottest, The Princess Punani: Quintessential Queen of Quim!"

Mr Fairclough's face was a study in apoplexy, but in fairness, that word was *also* in the OED, and he had used it himself once while struggling with a Q in Scrabble. But was it suitable content for an essay by a 15-yearold? No, it was not. *He* could get expelled, never mind *her*.

The class held its collective breath then a light *zapateado* became a fully-fledged fandango that caused his desk to judder. Macy flashed him a look that said: "I've got this!" and without waiting for his reply, ploughed on with the story.

"Yoni noted, with deepening satisfaction, that the other goddesses were touting their well-worn wares like hawkers at a fair. Although she heard the words 'Chav' and 'Slapper' spat in her direction, she knew her effusive fruits had made her fabulous.

To facilitate her adulation, she had herself raised onto a revolving dais, rather like a gâteau in a Parisian patisserie. It wasn't very comfortable, she had to admit, but that was a small price to pay for her rise from average to absolute. Ling, meanwhile, lay languidly on his chaise longue, strung out by the test to his testosterone. Envy and frustration gnawed at his…"

"Can I say 'nuts,' sir?"

This was somewhat academic considering what had gone before.

"It balances nicely with the word 'gnawed' and I couldn't find a better synonym."

Airey Fairclough surrendered. They were in the water now, they may as well swim. And it wouldn't do his cred any harm so long as no one drowned. Again, he nodded in consent.

"*Envy and frustration gnawed at his nuts like a horde of hungry hamsters.* (Giggles, guffaws, and an involuntary snort from the teacher himself.) *Had HE, Ling the Omnipotent, not been her mentor, her guru, her guide unto the path of righteousness? Was* this *how she repaid him? By turning herself into a pu-si-lla-nimous obscenity, milking her newfound fame with all the finesse of a barmaid milking a sacred cow? Ling came to a decision: Precocious little goddesses with delusions of 'glandeur' could not be allowed to survive. So, he retracted his incomplete appendices (for he hadn't quite managed the thousand and second) and he reached for his tome of last resort: The Lexicon of Devilish Castigation."*

Macy paused and turned the page. Her audience sat spellbound.

"*It began with a tiny itch, an innocuous little tickle just below the one on her left shoulder. Yoni couldn't reach it, which was bothersome enough, but it was a Friday afternoon and her slaves had gone home early. The crowds were gathering at the Gift Shop to stock up on something for the weekend and now she had an itch she couldn't scratch! She lay down on her dais and tried to bring the offending area into contact with the surface. As unobtrusively as possible, Yoni began to squirm. The squirm turned into a wiggle and the wiggle became a rub. Her devotees cheered and applauded, assuming these new moves were designed to inspire them and bring joy into their dull little lives.*

Yoni had barely managed to appease the first irritation when a second one erupted and then a third. It wasn't long until all of Yoni's floribundae were aflame with inflammation causing her to leap to her feet and start tearing herself to pieces with her bare hands."

"Bet she wished she had eight arms now," someone heckled. The class burst out laughing as one and even Mr Fairclough cracked a smile. For the first time ever, his group was united in a bond born of mutual appreciation. Macy recognised it too and something surged inside her. She raised her hand authoritatively and was instantly obeyed.

"The throng fell silent and stood aghast as they watched the degradation of their Adored One. As Yoni scratched, the stench of a thousand rotting sea creatures filled the air…"

"Ergghh!"
"Shhhh!"

"…spreading from her body like evil ectoplasm, polluting the atmosphere, corrupting all around. The people gagged, retching as they ran, falling over each other in their urge to get away. Yoni wriggled wretchedly atop her pedestal scratching like a rabid monkey. As she did so, all the sacred images, figurines and carvings created in her honour exploded in mid-air shooting shards of porcelain, jade, and crystal into the flesh of her absconding admirers. Some were blinded, others were stabbed through the heart. The destruction did not abate until everyone was dead.

Yoni clambered down from her pinnacle and waded through the bloody mire. She noted with relief that her one thousand and one vaginas had all but disappeared and she was left with just one, as virginal and intact as the day that she'd been born."

Mr Fairclough raised an eyebrow in soundless approbation.

"Ling smiled to himself. Yoni smiled too for she knew that as sure as time endured, that one *part of* WOMAN *would always hold more power in Heaven and on Earth than its equivalent in* MAN…*"*

"And so ends the legend of the greedy little goddess, Yoni," Macy explained, "which incidentally in Hindu means…"

Mr Fairclough had again leapt to his feet, this time coughing loudly.

"Thank you, Miss Lord!" He'd blustered, his blush bleeding up from beneath his collar to cover his neck and face. "An interesting if not er…*outré* interpretation of one of India's more exotic fables. Now please return to your seat."

Macy remembered closing her exercise book slowly, unwilling to step out of the spotlight. It had felt good up there, and she wasn't about to relinquish the moment by standing down too soon.

Not one classmate – *they'll be my mates now, won't they?* – wasn't either thumping their desk, standing with their gob smacked, or commenting incredulously to someone across the aisle.

Mr Fairclough stood at his desk like Christ the Redeemer, arms outstretched to calm the clamour. Eventually, the hype had died down and Macy had inclined her head in recognition of her public's adoration. It didn't take an expert in *Body Language: Causes and Effects* to analyse her swagger as she returned to her desk.

Total wipeout? Nah. Proper respect. Yeh! *PROPAH!*

*

Macy tossed her book aside and went over to the mirror. You've *got* to get that handbag, she urged herself. You've got to keep this…this power going, keep them liking you, admiring you, like they admire Zenith and all her…stuff.

She picked Pandy up and clutched him to her chest, inhaling the manky sleep smell of his unwashed fur.

"I'll steal the money if I have to," she whispered in his ear. "I'll steal Mum's measly stash and buy myself one, no, two! I'll buy myself TWO and I'll wear them every day, one on each shoulder, just to see her how…how…"

How what, Macy? Pandy seemed to say. *How loved they make you feel?*

*

Francine stared blindly into the fridge and wondered what had prompted this demand for a designer handbag, today's equivalent, she supposed, of those bell-bottom jeans she'd always hankered after. She'd loved skiving off on a Saturday afternoon to Kensington Market, rifling through the rails, pulling them off the hangers and holding them up against herself in the mirror. Of course, she'd never dared bring home a pair: Her father would have embarked on one of his lectures and then probably chopped them to pieces.

"The word *denim* comes from 'de Nîmes' – a town in France," she mimicked in her head. "And *jean* is an Anglicised version of the city of Genoa in Italy, renowned for its…sailors." This dirty word had to be spat rather than spoken. "Together they make up the name of that…*garment*," (another dirty word) "that shall *not* be worn in this house. They are made for, and BY! – convicted felons in United States *prisons* (another spit) and they arrive on these shores imbued with the essence of those EVIL MEN!"

Which was precisely why Francine wanted a pair.

She remembered replaying the last sentence of this lecture in her head as she lay in bed at night, sliding her hands down the smoothness of her thighs, imagining how her legs would feel encased in something a rough criminal had handled.

If she thought about it, she was denying Macy the thing she most wanted, the same way her father had denied her. But a designer handbag at her age and at that price? Absolutely not.

5

Macy lay on her bed picking her cuticles till they bled. Her insides were raging like a rip tide, yearning for respite from the fury that made her hate her mother more than she hated herself.

The spike in her popularity had been short-lived. When word got around that she'd used the 'V' word and got away with it, a world of opportunity had unfurled, soaring her reputation to unsustainable heights.

High-fives and fist pumps in the corridors from students she didn't know, chants of 'Racy Macy!', looks of envy and admiration from those she'd previously feared – she dared to see her future as a stairway to the stars.

Most Popular Girl in the School: MACY LORD.
Pupil with the Maximum Potential: MACY LORD.
Highest Achiever in the Realms of Academia: MACY LORD!

The positive feedback soon dissipated however, causing her to crash even lower than before. The story had grown in the telling and now she was confronted with fake gagging, exaggerated nudging, and people holding their noses whenever she walked past. Someone nicknamed her 'Fanny Girl' which stuck, and she was afraid to make eye contact or speak to anyone at all. She considered feigning illness so she wouldn't have to go to school but that would mean that they'd won. She would have liked to have discussed it with her mum, but the woman was definitely barmier since Dad had left and instead of being twice as nice, she was twice as nuts.

Macy's only pleasure was through fantasy: Doodling designer handbags, convinced that life would be immeasurably better if she could only have what Zenith had.

*

Zenith sashayed up and down her mother's walk-in wardrobe checking herself out in the floor to ceiling mirror. Another half-size growth and they'd fit. She wasn't sure how one managed to walk in them, especially the latest acquisition: A divine pair of green snakeskin Louboutins with six-inch heels. Unworn and pristine, they lay nose to tail, coiled inside their box like designer reptile twins. Pair upon pair of brightly coloured footwear hung suspended on brass racks across the length of the shoe closet, matching wallflowers waiting for a dance.

Zenith tried them on each in turn, fastening the buckles, lacing up the straps, pushing her toes forward to reach the toe caps. She wobbled up to standing and marvelled at how long and slender her legs looked, then tottered into her bedroom to find her camera wondering which of her wannabee hangers-on she could impress the most.

*

Francine sat on the edge of her bed staring at the floor. It was Sunday evening – Sunday bloody Sunday. She hadn't dressed or left the house all weekend. She hadn't cleaned it either.

She took the little plastic tub out of her bedside drawer and twisted the lid around and around. It made a clicking sound. She could speed it up or slow it down. That was the only thing she had control over. That and the cleaning.

She resisted pushing the lid down to release the little tablets unsure of where that may lead. Last night's glass of water waited on the bedside. Bubbles clung to the sides, suspended in liquid space. Stale, like everything else.

The looming menace that dominated her life for so long was no longer a threat, but the fear remained. Keeping Macy safe had been her *raison d'être*. Now, although physically together, they were mentally apart, unable to engage on any level. She'd hoped they would have grown closer, but it seemed *he* had been the catalyst that kept the unit unified. Was *she* of any use at all? She'd fought her father, she'd fought her husband, and now she was fighting her daughter. She was running out of fight, floundering in a mire of money worries, dyscopia and isolation. Flimsy, like chiffon near a flame. One gust…

Macy could hear the click-clicking coming from the other room. Same sound every night – doing her head in. She hadn't known what it was until she'd burst in one evening to find her mother quickly swallow something in the palm of her hand.

"Please knock, Macy. I don't come into your room without knocking."

"I'm trying to study, Mum!" Macy had growled. "Stop that bloody clicking!"

The next day Macy had gone into her mother's room and opened the bedside drawer. She pulled out the little jar and examined the label.

Zolpidem Tartrate

Take 1 tablet at bedtime for the treatment of insomnia.

Go on, she willed. *Go on, I dare you. Take them. Take the whole bloody lot of them and put us both out of your misery.*

6

Zenith's Rollerblade Party was unquestionably the worst night of Macy's life. She knew she'd only been invited because of her fleeting fame, and she arrived at the rink early so no one would see how she'd got there. It had taken her hours to get ready: Skirt, shorts, jeggings, leggings, mini-dress, crop top, over-the-knee socks, stripey tights…every single hideous, obsolete, cheap and nasty item of clothing she'd never wished to own had been torn out of the wardrobe and strewn around the room. Even now, after a hundred changes and colour combinations that would have made a rainbow blush, she hated the way she looked.

The EasyFix Blonde Extensions from PoundWorld made her look like she'd dunked her head in sheep dip and fallen into a threshing machine. Her make-up, hastily applied because of the fiasco with the hair, may as well have been put on by a blind beautician with Parkinson's. So, there she stood waiting for the others to arrive feeling like she didn't fit her own life never mind anyone else's.

Zenith pulled up in one of her father's flashiest cars: The burgundy Bentley Mulsanne with the tinted windows and silver coachwork that had a top speed of a squillion miles an hour. Macy knew the spec because she'd been told it several times.

Short arse, Macy thought, as Zenith swung her skinny Lycra leopard print legs out of the back seat.

"Hi-ii!" Macy forced brightly. "You look nii-ce!"

Zenith batted her black widow eyelashes. Compliments, like friends, came easy. She flicked her dark curtain of professionally straightened hair over her shoulder and delivered the next blow: A double-flap pewter leather handbag studded all over with skulls and dripping with tags, labels, and chains from a designer so exclusive, Macy had no idea know who it was!

"Tomorrow's vintage, dahling!" Zenith gushed, rubbing it in. "Isn't it just chim?"

"T-t-totally chim!" Macy replied resisting the urge to punch the girl in the mouth. "In fact, it's…"

She'd been about to say 'chimchimneychimchimneychimchimcheree' but luckily, the others started arriving in their various daddies' sports cars and people carriers, and once they'd finished insincerely air-kissing each other and being sycophantic about their various outfits, they all trouped into the Roller Dome. Macy stood alone in the outer circle wondering how soon she could decently leave.

They queued up to hire boots then set off to race around the rink. Zenith had her own skates of course: Fluorescent pink high-tops with silver wings on the sides. Most of the others rented the hard, blue plastic boots so at least Macy wasn't alone there.

The more confident girls hurtled across the hardwood surface aiming headlong into groups of boys, pretending they didn't know how to stop. They screamed as they crashed into the barriers, hoping to be picked up if they fell. The few more cautious ones, Macy among them, slid slowly along clutching the handrails like terrified tots. She managed to stay upright and was frankly relieved when the session was over so she could remove the agonising boots.

They all trouped into the Ladies Room to tart up their hair and lip gloss, then went next door into the café to share pizzas, Cokes, and gossip. Macy had nothing to bring to the party, so they ignored her. The conversation was exclusively about boys and nail varnish, neither of which much interested her. Once the meal was over, they shouldered their various handbags, air-kissed each other goodbye and gathered outside to await collection.

Macy stood awkwardly on the fringes of the group calling out: "Byee! See you Monday!" Into the ether. Not a single girl or parent offered her a lift home, and she would, in any case, have had to refuse. Life was bad enough without them seeing where she lived.

A black Range Rover whisked Zenith away and Macy waved lamely, pretending, to herself more than anyone else, that her father would soon be along in one of his gold Lamborghinis.

She walked to the bus stop with her head down, plotting which one of her 'lovely new friends' she'd like to kill first – and how.

7

Mr Fairclough left the marking of Macy's essay until last. It was his recompense for having had to wade through reams of banal narrative and anachronistic ineptitude. He had kept an eye on her since the reading, aware that she was a misfit, an outsider, ostracised now more than before. He'd developed a new respect for her, aware that her singularity may not serve her until later life.

"See me after class, Miss Lord," he said, when he handed the pupils back their books, then immediately regretted making so public a request. Negative interest drifted around the room like a bad spirit.

"Teacher's pet?" whispered one.

"Fishpaste fish face!" sneered another.

Macy studied the scratched woodgrain on her desk, and wondered how to make this stop.

A boy got up and brushed past her muttering: "My granddad's got a cute angina!"

She wished she could projectile vomit on demand rather than dignify the comment with a reply.

Once the room had fully emptied, Mr Fairclough spoke.

"Macy, you…er…you don't seem to integrate very well with the group." Macy gave an imperceptible shrug.

"This is not a criticism," he continued, "rather an observation of *their* lack of empathy and discernment. To be honest, I think they rather envy you."

"Envy me, sir? For what?"

My disjointed family, barking mother, absent father, council semi, no car, no cash, no clothes, no HANDBAGS?

"Your essay was outstanding, and I mean that literally: It stood out from all the rest. I can see that you enjoy the…um…the *art* of the written word and I wondered if you'd be interested in allowing me to put your name forward for an inter-school interfaith writing competition organised by the heads of the various Theology Departments."

A flicker of fire flared in Macy's eyes.

"It's a fairly broad church by way of subject," her teacher went on, "going under the heading of *Thou Shalt Not* – so it's Bible-based but not fundamentally religious."

Macy's mind was racing through its search engine.

"May I take your silence as a 'Yes'?"

"Yes!" Macy said, standing up abruptly. "Yes please, Mr Fairclough!"

"Excellent!" he replied. "One thousand five hundred words by…"

"Did anyone else get asked?" Macy interrupted.

"No, they did not. It was my choice who to nominate, and I chose you. As I said, fifteen hundred words to be handed in after the Easter holidays. I look forward to reading what you come up with but…er…"

"Keep it clean?" Macy asked, her mouth rising in a half smile.

"Well, no swear words," Mr Fairclough smiled back, "although don't stilt your imagination."

Macy made to leave but he stayed her with his hand.

"I…er…I've heard some rumours, Macy, and I just wondered: Is everything is alright at home? You seem…you don't seem…"

"Yes, it's fine, sir," she replied hurriedly. "And thank you. Thank you for having faith in me."

He nodded approvingly as she gathered up her books and left.

*

Mr Fairclough remained in the classroom contemplating the conversation. The girl was an enigma. He wished he could bypass the pupil-teacher divide and sit and talk to her like one adult to another. She obviously craved acceptance yet what she had done had resulted in alienation. He'd noticed the bullying, yet she retaliated by using her brain. Like him, she sought respect through individuality rather than convention. But did it make them happy? Probably not.

*

When she got home, Macy researched the term *Thou Shalt Not* in the Children's Encyclopaedia her grandad had bought her. She made some scribbled notes, listing The Ten Commandments as she understood them.

- No strange gods (they're all strange, aren't they?)
- No craven images *(craven? Isn't that a bird?)*
- No names to be taken in vain *(what, like Jesus H Christ?)*
- Honour the Sabbath Day and keep it holy *(Why? Nobody else does)*
- Honour thy father and thy mother (Really? Let them honour me then we'll talk about it)
- No killing (No comment)
- No adultery (No problem)
- No stealing (Too late)
- No bearing false witness (What's that?)
- No coveting thy neighbour's house, wife, ox, donkey, manservant, maidservant, or anything that is thy neighbour's (no mention of coveting thy best friend's handbag, so that was OK!)

Since this was the only 'Thou Shalt Not' Macy could relate to, she decided to base her story on Commandment Number Ten.

8

"Nanny Jean's coming this weekend."

Francine spoke from her position on all fours on the kitchen floor where she was torturing the lino with a Brillo pad. She expected an objection, but when none came, she continued.

"She'll want to go to church on Sunday and it would be nice if…"

Macy stepped over her and reached into the cupboard for a Wagon Wheel then went back upstairs. Francine thought she'd heard her say: "Fine", which was unlikely, so she redoubled her efforts with the wire wool.

Nanny Jean, at the age of 79, knew a thing or two about stroppy teenagers. She'd raised three boys, one of whom had grown up to be Macy's father. He was not what she would call her 'favourite son'.

When she arrived to visit on the Saturday morning, her granddaughter was, unsurprisingly, still in bed. Jean caught up with her daughter-in-law at the kitchen table over a cup of tea.

Francine was scrubbing as usual, standing on a chair giving the tops of the units the full benefit of her Vim and vigour. She listened to her mother-in-law wittering on about the pain of bunions and the price of onions, or maybe it was the other way around. Francine tried to put a brave face on it; at least now it was a brave unblemished face, unlike the one she'd sported while married to Jean's son.

Just before noon, Macy shuffled down in her pyjamas. She stood at the kitchen door stretching and yawning. Jean diffused any potential mother/daughter situation by struggling up to standing and going over to give her granddaughter a hug. While doing this, she pressed a £20 note into the girl's hand.

The new and improved Macy Lord lit up like a sparkler while still managing to glare pointedly at her mother as if to say: 'You see! It doesn't take much!'

This devil-to-angel act really pulled Francine's strings, but notwithstanding the hypocrisy, she was relieved to see the child cheerful for once.

"I'm saving up for something special, Nanny," Macy steamed in as she held the note against her heart to emphasise her love for it.

"What's that, dear?" Jean asked, moving slowly through to the living room.

"It's a very particular *handbag*, Nanny," Macy followed close behind, "not just *any* old handbag but something strong and er…sensible. It will last me a lifetime."

She knew that old people were big on sensible things that lasted a lifetime, something to do with deprivation during two world wars.

Encouraged by her own guile, Macy gazed devotedly at her grandmother and batted her eyelashes.

"Well maybe you'll be able to buy it now, dear," Jean said with satisfaction, sinking into the armchair.

Francine, who had followed close behind to keep tabs on the conversation, scuttled back to the kitchen when Jean said: "I hope lunch will be ready at one o'clock. You know I need to eat on the dot."

Macy now had her grandma's full attention. Bending down while holding her breath against any unpleasant odours, she lifted the old lady's feet onto the footstool then sank down beside her on the well-worn carpet. Arranging her face into that of someone whose puppy had just been run over by a steamroller, she said:

"But Nanny Jean, you see the thing is…the bag is, well, it's *really expensive* but of course it *has* to be because it's *so* well made and *ALL* my friends have got one and since Daddy left and Mum's gone loopy, I feel terribly left out." Francine re-entered just in time to stop her daughter mugging her grandma for more money.

"Nanny Jean's already been very generous, Macy," she said. "And your dad didn't *leave*, we…we…" She caved, deflating like a well-used blow-up doll. Macy, furious that her mother had killed the moment, burst into a tapestry of tears.

"You see, Nanny! She's horrible to me! I hate her! I hate my life! I want my daddy back! I wish I was dead!" And she fled back to her room.

The two women exchanged glances: Francine bit her lip. One did not come between a mother and her son, but it had always been a mystery to her how gentle Jean could have spawned nasty Nev.

The three of them sat down for a lunch of tinned mushroom soup, sliced ham, mashed potatoes, and peas, followed by tinned peaches. On the pretext of homework, Macy pecked her grandmother on the forehead and went upstairs, knowing Francine would stay with Jean.

To make up for the loss of earnings, she went into her mother's bedroom and pulled the shoebox out from under the bed. She rummaged around beneath the scrum of papers, letters and old photos and liberated the envelope. It wasn't much fatter than the last time she'd looked. She helped herself to a £20 note then swapped it for two tens and a five and slid the box back to its pathetic hiding place. That made the day's takings £45. Not bad but nowhere near enough.

Sometime in the early hours, long after her mother and gran had gone to bed, Macy rolled off the sofa and tiptoed upstairs. Nanny Jean was sleeping in her room – lying on her back, mouth agape, wheezing like a warthog. Macy wrinkled her nose then squinted around until she saw the large black patent handbag, squatting on her worktable like a panther in repose. She stretched her arm out, looped it through the handles, drew the bag towards her and tiptoed from the room.

Back downstairs, she switched the lamp on and began to ransack. Inside the bag was a higgledy-piggle of worthless objects:

- One lace handkerchief (crumpled)
- One cheque book (creased)
- Two biros (free from the bank)
- Three Werther's Originals (one half sucked!)
- One WH Smith diary (empty save for a few random names and numbers)
- One plastic photo holder containing two pictures: One of Macy as a baby and one of her dad and his brothers.

She peered at it closely and a churn of nostalgia threatened to distract her from her mission.

There was also a leatherette wallet containing a library card, a book of three second class stamps, a folded food receipt from The Co-op, a £5 Gift Voucher from Boots if you spent £30 on No. 7 Skincare, and £18.47 in notes and loose change.

Hardly what you'd call 'a haul'.

Irritated that her master plan was failing to come to fruition, Macy was about to replace the bag when she noticed a zip pocket in the lining in which there was:

A Gold American Express Card!!!!

Grinning like a lottery winner who'd just found the missing ticket, Macy slipped the precious piece of plastic into her pyjama pocket and tiptoed the bag back to its resting place.

Now all she needed was the old trout's pin number.

*

Macy came down early next morning wearing her school skirt – her school skirt! – a long-sleeved black top and black tights. She ate some cereal without milk and drank some generic, orange-coloured liquid masquerading as juice. Then they set off for church like three generations of a family of proper people. The service was as mind-numbing as it was pointless. Macy did, however, take a moment out from her scheming to glance up at the tragic figure on the cross and ask Him for assistance. After all, wasn't that what He was there for? She was just about to launch into pleading diatribe as to why it was imperative for her to get a designer handbag to fit in with the strata of society to which she wished to become attached, when she remembered she didn't actually believe in 'Him'. Any help she needed would only be realised through her own endeavours, but she'd heard said that God helped those who help themselves, and she'd certainly done that.

After the sermon, they visited the cemetery where the remains of Grandad lay rotting.

We fat all creatures else to fat us, and we fat ourselves for maggots. Hamlet. Act 4, Scene 3, thought Macy, remembering the gruesome quote. She had her grandfather to thank for knowing that: The old man had been alright to be fair, but the Trust Fund he'd left to pay for her private education was causing her more trouble than it was worth – why couldn't he just have left her the cash instead?

Mum and Nanny laid flowers on the grave then clung together in quiet contemplation. Macy respected the moment until she thought the mourning period had gone on long enough.

"Anyone hungry?" she asked.

Nanny Jean kissed the tips of her fingers and patted the kiss into the top of the tombstone.

"See you next time, Dick," she sighed, and they set off home.

*

"It's your birthday soon, isn't it, Nanny?" Macy asked over a Sunday lunch of cremated lamb chops, underdone roast potatoes and boiled to buggery broccoli. Why couldn't Mum ever get the timings right?

"No dear. It's just been," Jean answered indulgently. "But yours is coming up, isn't it?"

"Yes, it is!" Macy rejoiced, glad than her gran had taken the bait. "You know Nanny, when I'm old enough to have my own credit card, I'm not going to use my birthdate as my pin number like most people do." She was speaking as if to a child in a high-pitched unnatural octave.

Francine stopped masticating and narrowed her eyes. Had she heard correctly? Macy with a credit card? Where on earth did that idea come from? She would not be eligible until she was eighteen unless a parent guaranteed it and who exactly was about to do that?

"Oh, you have to have a very special, very secret number and not reveal it to anyone," Nanny Jean agreed, abandoning all efforts at gentility by picking up the chop and gnawing at it with her acrylic dentures. She was glad for the opportunity to dispense her years of accrued wisdom, none of which seemed to impress anybody these days, least of all the younger generation.

"There's jam roly-poly and custard for dessert," Francine said flatly, to change the subject.

The thought of dried-out pastry encasing a smear of gelatinous substance with bright yellow ooze on top had about as much appeal as licking the inner sole of her grandma's orthopaedic shoe, but Macy feigned interest in the ensuing culinary reverie.

"Oh, *my* Neville loved a bit of jam roly-poly," Jean reminisced, "but he always said *mine* was best. I used raspberry instead of strawberry jam, you see – gave it that extra edge."

He also loved a bit of GBH, Francine thought, as she cleared away the lunch plates.

"I'll probably use 1199 or something easy to remember," Macy reeled the conversation back in. "Or maybe 4774 like our phone number? What about you, Nanny?"

Nanny's famous jam roly-poly had led her straight to her historic spotted dick. but realising her granddaughter was waiting for an answer, she refocused.

"Oh…er…yes dear, but you must be a lot less obvious than that. What if you lost your card and the person who found it also found your phone number?"

"Well, you could reverse the numbers, couldn't you?" Macy said impatiently. "Then you…"

"Why are we having this conversation?" Francine demanded, carving the pudding into three bowls. "It's completely hypothetical as no one is getting a credit card!"

"Yes, but it's *really* important to know these things!" Macy shouted. "And it's…it's good for my maths to talk about numbers!"

Francine shot her a *Really?* and shook her head.

"Well, I had four brothers, and I used their birth dates," Nanny offered. Macy practically climbed across the table and into her lap. "The trouble was two were in double figures, so that made it a bit difficult, but I added those two numbers together then I…"

Macy wanted to put her hands around her grandma's scrawny neck and wring it hard until the numbers popped out through the hole in her face. Instead, she put her spoon down, and composed her features into a benign expression of absorbed fascination.

"So, what *is* your pin number, Nanny?" she asked, blinking coquettishly. "I could use the same one, then if ever I forgot mine, you could…"

"Best not, Jean!" Francine warned. "I wouldn't trust that girl further than I could…"

"MUM!" Macy leapt to her feet in outrage. "How could you be so…"

Jean caught hold of her granddaughter's arm and shot Francine a disapproving look.

"Now – now, dear," she said. "What is all this? You both need to calm down and be kinder to each other now that it's just the two of you. I am not going to give you my pin number, Macy, but I will set you a little test if you want to practice your maths. Now, listen carefully: I use the dates on which my oldest and youngest brothers were born. William was born on the fourth, and George was born on the ninth but since Henry, the youngest, was born on the twenty-fifth, I add those two numbers together to make one single digit."

4–9–7!!! Macy's mind had gone into overdrive. There must be a million combinations of these three numbers, and she was still missing the fourth! Jean was folding her napkin away and looking as satisfied as Pythagoras when he discovered the square of the hypotenuse was equal to the sum of the squares of the other two sides.

"But what was the date of your *other* brother's birthday?" Macy probed.

Jean simply tapped the side of her nose, got up from the table and waddled towards the armchair for her afternoon nap.

"What in hell's name are you up to?" Francine hissed as she tried to get a sheen on the aluminium saucepan.

"Nothing!" Macy snapped. "Can't I take an interest in the family?"

"The family? Your long-dead great-uncles who you never even met? Why now, all of a sudden?"

Macy deliberated.

"It's…it's for a history project I'm doing. First World War."

The answer seemed feasible, but Francine's doubted its authenticity.

"I'm going upstairs," she said. "When Nanny wakes up, make her a cup of tea. And no more cross-examination. She has come here for a quiet weekend because it's the anniversary of Grandad's death and the last thing she needs is you giving her the third degree."

Macy sat on the footstool at her grandmother's feet waiting for the old dear to wake up. Jean shifted in her seat, raised one buttock, and let out a series of pops like distant gunfire. Macy suppressed a gag.

"Poor George," Jean murmured. "Never stood a chance…"

"How *ooold* was he?" Macy intoned, invoking Madame Arcati in *Blithe Spirit*. "First day of Lent…" came the imprecise reply.

Macy's ensuing Q&A guided her sleeping grandma through Epiphany, Shrove Tuesday, Maundy Thursday, All Soul's Day, and the Episcopalian Feast of St. Joseph the Redeemer. To Macy, High Days and Holy Days were nothing but small print in a diary, but she needed to remember them in case they matched any relevant birth years. It occurred to her that it might be easier to return the bloody credit card to its zip pocket and forget she'd ever stolen it.

She would have to adopt a different tack. Jean was waking up, so she went to make her a strong cup of tea with three sugars and took it to her with a sheet of paper and a pencil.

"Hello, Nanny," she said putting the tea down gently on the side table. "Did you have a nice nap? I was wondering if you could you draw me a family tree for my history assignment?"

Jean took her time coming to which involved some minor readjustment of her top set, a good tug of her bra strap and a lot of hair patting, but once she was fully *compos mentis* and had sipped some tea, she embarked on the project with enthusiasm.

The result was an impossible maze which required Macy to produce three additional sheets of A4 paper and a roll of Sellotape with which to stick them together. Added to which she didn't really give a shit. Annoyingly, Jean had only written down her brothers' names without their actual birth dates, but eventually, after more quizzing, querying, and cajoling, Macy finally obtained the four digits she so desperately needed. Trouble was, there were twenty-four permutations.

Nanny Jean left the next morning oblivious to the fact that the precious piece of plastic she loved owning but had never used had been misappropriated from her handbag. She had also forgotten that she'd written her pin number on the signature strip in case she ever needed to remember it.

9

Airey Fairclough awoke in a cold sweat with something hard and pulsing in the palm of his hand. He let go with a start, much as one would a fizzing firework. He rolled onto one side, groaned, tried to be strong, failed, and returned – with some degree of uncontrollable dislike – to finish what he'd started.

He closed his eyes, better to claw back the dream dispelling in the dawn – so inappropriate yet so compelling. Had he been wearing a ram's head atop his naked torso, with sprites dancing around a cloven-hoofed behemoth with alarming eyebrows and a flaming red cloak? The otherworldly creatures taunted him with their translucent skin and androgynous features and Airey was hard pressed to resist the lure of his own temptation. He cried out in ecstasy, then jerked in horror as he realised Macy Lord had made a fleeting appearance at his moment of climax.

Mr Fairclough spilled out of bed and sank to his knees. Waking thoughts were manageable, but fantasies that occurred during sleep? He would surely be damned.

*

Macy stood in the bus shelter, coat hugged around her, legs jigging like Saint Vitus at a dance. It was pouring and she was in danger of arriving looking like a sewer rat.

As the bus approached, she hurried to the kerb, just close enough for the tyres to splash effluent all over her feet. She stamped angrily, elbowed her way on board, and stomped up the stairs. Condensation wept down the windows and she could feel her hair frizzing up – so much for the two hours she'd spent struggling with the straighteners.

A young guy plonked himself down next to her and Macy leant away, pressing her forehead against the cold, damp pane. She stared down at the

Saturday shoppers laden with carrier bags. A shiver of apprehension ran through her. Was she really doing this? Shouldn't she just go home?

The bus turned into Oxford Street and Macy's heart began to pound. They passed C&A on one side, then Littlewoods and Dolcis on the other – they were nearly there; she could barely swallow. The driver braked suddenly, and she shot forward, grabbing the handrail, knuckles white against the cold metal. The bus juddered off again and she fell back. The guy next to her continued drumming his thighs and deafening himself with his *douff-douff-douff*.

Through the smeary glass, Macy could see the store up ahead: Classical rows of stone columns – Ionic? Corinthian? – as far as the eye could see: A perspective in perfect symmetry. The bus came to a halt, and she stood up, clambered over the music nerd, and hurried down the spiral staircase. She jumped off and ran forward through the sheeting rain, and all at once, there she was: In the place of her dreams with the means to make those dreams come true.

A shard of lightning split the sky followed by a crash of thunder. Macy winced.

I do not believe it You, so You can stop that right now.

Macy was so taken with her own temerity that she revolved through the bevelled glass doors twice before spilling out into the store, where she stood overwhelmed by the assault of aromas: Perfumes for princesses, not *Charlie* girls like her. She inhaled deeply – how rich the scents. The hubbub of people behind her moved her forward, and glancing through towards the next department, her breath caught in her throat: Had she died and gone to handbag heaven? Gucci, Fendi, Dior, Céline, Prada, Saint Laurent, Chanel, Louis Vuitton: The brands swam before her like exotic fish in an affluent aquarium.

Customers and aspirants hovered around the counters, staring, stroking, reaching, wanting. The confident superrich swanned up and glibly picked them up, the two groups distinguished by the one great divide. You either had it or you did not.

Macy wandered warily through the department viewing each bag without daring to touch. Her mouth, so dry earlier, was now drooling. Just when she thought she'd seen the very one, she'd spot another, then a third. They were *all* so fabulous, beautiful, sophisticated…CHIM! She'd never be able to decide. She'd have to go home and think about them, come back another day.

Relieved at the thought of getting the hell out of there, Macy was suddenly arrested in her tracks, for there it was: The One. The Bag that stood out from the rest, a Bag that shouted Fashion yet whispered Class – The Bag she knew she had to have, if it was the last thing she did.

Over-sized, bold, and bedecked, the rich gold python skin glimmered in the store's fluorescent glow. I Am IT, The Bag proclaimed. Buy Me and You Too Will Have IT.

Macy circled the counter like an eagle orbiting a turtle's nest. She moved closer then backed away, but the bag drew her back, blinding her eyes to any other. She sauntered past feigning indifference, treating it like some bloke she might fancy but not enough to let him know.

A couple of six-foot amazons, designer-clad from top to toe, wandered up to the display. One of them poked The Bag with a long, crimson fingernail. The counter was busy now, people hustling around – she couldn't see it anymore! What if some rich bitch bought it before she had the chance!

Macy pushed through the throng and swooped, snatched the bag off the counter, dropped it on the floor, snatched it up again, then spun around, not knowing what to do next. Glamorous gazelles, speaking in tongues, laughed, and flounced away. Security on the sixth floor squinted at their screens.

If I'm going to do this, I need to do it now, Macy thought, searching left and right for a cash desk. She saw the sign and hurried towards it, the trophy clutched against her chest. A bazaar of burkas was waiting to pay. She looked around to see if there was another till. Ground Floor Security had her in his sights. He murmured into his headset, but he couldn't do anything unless she left the store without paying.

Three women in front of her completed their purchases and left. And then it was her turn.

"How would you like to pay?" asked the sales assistant brightly. "Lovely choice, by the way! I've had my eye on that one since it first came in!"

Macy's mouth felt like she had opened it and the Sahara had blown in. She fumbled for her purse, opened it, and handed over the credit card. Security stepped forward as the salesgirl caught his eye.

"Pin number, please?" she asked, not quite so friendly now. Macy held her breath and tapped in the numbers she knew by heart. One night, while twisting the card over and over in her hand, she'd spotted the four digits pencilled on the signature strip. She'd laughed out loud. *Good Old Nan!*

Macy wasn't laughing now. What if the numbers had nothing to do with the card at all? What if her bowels slid open all over Selfridges' marble floor? – but as the words 'Pin Accepted' appeared on the screen, her sphincter retracted like a tortoise head, and she was able to breathe again.

"There you go," the salesgirl said, charming once again. She winked at Security who melted away.

She tore off the receipt and handed it to Macy together with the credit card. The handbag was wrapped in its cream silk dust cover and placed into a shiny yellow carrier bag with big black lettering.

"Enjoy the rest of your day!" The girl said, calculating her commission, ready to serve the next customer.

"Th-thanks," croaked Macy, "you too…" and head down, she made for the nearest exit.

And then she stopped. She'd done it, hadn't she? She had bought the designer bag she wanted, and she wanted to use it right here, right now. Macy turned back to look for a Ladies Room.

Mumbling: "Sorry, I don't feel well," she jumped the queue and dived into a cubicle. Hanging the bright yellow carrier on the hook behind the door, she closed the toilet seat, sank down on it and dropped her head between her knees. *Christ! It worked.* No one had apprehended her. She hadn't been carted off and thrown in a cell. Maybe, she should go back and shop some more?

In a surge of excitement, Macy emptied the contents of her faux suede embarrassment into the Sacred New Bag, stuffed the old one into the yellow carrier, and headed out of the toilets feeling like Madonna going onstage at Wembley Stadium.

When she emerged onto Oxford Street, the rain had stopped. Rays of sunlight beamed through the oyster grey clouds pointing their gilded fingers at the golden bag. She could almost hear them saying: "Ooh! Hell-oo!"

The bag caught the eye of a smartly dressed lady en route to a matinée; she turned her nose up at such tasteless bling, but an Essex girl heading home to Romford, ogled it with envy.

Macy strode towards Hyde Park. She needed some fresh air, needed to regroup, think things through. With the empowerment of the Gold American Express Card, the possibilities were endless. A fantasy of international boutiques would open their doors to her, fawning sales assistants beckoning like sirens from the rocks.

Those so-called friends of hers – what would they think now? She'd no longer be the girl who wrote 'that filthy essay'. She'd be The Girl with the Golden Bag.

10

It lived a vampire's life, denied the light of day, concealed at the back of the wardrobe, coming out, only briefly, very late at night. No opportunity had arisen to use it, except one wretched afternoon when she released it from its dust cover and insulted it by stuffing it into a Tesco carrier before leaving home. Outside her house, Macy reversed the action, hiding the dust bag and the carrier inside The Golden Bag. She got little pleasure out of that, terrified she might bump into someone who would question where it came from, or worse still, assume it was a fake. So much for: *To the victor the spoils…*

The school term dragged on with little improvement to her social life. Parties seemed to have dwindled – or maybe they were going on without her, no change there, then. She couldn't have a party for obvious reasons, and even if she did, she'd look a bit daft carrying a handbag in her own home. Like someone who longed for a nose job convinced it would improve their life, Macy realised that *owning* a designer bag had failed to change hers.

Part of her longed to show it to her mum so she could say: "See, Mum? *Now* do you get it?"

To share the honour of its presence in the house, to be able to leave it openly on her bed, but how could she explain where it came from? Would Francine believe her if she said Zenith had gifted it to her? Would she call Zenith's mum to make sure it hadn't been 'borrowed' from her wardrobe?

And so, it languished, loved yet alone, going out of style faster than you could say: "Hands up! It's the fashion police."

*

Macy sat doodling a horse with a swishy tail. She had a story in mind for Mr Fairclough's writing competition but had yet to write a single word. She got up and went to the wardrobe: Maybe the bag would give her inspiration. She was just smoothing her hand over its surface when her mother walked in.

"Have you seen my…?"

Francine stared at the handbag as she would at an intruder. Macy struggled to stuff it back inside its cover.

"Where did you get that from?" Francine asked.

"It's a…it's a…" Macy laughed nervously. "I…er…you've…er…it's a present! For you. And now you've spoilt the surprise!"

Macy shoved the bag back inside the wardrobe and slammed the door. She leant against it as if the bag might escape and explain itself.

"Where did you get the money to buy a thing like that?"

"A thing like what?" Macy blurted. "It's a…a copy! A cheap knock off! Ten quid down the market! Amazing what the Chinese can do! It's all I could afford. I bought it with the money Nanny Jean gave me and it was going to be for your birthday but of course you've ruined that now. Is supper ready?"

Francine pressed her index finger into the dent at her temple.

"Supper will be another ten minutes. And my birthday's not for another eight months. Bit premature to shop so far in advance since you often forget, or leave it 'til the last minute, or even the week after?"

Mother and daughter stared at each other in awkward silence. The younger decided it was time to shut up and the elder left the room forgetting what she'd gone in for.

Macy put a circle around the word LIE on her Thou Shalt Not list, distraught that she'd now have to donate her precious purchase to a most unworthy cause.

*

As soon as she left for school the next morning, Francine unearthed the bag and examined it closely. It certainly looked, felt, and smelled like an expensive item. The finish was excellent: The stitching professional, the handles well-fitted, the skin exotic – but the gold? All that tasteless gold? No wonder it only cost ten pounds. Macy must have bought it with the sole intention of borrowing it back, knowing her mother would never use it. Conniving little cow.

Francine returned the bag to its hiding-place. Her daughter was definitely lying, probably shoplifting, and would turn out as worthless as she was.

11

Macy spent half an hour mucking about with fonts, layouts, designs, and colours before typing a single word. Every time she opened the document, she went through the same ritual until eventually, late one night, long after her mother had gone to bed, the story that had been nudging at her brain finally found release through her fingers.

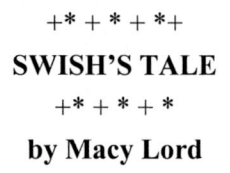

+* + * + *+

SWISH'S TALE

+* + * + *

by Macy Lord

"How much d'ya want for it?"
"IT is a HE and he's not for sale."
"Everything is for sale. Whaddya want for it?"
"I said HE's NOT for sale. And I wouldn't do business with you if you were the last merchant on earth."
"We'll see about that…"

o – o – o

I listened to this exchange with a sense of apprehension. Snodgrass was a lowlife and a bully – I saw how badly he treated others of my kind. I trusted my master: He was a good and honest man, and I knew how much he valued me. There must have been better deals on the market the morning he took me on, yet he'd seen fit to put his faith in me.

Although I'd been born to a good family, I'd been unlucky with my employers. If I'd had my way, I would never have gone to the city at all.

I'd been born in Hertfordshire near a little village called Redbourn. My parents were farm workers, and they had a lot of offspring. It must have been a wrench to let us go, but that was their lot in life and also ours.

When I first began to travel, I dreamed of a fine future. If I had to live in a city, my choice would have been London, serving a high-ranking family. I would be matched with others of my colour and size, placed between the shafts of an elegant carriage.

It soon became apparent that this was not to be; far from becoming a West Ender, I became an East Ender through and through.

Although I wasn't one of those thick-legged, wide-rumped beasts, I was expected to perform labours far beyond my capabilities, labours more suited to those of a stockier stature. I worked for a milkman at first: That was all stop-start, uphill, and down dale. Just as I'd get into my stride, I'd be whoa-ed again and I'd be obliged to wait while he lifted the crates off the cart, delivering to the various doorsteps. He used to stop longer at one address and would emerge whistling with his clothes askew. Heaven knows what that was about, because how long could it take to drop off two gold tops and a pound of butter? I grew strong in that job and was soon sold on to a coal merchant.

Oh, what dirty work that was! My smart grey coat became ingrained with coal dust, and I never felt clean no matter how much they hosed me down. The gentry's ponies would trot past with their noses in the air – those mares were so haughty, and never gave me a second glance – well, they wouldn't, would they? No highfalutin' mount would fancy a bit of rough like me, yet I longed for love like any other creature.

Next, I got sold to a brewery: Back-breaking work and I got drunk on the beer fumes! I faltered in my step sometimes, and once sank to my knees and brought the barrels down with me. I was whipped so hard, so they let me go, moved me on again. Through all those jobs, I never once had a roof over my head. I lived outdoors, no matter the season, in varying degrees of discomfort.

Eventually I ended up at the cemetery in Edmonton lugging stones and earth around. Sometimes I would drag the carts that bore the coffins to their final resting place. That was depressing work, I can tell you – listening to the mourners wailing, having to stand for hours on end in the driving rain while graves were dug, and funerals conducted. I could guess from the weight of the cart what sort of soul had passed...it broke my heart when the load was light.

Then one day, I trod on something, and my foot grew very sore. I took to limping – I could not help it. Without even bothering to check, they dragged me to the marketplace and hung a piece of card around my neck. Different men came by and pulled my lips apart as if my teeth would tell them I had a nail stuck in my foot. It was agony and it must have got infected. Some punters got down on one knee and lifted my fetlocks, but if only one of them had looked a little closer, they'd have noticed what was ailing me. I stood there glumly – no energy to make a fuss. They hadn't fed me well and I'd developed a wracking cough – I was a hoarse horse!

As I awaited my fate, fearing what it might be, I heard voices raised and an argument broke out. Eventually, whoever won took hold of my reins and handed over some coins, so I knew a deal had been done.

I prayed it wasn't the glue factory – I wasn't ready to be 'ockamatutt' just yet. I'd heard of pals of mine going down that route: Their bones melted and mixed with shellac to make jewellery and buttons – not the greatest end but given a new lease of life, nonetheless.

A firm but gentle hand patted me on the neck and a kindly voice whispered: "Come on, old boy. Let's get you home." I couldn't believe it. He actually sounded like a gentleman.

My new boss, Mr Zelig, was very good to me. The first thing he did was to see to my poor foot: It wasn't a nail from a coffin as I'd thought, but a stone trapped beneath my shoe. Then he installed me – and now I understand where that word comes from – if not exactly in a 'stall', at least beneath a flat roof in the yard behind his dwelling. There was hay to eat and water to drink. What luxury! The following morning, he tethered me to his cart and led me off to start my new career.

I enjoyed this work more than anything I'd done before. The smell was pleasant for a start: The cart, fully laden, was weighty, but the aroma of fresh fruit and vegetables wafted over me when the wind blew right. At the end of each day, I got a few apples and some carrots to eat. They were probably bruised but what did I care? I built my strength back up and became quite fit again – which brings me to the point of the nasty neighbour who wanted to take me on.

Hoxton, where we lived, was a rough, tough tumbledown old place populated by Jewish refugees. Although they worked all the hours God gave, they were poor as church mice, or synagogue mice, if you get my drift. The Jewish race, apparently, were God's Chosen People, but they always used to joke: "God! Do us a favour and choose someone else!" The nearby docks where the immigrant ships came in 'welcomed' the settlers like so much flotsam washed up by the tide. Those poor people landed in untidy heaps, lugging their dreams in bags and bundles, landsick from their gruelling sea voyage. They were the rejected refuse from Eastern Europe and beyond, denigrated and dispersed from all their native lands. Bedraggled children clutched their mothers' skirts, all of them surely wondering: "What happens next?"

My master was a wise and gentle man. He knew what was needed – he'd made that trip himself – and had also suffered the deprivation of all things fresh and green. Even before sunrise, we would stock up at the wholesalers then set up shop on the dock to offer the new arrivals the chance to eat well on the cheap.

Carrots, celery, parsnips, swedes, turnips, onions – all roots that made a tasty, wholesome soup. Once the docks cleared out, we'd pitch up at the street market in Shoreditch for another influx of customers. I just had to stand there, it was not exactly taxing work, and I liked it when the children came along and patted my nose or rubbed their sticky hands along my flank. No one had ever ridden me of course, and that was a regret. I'd have loved, just once, to gallop across a meadow with the wild wind in my mane, my tail billowing out behind me like some romantic steed. I guess that will never happen now, but I can dream, can't I?

So, on that particular morning, that bastard Snodgrass came by and made some snide comment to the mild-mannered Mr Zelig.

"Not much business today!" he said squeezing some bananas much too hard. "I wouldn't buy from you anyway – it all looks rotten to me!"

His voice was loud enough for the customers to hear. I snorted at him and pawed the ground but Mr Zelig kept his dignity and carried on with business.

I must just tell you, in passing, the first summer when it grew hot, he made sure I had enough water to last the day and even got me a straw hat to wear. His lady wife cut holes in an old one of hers and made it fit so my ears could poke through. I felt quite jaunty! – if I'd had a pair of sunglasses, I could have trotted down to Westcliff and had a stroll along the beach – eaten some ice cream, maybe! Also, that winter, when it got really cold, Mr Zelig threw an old grey blanket across my back; it felt a bit scratchy at first, but it did keep me warm. I felt quite posh – not many East End nags sported their own overcoats.

Life continued smoothly until that fateful day when 'Robber' Snodgrass came by and asked to buy me again.

"I've already told you! He's not for sale!" said Zelig firmly.

"Two quid! I'll give you two quid for him! He's not worth more than 30 bob!"

"Go and annoy someone else, Snodgrass. This horse is mine and will remain so for the foreseeable future. Thanks, but no thanks!"

As we walked home that evening, the sky darkened, and thunderclouds rolled overhead. My boss led me down the alley and tied me up in the back yard, but I felt a strange presentiment of doom. It made me shiver in my stall.

The rain began around suppertime and continued relentlessly through the evening, interspersed with flashes and crashes like Mars and Neptune come to blows. I huddled beneath my corrugated roof feeling chilled and apprehensive.

It must have been around midnight when I first heard the scraping. At first, I thought it was rats: Those little beggars often sniff around looking for scraps. I usually let out a tremendous fart which scares them off but this time it didn't so I knew it wasn't rats.

Then I heard the unmistakeable creak of the gate being opened. I pricked up my ears. Despite the rain lashing down, I could hear footsteps coming in my direction, so I reversed back against the wall. I don't know why I did that – it's not like I could make myself invisible or anything. Suddenly, whoever it was tripped over the tin bath which clattered across the cobbles with a terrible crash.

Upstairs, unbeknown to me, Mrs Zelig shot bolt upright in bed.

"What's that?" she asked, shaking her husband awake. "There's something happening in the yard!"

My boss must have grunted and rolled over but his wife lit a candle and got out of bed. I could see the glow flickering in the window, and it brought me comfort to know I was not alone. My reassurance was short-lived, however, as a hand suddenly snatched my mane causing my neck to jerk awkwardly to one side.

A rough voice whispered: "Come on, you ol' donkey. Doesn't wanna sell you, eh? Well, you're coming with me just the same! For nothing!"

Snodgrass – who else? – tried to yank me towards the open gate but I stood my ground and refused to budge. I lifted my tail and expelled a great heap of steaming manure hoping it would turn him away. Then a sharp pain stung me on the rump as a leather lash whipped across my back. I lifted my head and whinnied for all I was worth. The rain gained in intensity...

Mr Zelig didn't bother with his slippers or his robe, neither did he don his black hat or coat to shield him from the storm. He hurried down the stairs and tore open the back door just in time to see me rise on my hind legs like a Lippizaner from the Spanish Riding School and kick his nemesis in the face. As if in slow motion, my feet returned to earth, but I took the opportunity en route to kick Snodgrass where it would hurt. He went down, blood pouring from his mouth, hands clutched between his legs!

"You fucking mule!" he shouted. "You'll pay for this!" Then he staggered up to standing with his whip raised in his fist.

Macy stopped typing. She wanted to use the words Snodgrass would have used but Mr Fairclough had said: "No bad language."

She replaced the 'u, c and k' with asterisks. They would get the gist. She was on a roll now and wanted to reach the end. Her bedside clock said 02:16.

My boss was outside by this time, and he grabbed Snodgrass by the wrist and twisted him away to deflect the lash. Then he reached for the spade he used to shovel clean my stall and swung it hard against the side of the assailant's head. This blow, added to the wounds already inflicted by Yours Truly, sent the attacker flying back against the wall. His legs slipped out from under him, and he crashed down on his arse. He sat there stunned for a moment, limbs twitching like a crushed roach, then he let out a long, low groan and slumped sideways to the ground.

My employer stood there in the pouring rain, pyjamas soaked and sagging. I whinnied my thanks and nuzzled his neck. He did not go back inside but stood there in the cold patting my flank and whispering: "It's OK, boy…you done good – he won't bother us again."

He filled my nosebag with fresh hay and stayed there until I settled; I could feel him trembling with cold while I felt like the adored horse of Emperor Caligula. Legend has it that the famous *Incitatus*, for such was his name, had an ivory manger, purple blankets and a collar of precious stones. He was attended by his own servants and fed on oats mixed with gold flake, but he could not have felt more appreciated than I did that night.

My beloved master never stood trial for murder or any other crime. The chill he caught that night trying to protect me went to his chest and then his lungs and the dear man passed away on 11 August 1905 in the London Hospital, Whitechapel from an attack of pneumonia. He was only 38 years old and left a wife and five children.

I should have dealt with Snodgrass myself and let poor Mr Zelig stay in bed. Although what happened was not my fault, I suffered the guilt for the rest of my life.

Macy typed the last full stop and slumped back in her chair. It was probably over the word count, but she'd edit it tomorrow. It was quarter to three in the morning, and she'd been working flat out since ten. She had no idea where the story came from – some apocryphal tale of a long dead great-grandfather? – but it *was* to do with coveting, stealing, and killing which were three of the Thou Shalt Nots. She rubbed her tired eyes, switched off her computer, got undressed and went to bed.

12

"What you lookin' at me like that for?"

"Because you look…"

"Look what? Go on say it!"

Francine turned away and continued wiping out the hydrator compartment in the fridge.

"10:30 please, Macy. No later. I'll wait up."

"God Almighty, Mum! One night in my life! Anyone would think…you're not my *dad*, you know!"

"That's quite lucky, isn't it? I don't think he'd have let you go out dressed like that."

Macy threw her eyes skywards, adopted the expression of Our Lady of the Everlasting Agonies, and headed in the direction of 'out'.

"What's in the carrier?" Francine's called but the question got lost between the opening and slamming of the front door.

Francine went over to the window to watch her daughter leave. Her emotions were dissolving like jelly in hot water. Where had her little girl gone? If only Macy had consulted her, she would not have let her go out looking like that. She would have loved to help her choose what clothes to wear, put on a little make-up, style her hair. Instead, she was left feeling like a corroded colander, every effort she put in just drained away.

Francine was just about to let the curtain fall back when she saw Macy stop at the end of the path and remove something from the Tesco carrier. The gold bag! – *of course*, followed by a pair of tacky fuchsia stilettos. The scuffed pumps she'd been wearing when she left home were stuffed into the carrier which in turn was stuffed behind the bins. Francine watched in despair as Macy wriggled her teenage toes into shoes befitting a pole-dancer, then she shouldered the gold monstrosity and teetered off down the road.

Francine returned to the kitchen and picked up the rubber gloves. She stared into the sink like the answer lay somewhere between the dirty dishes. She let the Marigolds slide to the floor, then turned and walked upstairs to her bedroom and the salvation that waited inside her bedside drawer.

*

For Macy to be included in one of Zenith's Saturday Nights Out was truly EPIC. She didn't know how it had come about: just being in the right place at the right time, she guessed. She was certain that tonight, at last, The Golden Bag would come into its own and secure her future as part of 'the in crowd'.

Despite the platform shoes making her walk like she had rocker blotters on her feet, she managed to get to the bus stop without falling over. She wished she'd kept her pumps with her because how she was going to get through the evening in these instruments of torture, God only knew.

Macy caught her reflection in a shop window and stopped to flick a heavily lacquered shank of mousey brown hair over to the left. Then she flicked it back over to the right. It still didn't work.

The bus arrived and Macy struggled to step aboard. As soon as she sat down, her tight skirt crept up her thighs. The man opposite smeared his gaze all over her, stopping only to focus on the dark area between her legs. She felt her discomfort rise. She yanked the skirt down then bent forward to adjust the painful shoes, which caused her breasts to spill forward. The man hawked a gob of phlegm up his nose and moved it around his mouth. He spread his legs wider to accommodate whatever was going on in his pants.

Macy didn't dare move seats because she'd slipped her shoes off and would have to lean forward to get them on again. She hoicked her skirt down and her top up and turned her head away. What right did this toe rag have to use her as his paedo fantasy?

*

Swanky's was mobbed. Macy's too much make-up and jailbait outfit got her past the bouncers, but once she was inside, she had no idea where to go.

The walls were black. The ceiling was black. The floor was black. Tinted mirrors made the space seem bigger so you couldn't tell where the room ended, and a black eye began. Strobe lights pierced the darkness endangering the wellbeing of any epileptics out for a fun time.

Macy followed a gaggle of girls towards the bar shielding her precious bag beneath her arm. It had to be protected. No one had seen it yet. She was relieved to spot Zenith perched on a bar stool flashing her tits at the barman. He was busy showing off his mixology skills and didn't bother to check IDs – if they'd got past the bouncers, they could get past him.

Macy fought her way to Zenith's side.

"Hiya!" she said like it was perfectly normal for her to be out clubbing on a Saturday night. Zenith shot a cursory glance in her direction making Macy feel like prosecco at a champagne party. One of Zenith's minions, a girl Macy didn't know, whispered something in the queen bee's ear, and her head shot around. She peered inquisitively at the golden bag.

"Zat real?" Zenith asked.

"Y-yes?" Macy answered, as if trying to convince herself.

"Cool!" came the reply.

Before she could process the thrill of acceptance, Macy was elbowed sideways by a tribe of mingers dressed in t-shirts printed with the logo:

VIRGIN
ON THE RIDICULOUS

and much to her annoyance, the 'Discuss the Bag' moment got lost in the fray.

Once Zenith and her coterie had been served, they moved away from the bar and stood sipping dayglow cocktails through fancy straws. Macy managed to order a cranberry juice on the rocks – *all rocks and no cranberry* – then moved uncertainly across to join them. They had obviously managed to buy alcohol – or bring it in with them – as they were already talking fluent vodka and falling about like they'd just heard The World's Funniest Joke.

One of the older girls, substantially rounder than the rest, started dancing on her own. Any potential wobble of her Michelin-tyred middle was restrained in a tourniquet of Lycra. Her face was pretty in a piggy sort of way: Deep set eyes, rosy cheeks, a turned-up snout, and a joker's mouth slashed with what Macy guessed to be Revlon's *Wild Obsession.*

"Go Prinny!" Zenith encouraged. Prinny's generous boobs bounced up and down like Pinky and Perky on a trampoline, and her thighs, freed from the confines of thick school tights, flashed their flesh in the faces of anyone within flashing distance.

Having looked forward to this evening all week and dished out an extra dollop of vileness to her mother to be able to leave the house without being challenged, Macy realised she wasn't actually enjoying herself. Maybe she also needed a *proper* drink. Erasing the memory of throwing up after her dad had plied her with beer and cigarettes at the age of nine, she elbowed her way back to the bar.

"Vodka and orange please!" she shouted, sliding the Amex card across the counter.

"Scroo-derr-rriiiverr, bebey!"

The barman, all slim hips and fake American accent, made a show of shaking and pouring before picking up the card.

"Wanna start a tab?" He flipped the piece of plastic across his fingers like a card sharp, swapped hands behind his back, then spun it in the air and caught it between his teeth. Macy watched in alarm. If this tosser mislaid her card…

She had no idea what a 'tab' was, but she knew she didn't want one, so she shook her head vehemently and snatched the card away the minute the screen told her to. She thrust it deep inside the interior pocket of the golden bag, picked up her drink and left, stopping just long enough to take a long slug. It tasted good. Sweet and…different. Clutching the glass, she headed back to find her 'crew'.

The crowd swallowed her up and spat her out on the edge of the dance floor.

*

The man in the 1960s outfit observed Macy from behind a pillar. Against the black background, in his black jeans, black polo neck and black-rimmed spectacles, he was barely visible. His hair was unrestrained, flopping forward over his eyes instead of parted on the right-hand side and smarmed down with Brylcreem.

When he'd first entered the club, he'd been daunted by the thump of the music and the chaos of the crowd. He'd never been in a place like this before and he wanted to leave immediately, but having overheard the arrangements being made, he felt it his responsibility to do some off-duty sleuthing. They were all underage and some of them might consider drinking.

From his observation point *in tenebris,* he sipped a glass of sparkling water one drop at a time. He wondered about his actual motives in being there: Was there a deep-rooted emotional reason for wanting to keep an eye on them, or on one of them in particular? Everything in his life so far had pointed inward but he was young-ish – and it was the weekend, so wasn't this the sort of place he was meant to be rather than home alone with Homer – and not the one called Simpson?

A flashily attired buxom blonde appeared suddenly from around the pillar making him jump.

"Not dancin'?" she shouted, then immediately turned her back on him and began making circular motions with her rump in time to the music. With every gyration, she reversed closer to him until his polo neck, jeans, vest, pants, shoes, and socks seemed superfluous and stifling.

"All on yer tod then?" she asked, but before he had the chance to answer, she turned and shimmied her shoulders at him, inviting him to partake of her glorious décolletage. Smiling stiffly, the only thing he was certain of was his own uncertainty. The woman was dancing very close to him. Societal rules regarding respect for personal space clearly did not apply here, but he was in a dance club, and so he began, tentatively at first and then with a little more élan, to loosen his legs in time to the tempo.

"'aven't seen you in 'ere before!" She leaned in and yelled against his ear. A spray of spittle moistened his lobe sending a bizarre thrill through him. He shook and nodded his head at the same time, like a fuzzy bulldog in the back window of a Ford Cortina.

The woman took hold of his hands and placed them firmly on her swaying hips. He was beguiled, albeit through fabric, to experience the feel of female flesh beneath his palms. They rocked together for a while, his eyes mesmerised by the body glitter that ran in rivulets between her bobbing breasts.

"Fancy another drink?" She shouted, and without waiting for a reply, grabbed him by the hand and dragged him towards the bar. He kept his head down but was powerless to do anything but follow.

He bought her a Cosmopolitan which she sipped genteelly at first then necked like a navvy.

"Let's get some air," she bellowed above the blare of the music, and grabbing his hand once more, tugged him towards the exit. He hesitated and turned, craning his neck to scan for the girls but he couldn't see them anywhere. *Oh well,* he thought, and held the door open for her like the gentleman he was.

"Blimey!" she gushed. "Nice manners!" and they spilled out into the night.

She linked her arm through his and staggered him across the car park towards a clump of trees.

"Bleedin' punishment, these are!" she cursed and took off her shoes. She bent down to rub her feet paying special attention to a nasty bunion. He averted his gaze. Now was his chance to escape, but did he?

"Talk about suff'ring for beau'y, eh!" she squawked, her accent grating like a raw onion.

He allowed himself to be led into the darkness of whatever she had in mind, knowing this was wrong on so many levels.

She walked him backwards against a tree and once he was pinioned, plunged forward, teasing his lips open with her tongue. It was disgusting, yet delicious. He savoured her flavour: Ambrosial, limey, with a hint of lanolin and nicotine, like a complex cocktail yet to be invented.

"Oo-er!" She flattered groping him through his jeans. "'oo's a big boy then?" The brain over which he once had control struggled to answer this simple, though rhetorical, question.

She soon figured out his flies were buttoned not zipped, so she slid her fingers through the gaps. His knees buckled like a *puppetmeister* had cut his strings and, liberated of all conscience, he pushed forward with his hips.

With the deftness of a prestidigitator, she flicked open the fly buttons and released him through the opening in his Y-fronts. Despite his arousal, he was mortified. His penis had never been out in public before, certainly not *al fresco* and especially not *in flagrante erecto*!

"Anywhere I hang my hat, babe!" She tittered, and without so much as a by-your-leave, she sank to her knees and wrapped her lips around him.

A thousand diseases flashed through his medical records, but he was too far gone to care. Unable to contain his urgency, the speed with which he climaxed both shocked and shamed him. She took him in her stride – on the chin – then chortled: "Speedy Gonzales, eh! My turn!"

She started to pump him in the hollow of her hand, and he hardened again in quick response. She hoisted up her skirt and cocked her leg to slide him in. And there he stood, manhood encased – for the first time ever – inside a woman's flesh. She grasped his buttocks and thrust, grunting like a hog in heat, cursing loudly as she came. He kept going, lost in divine violation, praying for mercy at the altar of her ecstasy.

"I'm Charmaine by the way," she said, adjusting her knickers and yanking her skirt down.

"And I'm…J-J-John," he fibbed. "P…pleased to…"

Before he could compose the appropriate small talk to suit the occasion, she pecked him on the cheek and was off.

"Ta-ta, love!" She waved in the air as she wobbled away across the tarmac. "Thanks for coming!"

With a mixture of exhilaration and mortification, he mouthed the words: *Thank you for having me.*

And forever after, Mr Fairclough would recall his first carnal encounter as: That Curious Incident…(of the shag in the car park).

13

By the time the remaining girls spilled out of the club, it was gone midnight: Two hours past Macy's curfew. The group had eventually bonded through dance + alcohol, a freedom fest the likes of which she'd never known. She put her success down to the power of The Golden Bag. If cachet was the word, she had it with knobs on.

Halfway home, the misty-eyed and freshly-deflowered Mr Fairclough suddenly remembered the reason he'd gone out that night: Not to 'get laid' – *how brash to be able to say that and know what it meant!* – but to keep an eye on his juvenile pupils, specifically Macy Lord. He decided to head back to the club to make sure they were OK.

Groups of kids loitered on the pavement. He didn't recognise any of them and was just about to re-negotiate the bouncers when his girls emerged looking somewhat the worse for wear. He stepped back into the shadows as they said their goodnights and watched them climb into two minicabs. Macy was in the second cab. He hailed the next one and told it to follow.

"If we each give you a fiver, can you pay at the end 'cause you live the furthest?" one of the girls asked. Macy nodded, trying to calculate where this might leave her money-wise.

The girls got out one by one, called: "Ni-ight…" and were gone, leaving her alone.

"Have fun, then?" The driver asked, suddenly friendly. "Been dancing?"

Macy grunted. She was feeling sick, trying to stay focused. Her mum was going to give her hell. Hopefully, she'd be asleep.

They turned into her road and the driver braked hard and pulled up sharply a fair distance from her house.

"Just gimme ten quid and get out quick," he hissed.

Macy leant forward, threw two fivers at him, and jumped out. He floored the pedal and sped off.

She stood on the pavement swaying slightly, looking at the notes in her hand. She hadn't paid her fare and she'd made a profit. The night just got better! She didn't notice the other cab purring behind her, but as she began walking, she was drawn to a commotion up ahead: An ambulance and two police cars with their lights flashing. A knot of nosy neighbours, many in their nightclothes, were rubber necking... her own front door! Their faces were illuminated by the revolving blue lights, as cold and cerulean as a scene from *Close Encounters*.

A stretcher was being carried out of her house with someone on it wrapped in a red blanket. Macy ran forward, suddenly sober, and very scared.

"What's going on!" She shrieked at the paramedic. "Who...*is* that?"

"Stand back please, miss," he answered, but Macy flew at him crying: "That might be my mum! I think it's my MUM!!!"

A policewoman stepped forward and took Macy by the arm, steering her away as the stretcher was slid into the back of the ambulance.

"I want to go with! It might be my MUM!!!" Macy's hand shot up to her mouth and she dry-retched. "What's happened to her?"

The doors were slammed shut and the vehicle sped away, siren wailing.

"Come on, love," the WPC said gently, leading her to a squad car. "We'll follow behind. Can you give me you and your mum's names and tell me if there's anyone you'd like us to call?"

"I..." Macy stammered, "IthinkI'mgoingtobe..." and she launched a torrent of orange spew all down herself and her tarty shoes.

*

In the final analysis, it may have been better if Francine's cry for help had not been heard. The chemicals had dissolved in her stomach then seeped their toxins upwards, through her veins and into her brain. She'd just had enough time to call 999 before she lost consciousness.

Macy sat in the family room in a state of arrested mobility. Her clothes stank and she'd kicked her shoes off and left them in the gutter. The golden bag had survived the onslaught.

She'd answered all the questions except: "Was your mother depressed?" and "Do you have any idea why she may have taken an overdose?" because if she answered that one, she may as well confess to her mother's murder.

The police said they would like to question her again 'in the morning' and left her 'in the capable hands of the nursing staff'. There were obviously more important emergencies to attend to, as they'd gone off mumbling into their walkie-talkies.

Someone had brought her a polystyrene cup filled with hot, sweet tea but she'd left it to get cold. She'd grabbed some paper towels in the loo and wet them to swab herself down. How could such a fantastic evening end like this? She'd been so happy an hour ago and now she was in a hospital waiting room, smelling like a skunk, and waiting…for what? If her mum came around, she'd have a massive go at her – and if she didn't…Macy couldn't get that far.

Maybe this was a bad dream. Maybe she was in bed fast asleep, and she'd wake up in the morning with a thumping headache having learned her limitations regarding vodka. Every action etc.

But what if her mum really had…what they said? No. She couldn't have. She *wouldn't* have. She had *me* to look after. She was probably having her stomach pumped and they'd give her some strong coffee and walk her around for a bit and she'd be fine. But why hadn't they come to tell her anything? How could they leave her – a child! – sitting alone like this?

She stood up, opened the door to the family room and peered out. A nurse hurried past on some urgent mission, leaving an unasked question lingering on Macy's lips. She went back inside. She felt safe there. They'd come in soon enough and ask her to bring her mum a nightie or something or arrange to call a minicab to take them home.

Francine lay behind a curtain in RESUS. They were working on her, like a frenzied orchestra trying to complete an unfinished symphony. Later she would be hooked up to an electroencephalogram to monitor the ionic currents flowing through the neurons of her brain. Small sensors would be attached to her scalp to pick up any electrical signals produced when brain cells send messages to each other. The results would prove inconclusive.

Macy's emotional compass continued to lurch between anger, denial, shock, and disbelief. The azimuth had yet to reach bargaining, guilt, depression, and acceptance, but she suddenly knew she *had* to find her mum. She wrenched open the door and ran out into the corridor. She'd give her a hug and apologise. She'd tell her everything would be alright, and that she…she *loved* her. Yes. She'd tell her mum she loved her and that she'd behave better in future and then everything would be alright. She would tell her that she loved her and say she was sorry, and everything would be alright.

Between Saturday night and Sunday morning, A&E was at its busiest. Paramedics rushed trolleys towards AAU bearing casualties in neck braces or hooked up to drips. Heart rates and blood pressures were called out like bingo numbers. Walking wounded, drunks and the low priority injured hung around or sat catatonic on chairs, like extras in a zombie film. Open-curtained cubicles displayed a freak show of bleeding bodies and broken limbs groaning for attention. It was like the set of *Casualty* following a major RTA.

No one took much notice of the scruffy young girl looking for her mother. Every time she tried to waylay someone, they would say: "Ask at Reception" and hurry past. Eventually, she found the main desk and the distress in her voice drew their attention.

"I need to find my mum," she implored. "Francine Lord? She...we came in earlier – I don't know what they've done with her?"

The triage nurse looked at the notes.

"I thought the police were with you. Have they left? It is best you wait in the relatives' room, dear. We're awfully busy tonight and someone will come and find you when they've got some news."

Macy's head drooped and she caught sight of herself. She was covered in dried sick, barefoot, with smudged make-up, sweaty hair, and probably stinking of booze. No wonder no one wanted to help her. She slunk back from whence she came.

Time ticked past like a detonator – yet still, no news. No good news, but no bad news either. Just no news. And no news was good news, wasn't it?

Macy dropped her head back and stared at the ceiling. The colour, if you could call it that, had been chosen after weeks of consultation with a colour psychologist who decreed that *'certain tones create an emotional, mental and physical response as well as a feeling of cleanliness and healing'*.

It was beige.

For an additional fee, the report had stated that *'natural daylight is key to a hospital environment as it contains all the colours of the spectrum and is absorbed through the eyes and skin. Patients' recovery time is shortened because of being able to look out into nature. Lush greens bring us back to a state of balance & harmony'*.

The room had no windows.

She picked up and discarded a dog-eared magazine. She was dying for a wee but didn't dare leave in case they came to find her. She'd read the notice board and health leaflets without seeing a word, and now her head was pounding. She slumped back against the wall and wondered who to call.

Nanny Jean, obviously, but it was the middle of the night and what would she tell her anyway? Her new friends would all be fast asleep in their king-size beds in their five-star houses and wouldn't give a...

DAD! What about her dad? Then she remembered her Mum had never, for some reason, given her his phone number.

Macy was just about to start pacing again when the door to the family room began to open very slowly. Her eyes widened and she shrank back as a sombre-faced man all dressed in black came in. Macy instinctively covered her face with her hands. It was The Grim Reaper, and she did not want to hear what *he* had to say.

"Macy?" The voice was tentative yet known to her. "Are you alright? I just wanted you to know that I'm here. If you need me."

She peeled open her fingers and Mr Fairclough's familiar features blurred into view. Macy couldn't place him in this context. This was her RS teacher. From school. What was he doing here? At the hospital.

He sat down next to her and patted her hand.

"I...er...I heard what happened. Is there any news at all?"

"Who...who did you hear it from?" she asked. "Who told you?"

"The police rang the school," he lied. "The call was diverted to me. I thought you might need some..."

A door swung open in Macy's heart and all her pent-up emotions tumbled out. She fell against Mr Fairclough and started sobbing.

Mindful of their teacher/pupil relationship, he hesitated in putting his arms around her then changed his mind. The night had gone from bizarre to surreal to back again so what difference would it make if he was caught comforting a distraught teenager in a way *he* would describe as 'caring', but a Court might see as 'taking advantage of a minor'? Frankly, he didn't give a damn.

The girl currently burrowing in the clammy consolation of his cashmere-clad armpit, was in dire need of some TLC, and in the absence of a parent or guardian, with him being the only responsible adult present, the solace should not be misconstrued as 'inappropriate behaviour' but as a basic human response. Having presented, argued, and won his case, Mr Fairclough regretted not having come to the hospital sooner. The poor child had been sitting here for hours, no doubt sick with worry, after suffering the ordeal of being driven in a police car behind an ambulance containing her unconscious mother. She would have been questioned, which would have been traumatic enough, and he should have been here to support her, but instead of asking his cab to follow the police car that was following the ambulance, he'd asked it to take him home. The evening – and all that it entailed – had been a bit much. What with That Curious Incident…which would take time to process, and the fact that he could, if found out, be accused of stalking his pupils, he had gone home to make himself a nice cup of tea. He then phoned around the hospitals to find out which one they'd been taken to, booked another minicab which took time to arrive, and by the time he'd got there a couple of hours had passed, hours during which Macy would have appreciated having him there.

When the ward sister came in a little later, she found the girl asleep on the man's shoulder. She was glad she had someone with her. It was not going to be easy giving her the news.

14

6 months later.

03:46. Pitch dark. Barely daring to breathe, she slides out of bed and tiptoes to the door. Pressing her ear against it, she hears his snoring ebb and flow like gravel in a cement mixer.

She pulls on her jeans, hoodie and denim jacket, rummages for Pandy beneath the covers, and inhales his grubby greyness. His once white fur is tainted with her sweat, snot, and tears. She stuffs him into the front pocket of her rucksack and shoulders the bag. She listens again, senses prickling like nettles.

Come on. You can do this. You MUST do this.

She grits her teeth and twists the doorknob slowly before easing it open. She steps onto the landing. A floorboard winces and she recoils like a discharged gun. A loud snort rockets up from below. Knuckles white, heart hammering, she counts the seconds till the droning starts again, regular and even, then she creeps downstairs, well-practised at avoiding those that creak.

She sneaks along the hallway and leans forward to peer into the front room. Splattered on the sofa, hole-ridden vest stretched across his bulging belly, lays her father, slack-jawed, teeth like weathered gravestones in an abandoned graveyard. Empty beer cans idle on the rug, staining the stains with their remains. The smell of farts and fag-ends toxify the air.

She flattens her hand against the living-room door and pushes it open as far as it will go. He snorts again, grunts, and turns onto his side. She flinches backwards then moves swiftly towards the kitchen.

Macy stands for a second, gazing upward. Her eyes soften and she closes them as if in prayer. She scans the windows to make sure they're tightly closed then turns each knob to maximum and opens the oven door.

She lifts her trainers off the mat and exits through the back door, locking it from the outside. She lets the key slide down the drain, then belts along the alley onto the silent street. She drops down to pull her shoes on, twists the laces into clumsy knots. She charges off, flipping her hood up as a milk float grinds past on its rounds.

Scrambling up the grassy bank, she pounds towards the footbridge that spans the motorway between Leicester and London. Two at a time, she careens across then down the other side, whipping around to face the traffic flow, arm outstretched, thumb cocked. A speeding lorry thunders past gusting dust into her face.

Macy keeps running, thumbing, until finally a truck shudders to a halt. She rushes at it and climbs aboard, folding into the seat to make herself invisible. The trucker stares at her and gets nothing in return.

"Where to, Miss?" he asks, sardonically.

"Wherever you're going…" she mumbles. "Further and faster the better."

She pulls her hoodie more tightly around her face and clutches her knees to stop them trembling. Her body language warns him: *Do not talk to me. Don't even think about it.*

"Put your seatbelt on then," he says and guns the engine. She's not his problem. Delivering on time is.

"Want something to eat?" He asks, fifty miles later, shooting her an enquiring glance. She hasn't spoken, not a syllable. He's tried but given up.

"'m alright, thanks," she answers.

"Well, I've had Sod all since Grimsby – Mars bar and a packet of crisps. I need some grub."

He pulls into the next service station, and they judder to a halt. "You sure?" he asks.

She nods then murmurs: "Thanks."

"Suit yourself. I'll have to lock up, though. Comp'ny rules." She shrugs.

He jumps down from the cab, clicks the remote, hoicks up his trousers and walks towards the caff. Bleeding runaways. Never should have picked her up.

Macy unbuckles her seat belt and caves forward across the dashboard. She holds out her hands then tucks them back under opposite armpits. If only they would stop shaking. She leans back against the seat and gulps mouthfuls of air, trying to calm herself.

The trucker comes back clutching a paper bag. "'ere y'are."

She shakes her head.

"Go on, eat it. It won't *kill* you."

She glares at him and takes the bag, unpeels the wrapper and sinks her teeth into the greasy burger.

They plough on through undulating countryside past farmhouses fiercely guarding the land on which they stand.

At 7 am, the news comes on. Macy stiffens and cranes forward. He turns the volume up. *No news is good news.* She'd thought that once before and look how that turned out.

"So, what you plannin' to do in London, then?" The trucker asks, bored with the boredom.

"V-visit my aunt" she lies.

"Where's that then?"

"West End," she says. "Marble Arch."

"Been there before, 'ave you?"

"Er…yeah…before my mum…"

He dares not ask: "…before your mum what?"

Her head lolls forward and she appears to doze, twitching through video clips of her father stirring and reaching for his fags. The house goes up like a firebomb. *Job done.* She wakes up gagging.

"I'mgonnabe…!"

She heaves into her hand, and he wrenches the steering wheel left, routing the truck off the road, screeching to a halt on the hard shoulder. The driver behind him slams his horn as he speeds past. The sound fades into the future like a howling wolf.

Macy jumps from the cab and retches into the hedge. The trucker climbs down and hovers nearby, ineffectual, shuffling his feet.

"My fault," he consoles, taking responsibility. "Dodgy burger."

She spits up the last of it, rummages in her pockets for a tissue then wipes her mouth on her sleeve. She clambers back inside the cab. They carry on in silence till they reach a filling station.

"Want the toilet?" he asks. He's got kids at home. "Yes, please."

The ghost of a girl who once had peachy skin stares back at her through the dirt-streaked mirror. She stares back, trying to remember how to breathe properly. Maybe she should have topped *herself* instead of them. Would have been easier.

She cups some water in her hand, slurps, gargles, then spits. She wets her hands again and slicks them through her lifeless hair. She tugs her top down and her jeans up and strides back to the truck.

"Let's go," she says with renewed determination.

They hit the road again and arrive in Central London in time for rush hour.

"I can find my way from here," she says, reaching for her rucksack. The driver is about to speak, thinks better of it, then says it anyway.

"Look, love, I don't know what you're runnin' from – or to – but you might wanna think about letting someone know? When kids go missing, their parents worry, y'know what I mean? This, er, this aunt of yours? She expecting you?"

Macy does not want to be questioned, now or ever. When the news breaks, he'll realise soon enough. The least time spent chatting the better.

"I'll be fine," she says brusquely. "Could you please just stop so I can get out?"

"I just thought…"

"Look, I needed a lift, and you gave me a lift. End of. I really must go now."

"Suit yerself," he says again and pulls up where it's safe.

She jumps down from the cab.

"Thanks!" she mouths, as he pulls away.

Another bridge crossed. Or is it burnt?

Head bowed, she goes into the nearest newsagent to scan the headlines. No reports of any fatal gas explosions in the Leicester area does not necessarily mean there haven't been any. It is only 9 am. Papers get printed during the night, don't they?

15

She exits the newsagents and spots a McDonald's across the road. Despite having brought up the last burger, she walks in and orders breakfast: Bacon and egg McMuffin and a chocolate milk shake. The mirror behind the counter reflects the pallid features she witnessed in the filling-station. But she's back in the city now. Easier to disappear. A hot spring of expectation bubbles up inside her. She's free. At least for now.

She heads into a discount store and makes her face up from the samples on display. She considers nicking some, but that would be idiotic, wouldn't it? To be hung for a lamb when you've slaughtered a sheep.

She picks out a brown eyeliner, black mascara, pink lip gloss and a rosy blusher. She digs deep into her bag and peels off a tenner from her bankroll. At the checkout, she adds a shampoo on Special Offer, then returns to the ethnic anonymity of Edgware Road.

Macy turns her back on Marble Arch and heads northwest towards Kilburn. She more or less knows where she is. A bus goes past on the other side of the road heading towards Oxford Street – the same bus she would have caught…Was it only a few months ago that she bought the golden bag? Seems like a lifetime.

A police siren sends her diving into a doorway. *Is this how I must live now? Like a fugitive?*

The squad car speeds past, and a surge of relief overwhelms her. She steps back onto the street and continues on her way.

They shouldn't be after me anyway. All I did was defend my human rights.

She carries on walking for a mile or so until her bag grows cumbersome; exhaustion slows her step. She hasn't slept properly for weeks. How could she? She sees a bench up ahead and sits down. There's a Woolworths opposite and a street market selling exotic fruit and veg. A shoe repairer, a kebab shop, a stationer and a fashion outlet proclaiming Everything £5 line the pavement. An eclectic mix of blacks, whites and Asians mill about. Seems like a good neighbourhood to get lost in.

Macy heaves her bag back onto her shoulder and turns left off the high road. The tall, stucco houses, built for individual occupancy look shabby and rundown. Peeling paintwork and grimy net curtains testify to multiple occupancy. Washing lies draped out to dry on dusty windowsills. She must find somewhere to stay and think about what to do next. This isn't it.

She carries on walking and turns another corner where the properties are smaller, neater – low-built terraced houses. The street is leafy and residential. She stops to swing her bag from one shoulder to the other and something catches her eye: A square white oasis in a desert of glass panes, a hand-written sign in the window:

ROOM FOR RENT APPLY WITHIN

Without hesitating, Macy walks up the path and rings the bell. A curtain twitches in a ground floor window, then a shadow appears behind the frosted glass panel in the front door.

"Who's there?" A lilting Irish voice asks.

"You have a room to rent?"

The door opens a few inches to reveal a short, plump lady in a floral overall and carpet slippers with pompoms on.

"Yes, dear," she says, "I do," and she steps aside to let Macy in.

16

The room had pink cabbage rose paper on the walls and a pink crocheted bedspread on the bed. The house was warm, clean, and tidy and unavoidably chintzy, a complete contrast to the decor and ambience in which she had been living for the past six months. Best of all, though, apart from the kindly landlady, was no sight, sound or smell of men.

Mrs Reilly welcomed the tired-looking girl into the hallway and nodded her approval. A young (albeit rather skinny) female was exactly what she had been hoping for.

"This is the bathroom, dear," she gestured as she showed Macy around. "We only have the one, so we'll have to share, but there is always plenty of hot water. Breakfast can be between seven and nine and will be served in the kitchen."

Macy didn't trust herself to speak. The lump in her throat outdid an ostrich egg. The lady seemed so gentle, so nice. Macy had not been treated with humanity since she knew not when. On reflection, she did know when: The night Mr Fairclough came to the hospital and stayed with her till they got the news.

"And how long might you be thinking of staying?" Mrs Reilly asked.

Although Macy was vague about this – she'd been on her guard for so long – she welcomed the chance to have a normal conversation with someone who seemed like a normal person.

"I'm sorry to ask this, dear," Mrs Reilly went on, "but do you have a little job in the pipeline, for the rent, you see? And might you be able to provide any references? Just to be on the safe side? One can't be too careful these days if you know what I mean?"

Macy felt the panic rise. The make-up she'd applied may have added a few years to her appearance, but she hadn't factored in needing references. Money was not an issue though, and money talked, didn't it? She quickly dug into her rucksack and produced a bunch of notes.

"I don't actually have anything in writing as a reference," she said, "but if I give you three months' rent in advance, would that do?"

It did very well.

"I'll give you a set of keys and leave you to get settled," said Mrs Reilly, tucking the notes into her apron pocket before bustling off downstairs.

Macy closed the door to her new bedroom, unpacked Pandy from her rucksack, curled up on the bed and began to cry, but no matter how many tears washed down her cheeks, they could never wash away the guilt and shame.

Shattered by the events of the past night and day, Macy slept soundly for the first time in months. When she awoke and it all came flooding back, she burrowed into the pillow to negate what she had done. Eventually, she got up, unpacked, showered, washed her hair, and got dressed. She applied fresh make-up, put a few items in the golden bag and went downstairs. It was ten to five in the afternoon and although outwardly calm, her mind was jumping like a field full of grasshoppers. She needed to buy a newspaper. She had to know. But then again, if she didn't see or hear any news, she could kid herself nothing had happened. She might be safe here. No one knew where or who she was, and there were aromas wafting along the passageway that teased her nostrils like a Bistokid's.

She knocked on the kitchen door and went in. Mrs Reilly was at the stove.

"Ah, there you are, my love," she said brightly. "There'll be an Irish stew at half past six, as it's your first night."

"That's *so* kind of you," Macy answered, and she wondered fleetingly, if she and her mother had ever talked like this, she may not be an orphan now.

With the excuse of wanting to find the nearest library, Macy left the house in search of newspapers. Nothing. Not on the front pages anyway. She then decided to actually go to the library where the Notice Board yielded various small ads for babysitters, English tuition and yoga classes. At the bottom, just like the Room for Rent sign – *which Good God wrote this?* – was a typed card that read:

Part-time computer literate male/female required to teach senior citizens computer skills. Apply in person at the front desk.

Macy Lord filled out the forms and bluffed her way through a short interview. Twenty minutes later, reinvented as an '18-year-old student taking a gap year before reading English and Classics at the University of Bristol' was gainfully and miraculously employed.

17

Runaway teenagers only become Missing Persons when someone pesters the police sufficiently to find them. In the absence of such harassment, Macy slipped seamlessly into a well-ordered existence without fuss or bother. The Leicester neighbours were more concerned about the fallout from the blast than what might have happened to that nasty fat bloke and his surly daughter.

A mantle of mild-mannered mundanity settled on Macy's shoulders like a warm and cosy shawl: Breakfast in the kitchen with Mrs R, pigeons cooing on the window ledge, Magic FM crooning on the counter; daytimes in the library handholding struggling seniors through the 'wild world intranet', and after school hours helping children with their revision, or reading to the little ones at a Kiddies' Klub that she'd created.

She ate, slept, worked, read, and wrote, kept her head down and her mouth shut. Her sixteenth birthday came and went with no fuss or fanfare – not so much as a candle or a card. That upset her a bit, but who cared?

Mrs Reilly never bought a newspaper. "Celebrity rubbish and lies!" She opined which supported Macy's denial of what had happened and compounded her false sense of security. At work, her fingers occasionally hovered over the search engine itching to type in the words 'gas explosion in Leicester' but she always resisted. After all, to what end? Some things were better left alone.

Macy was in control of her life except for one thing: Her conscience. It pricked her like the needle on a spinning wheel without the benefit of a 100-year sleep. Some nights, in that twilight zone between restiveness and sleep, the demons came to call, raking the bad memories from the lockups in her brain: Her mother, distraught, desolate, cleaning away the pain, fading like an old fax as her substance slipped away; her father, fat, foul-mouthed and farty, pushing his filthy fingers where they never should have gone.

Some of the scars would not heal but Macy managed them like a chronic skin complaint: She covered them with the ointment of the ordinary and tried not to pick the scabs.

On nights when sleep refused to come and every creak or breath of wind signalled the arrival of the Devil himself, she huddled beneath the blanket like an unwanted foetus, expecting to be aborted at any moment. Every footstep on the pavement or tyre swishing past signified her imminent arrest. She had been free for seven weeks now – Seven Weeks! – but how long could she realistically remain in this bogus bubble before the truth came out and sent her straight to Hell?

Dawn, and the gift of one more day, brought a temporary respite, and with it, Mrs Reilly's cup of English Breakfast tea, steeped with extra sugar, like she knew and understood.

During her time off at the weekend, Macy explored the metropolis. She'd lived in East London with her mother but had never really visited the royal parks and garden squares, the heritage sights, museums, memorials and monuments of the West End and the City. She rarely made eye contact, especially not with those in authority. Uniforms freaked her out – parking attendants and postmen were no exception.

One sunny Sunday afternoon, walking along the south bank of the river Thames, she felt a nudge against her back and whipped around, heart leaping. Something was going on right behind her. A man up close to her shouted:

"Oy! What do you think you're doing?"

He wasn't shouting at her but was challenging another guy who pointed his finger at him like a loaded gun then ran off. Macy couldn't move since the man who'd been shouting was holding on to her rucksack.

"Let go of my bag!" she said angrily, trying to shrug him off.

"That kid was trying to rob you," he explained. "I stopped him. You should wear your bag in front in future."

"Why would I do that?" she retorted.

"So you can keep an eye on your stuff?"

Macy went to walk away then remembered her manners.

"Thanks," she said, "for…"

"No worries," and he fell into step beside her.

Macy stopped. She was not used to company, not this kind, anyway.

"Where're you off to?" he asked amiably. They were heading along Bankside. "I'm not sure," she said warily. "I've never been this way before."

"It's an interesting part of London. Where you are from?"

"Not far. You?"

She'd been quick to learn the subtle art of evasion. People mostly liked to talk about themselves so you could easily turn a question back on them without revealing anything of yourself. Mrs Reilly knew very little about her although they lived under the same roof. In contrast, she knew *everything* about Mrs Reilly: Her childhood in Killarney, how she had met her late husband, where her children lived, how and where the grandkids were.

Macy had no option but to carry on walking, and the young man continued at her side until they reached the Globe Theatre. A promenade performance was taking place on the forecourt. Macy hung back to watch.

"Dispute not with her: She is lunatic."

She smiled in recognition. *Richard III*. And that had always been her favourite line! Although she tried not to dwell on it, she regretted the loss – or theft – of her education. But at least now she had free access to the library. There were times, though, when she hankered to be back in class, especially with Mr Fairclough.

He would have loved this, she thought, as they stood listening to the players. An unexpected spasm squeezed her heart. What an idiot she'd been, plotting to impress Zenith and her useless bunch of frenemies. She should have concentrated on her studies better.

A lifelong dream of Macy's had been to see a Shakespeare play at Stratford – upon – Avon, but this was almost as good. She stood watching with the young man at her side and when it finished, he turned and asked if she fancied a pizza. Her immediate reaction to say "No!" came out, to her surprise, as: "OK!"

*

Lee Watkins decided not to tell the pretty young girl what he did for a living. Coppers didn't always get the best press: People either acted guilty around them even when they hadn't done anything, or thought they were a bunch of power-crazed tossers. He'd heard it said that anyone who actually *wanted* to join the force should not be allowed to. He'd joined in memory of his father who'd given his life for a few quid stolen from an off licence.

In the aftermath of the tragedy, you would have thought becoming a police officer was the last thing on his mind, but Lee felt an obligation to continue the good works his father had started and try to make a better fist of them.

Macy wanted to go halves on the pizza, but Lee insisted on paying. They left the restaurant, and he walked her north across Tower Bridge. They stopped to admire the view. The sun was setting, and the river glowed and rippled in the evening light. It seemed only natural for him to lean in to kiss her.

Her reaction was so alarmed you'd have thought he'd sprouted fangs and was heading for her neck. Her eyes widened in terror, and she literally jumped backwards away from him. He held his hands up in surrender.

"Whoa! OK. Bit soon? I don't bite, you know," and then with irony: "I suppose that means you don't want to meet up again?"

Macy seemed floored by this suggestion. It was not a question she could field with another question.

"We had a good time today, didn't we?" Lee reasoned. "After I *saved you* from the mugger?" He flashed her his most engaging smile.

Macy bit her lip and sort of nodded. "Then please may I call you?"

She shrugged one shoulder, shuffled her feet, and said she didn't have a phone. "You haven't got a mobile?" he asked disbelievingly.

"No. Y-e-es." She hesitated. "But sometimes I forget to…to charge it."

"Well give me the number anyway and I'll keep trying."

Macy stared at him uncomprehendingly. Why was he being so nice to her? They had had a *nice* afternoon. It was *nice* to be in his company, and it made a *nice* change from Mrs Reilly, the school kids, and the oldies. The conversation had been a bit stilted, but that said more about her than it did about him.

"07605 830831," she blurted.

"I'll be in touch then," he said without writing it down. "Safe home."

And he turned and walked away.

Interesting, thought Lee, as he headed south across the river. Innocent with just a touch of guilty.

18

It didn't matter that she had given him a fake number: He'd known that straight away. No mobiles began with 076 – that prefix was reserved for pagers. He didn't need the number anyway because when she'd opened her rucksack, he'd spotted the plastic label holder with her address on it.

Mrs Reilly had insisted: "…in case you ever lose it or get lost yourself, being new to London 'n all."

Macy was not keen to have the shamrock shaped luggage tag Mrs R had offered hanging off her bag, but she did agree to writing the address down and keeping it tucked inside. When she'd needed a tissue to wipe her nose when Lee was playing the name game, he'd scanned the address into his mental phonebook.

The name 'Honour' had been a paradox on her part, a sick take on the commandment 'Honour thy father and thy mother'. When Lee Watkins had introduced himself properly in the restaurant, he thought she was joking when she'd refused to reciprocate.

"Guess!" she had said, by way of a delaying tactic.

As they waited for their pizzas, Lee went through the alphabet from A to Z. He made her giggle with his off-the-wall suggestions ranging from Amaryllis to Zinnia with Edelweiss, Pyracantha and Wisteria thrown in.

"You sound like you've swallowed a gardening catalogue and you're regurgitating it plant by plant!" Macy teased. She couldn't remember when she'd laughed so much – she couldn't actually remember when she'd laughed at all.

Eventually, she came clean – or didn't – and said her name was Honour Lawless – her own private joke. She had no siblings, which was true, neither was she much in touch with her parents as they lived: "In Spain, near Alicante." Since 'bragging about self' was man's default setting, she managed to field his other questions with questions of her own.

Tucked up in bed that night, Macy replayed the day and tried to analyse her mixed feelings. Receiving *positive* male attention was a new experience for her and she would be lying if she said she had not enjoyed it. He'd saved her from having her bag rifled and then treated her to a meal in a restaurant. She'd felt protected and special – a different kind of special to what her father called her. She didn't dare take these positive thoughts further, however, as having a 'boyfriend' was hardly on her radar. How could she? She was…she wasn't good enough.

Notwithstanding this, Macy's research informed her that if she allowed her father's actions to define her, it meant that he had won. It was bad enough he had ruined her past; she didn't need him corrupting her present or polluting her future.

'Happy' was not an emotion Macy was familiar with, yet this afternoon, a tall, good-looking young man had come into her life and made her feel…could she even describe it? 'Happy' was the only word that came to mind. Plus, he seemed genuine. Of course, Mrs R and the people at the library were also nice, but Lee seemed like a different kind of nice: A Mr Fairclough kind of nice.

Then, as so often happened, she flipped it on its head and the negativity kicked back in. What was the point in even thinking about him? She would never hear from him again and that was probably for the best. She wasn't entitled to this, and besides, what did she have to offer? She was nothing but a sixteen-year-old murderer.

Macy continued her orgy of self-flagellation until eventually, she drifted down through the first layer of sleep.

The bridge stretched out before her like a long black ribbon spanning a canyon that separated day from night. She teetered on the dark side, fearful of the crackling noise below: The sound of an enormous fire. There were trees on the light side, lush green trees with flowers at their roots, swaying gently against a bright blue sky. Rabbits and squirrels gambolled around the trunks and bluebirds chirruped in the branches: The scene from *Bambi* before it all went wrong.

Every time Macy set foot on the bridge to walk towards the light, it creaked and swayed like a schooner in a storm, threatening to plunge her into Hell below. She somehow managed, one step at a time, to almost reach the other side, then some unknown force dragged her back. She could smell burning –

were the flames already at her feet? – and then she was falling…falling into noise! What was that strident sound?

Macy awoke, wet with sweat, nostrils flaring. There was a charred smell in the air – the fires of hell! – but then she realised – as often happened – that Mrs Reilly had set the smoke alarm off grilling the breakfast bacon. Relief washed over her, and she shook her head to erase the dream. Lee re-entered her mind and she berated herself for not having given him the right number.

*

"I'm sorry, but there's nobody called Honour at this address."

Mrs Reilly was just about to hang up when Macy came skidding out the kitchen like Roadrunner and grabbed the phone.

"Hello?" she gasped.

"Hey," said Lee. "You free this weekend?"

They saw each other most Sundays after that. He'd had to cajole at first, and he was taking it a lot slower than his primal urges dictated. She often seemed on edge, especially when he became tactile, but he made allowances knowing this was no ordinary girl.

One Sunday, they had been for a walk in Regent's Park then to an Italian restaurant for lunch. Mrs Reilly was away, visiting relatives in Ireland. Lee knew this, and Macy/Honour knew that he knew. She had drunk a glass of wine with her pasta – which broken *Thou Shalt Not* was that? – and she was actually quite tipsy. They'd been 'going out' for a month now and something had to give or be given back. She wasn't sure she could. It would be too traumatic, too distressful, too…the thought of it made her shudder.

Lee paced around her bedroom, thrumming his thigh in time to the music. He couldn't decide whether to make a move or not. So far, all he'd managed was one chaste kiss: Every time he thought *tonight's the night*, she'd freeze, leaving him edgy and frustrated. Was it possible that she just didn't fancy him? He knew he was good-looking – he saw that in the mirror – and he'd never had problems with women before. OK, she was young, 18 (*16 actually*), but he really liked her and was sure she liked him. He'd studied enough psychology to know there was more going on behind those baby blues than she was letting on.

Elusion was a game she played. Whenever he asked her a personal question, the shadow of something off beam flickered in her eyes. Why was she so reticent to engage? What had happened that she did not want to share? That was what intrigued him.

"D'you want a cup of tea?" Macy asked trying to defuse the tension in the room. She could hear Lee's mind ticking like a time bomb and she knew it would soon explode. She never should have invited him back. She felt trapped, and it frightened her.

He sat down on her bed and held out his hand.

"Come here," he said, patting the bedspread.

She took the long way around – which wasn't easy in a 12' x 9' room – and alighted near him like a nervous butterfly. Lee floated his hand over her lap. Macy tapped it away.

"Look," he said, standing up. "I'm a normal red-blooded male. You're a pretty gorgeous girl. I've wanted you since the first moment I saw you. That's what happens when X meets Y! I know you've been hurt or whatever – and I have tried to make allowances for that, but I just don't know how to be around you anymore."

Macy bit her lip. She went to stand up, but Lee caught her by the wrist. "If you won't tell me what happened, how can I help you get over it?"

"It's not that simple…"

He pulled her harshly towards him.

"You're driving me nuts," he rasped into her face. "How much longer do I have to wait? Either this moves forward, or we're done."

Macy jerked free with a force that surprised them both. "Then we're done!"

She stormed over to the farthest corner of the room, turned her back on him and folded her arms across her chest. Why should she give him the satisfaction of seeing her cry let alone anything else!

Lee got up, yanked the door open and left.

As he marched off down the street, he vowed to find the bastard who had done this to her and when he did, he'd give him a bloody good thrashing.

19

Macy lay on her bed snuffling Pandy, trying to ease an ache she had never felt before. Losing her mother, loathing her father – these were emotions she was learning to deal with. She would lock them in a box, but they'd creep out sometimes through the gaps in the hinges. She let them rampage through her brain until they found their own level but this…this lovesickness? This was different: A gut-wrenching intensity that clawed at her heart, shredded it into pieces and fried the pieces in boiling oil.

For the first time ever, she understood the power of all those wretched love songs. She asked Mrs Reilly if she minded retuning the dial because she could not cope with Melody FM anymore. How come Barry Manilow and Whitney Houston knew exactly how she was feeling? They sang every song, every line, every lyric, just for her. How could they be so cruel?

If all it took to get Lee back was to sleep with him, then why couldn't she just do it? People did it all the time…and at least with him it might be tender. But if she made that call, she would have to follow it through. And where was it written that females had to offer sex in exchange for food?

He'd probably met someone else by now – isn't that what blokes did? Plenty more fish n' all that? He was probably shagging someone right now and anyway, why *should* she give in? If he couldn't just enjoy her company and respect her boundaries, then was it worth pursuing?

As often happened, Mr Fairclough came to mind. How she wished she could speak to him, let him know what had happened, how her life was now. He had supported her through so much turmoil: The only person who seemed to empathise. He had encouraged her when no one else cared, taught her how to process stuff, write it down. In fact, maybe she should be writing now.

*

Thursday 5 September 1986

Lee Watkins lied to me as I had lied to him, so I guess in that way, we were even. I'd added 2 ½ years to my age and given him a false name and told him I'd come to London to get over a bad relationship.

Although that wasn't a million miles from the truth, it wasn't the truth, the whole truth and nothing but the truth. In fact, it was nothing like the truth. It was just an excuse to delay the inevitable, i.e., the progress of our friendship into a relationship. I said I'd been mucked about, and I wasn't prepared for it to happen again, and he said he'd never muck me about and he'd leave it to me to dictate the pace. Yeah. Right.

It was OK for a while, in fact more than OK. I couldn't wait for the weekends, and he seemed happy to just hang out, go to films, to a museum or for a meal. He'd never let me pay although I could have, and it felt really grown up to be 'dating'. I began to trust him like a proper boyfriend. He did try it on once or twice, but my reaction was so obvious that luckily, he backed off. The silly thing was I did quite fancy him. Or at least I thought I did. I didn't really get that whole male/female/sex thing – it was ingrained in my psyche as something dirty, painful, and wrong.

It wasn't so much his attitude that upset me, it was more the fact that he, like my father, thought it was his right. Although I didn't have any sexual experience as such, I knew there must some sort of technique beyond what had happened to me that made women willing. I was blocked by what had gone before and Lee's persistence had the reverse effect to what he hoped, blindsiding me into a horrible sense of déjà vu. *I just could not get past that and although I felt sick at the thought of losing him, I felt sicker at the thought of having to give him what he wanted.*

Macy concluded not to phone Lee. What was the point? She was riding the waves of her misery one breaker at a time, praying her little skiff wouldn't get dashed against the rocks and may, someday, wash up somewhere safe.

20

The Leicester Police Department failed to connect the dots between the 'Honour Lawless' Lee was researching and the Macy Lord she was. Missing Persons for around the time 'Honour' had moved to London shed no light on the matter and no one who matched her description had been reported lost or stolen.

In the way the internet has of unpeeling the layers, Lee found himself researching births and deaths. There was a Hannah Dawson born in 1988 in Fife but that clearly wasn't her. He clicked on one or two other names – one being an Anna Lawes, but she would only be about 15. His Honour was 18 and had been in London for…how long exactly? Had he ever known?

He regretted his impetuous exit from her bedroom that day because it denied him any chance of further questioning. He could, of course, just pick up the phone, apologise and promise to be good in future but the trouble was, he didn't want to be good in future.

She was one girl in a city of millions, but he wanted her – quite a lot, as it turned out. And he needed to get laid. He'd been horny for over a month now and if she wasn't going to deliver the goods, he'd find someone who would.

Lee got up and paced the floor then sat back down again. He fancied a cigarette but had long since given up. He poured himself a shot of tequila and knocked it back. How dare she refuse him? He'd have her if it were the last thing he did.

Later that night, Lee lay on his bed replaying their conversations.

- Honour always clammed up when he asked about her family.
- First time she said they were near Alicante, second time Costa Brava and that they'd 'sort of lost touch'.

To be a good liar, you had to have a good memory. Had they really lost touch? And if so, why would a lovely girl like that fall out with her parents? Unless it was over that bloody bloke?

Lee went back to his scrolling, and it was past 2 am when he shut it down again. It was irritating not being able to crack this, especially with his detective training. With a goal of DCI or even Super, you would think he'd be able to find out where some stupid girl had come from without this much hassle.

He lay in the dark wondering if she was worth it. He'd probably go off her once he'd had her – that was his usual MO – but deep down he was annoyed for having broken own rule: *Always let the girl dictate the pace.* She'd made it perfectly clear she didn't want to though, but did women ever really mean what they said? If he could fathom that, he could fathom anything.

In spite or maybe because of his frustration, Lee sought and found a lonely relief before oblivion took pity on him and flipped his switch to OFF.

*

The obvious starting point in any investigation is to get a photo of the suspect. Every time Lee had tried to take 'Honour's' picture in the past, she had slammed her hand over the lens or covered her face and turned away. He hadn't noticed any photos in her room, but that hadn't exactly been the main thing on his mind. As Macy left for work the next morning, she heard raised voices coming from across the street. It wasn't unusual for some of the neighbours to be shouting, so she ignored it and carried on her way.

Lee, lurking in the shelter of someone's porch, jumped when the front door of his haven was flung open, and the inhabitant yelled:

"Whadd'ya think you're doing? Gedoutofit or I'll call the filth!"

His desire to reply: "I *am* the filth!" – was silenced by a kick up the arse that sent him sprawling headlong down the path. Shocked and winded, he remained there for a few moments before getting up and running down the street. 'Honour' had disappeared around the corner. He legged it in the opposite direction hoping to head her off up the road. For someone supposedly trained in 'maintaining discretion during investigative observation', he'd certainly made a pig's bollock of this one.

21

Since becoming a man 'of the flesh' rather than 'of the cloth', Airey's only regret was that he had not done it sooner and more often. A passing interest in the priesthood had been rejected at the age of twenty-one as too binding for a man with a yet unexplored libido. Teaching Religious Studies seemed a reasonable alternative, but the mercury on the barometer of his job satisfaction was now hovering somewhere between Severe Northeast Gales and Heavy Snow. His star pupil's sudden departure had left him feeling non-productive and superfluous.

So, if not teaching, where would he set his vocational sights? Personal Development? Creative Consultancy? What did those labels mean? Should he aim higher, or better still, lower? Help the underbelly of society his pupils might turn into if left to their own devices?

But before he did anything, Airey was determined to take a break and re-invent himself because a limp handshake and faded corduroys did not a 'cool dude' make. He would work the year out then hand in his notice and spread his wings in search of cred. Oh, and he would change his name. To Aaron. That sounded better for a start.

*

Sunday 8 September 1986
Six months since D-D-Day. Dad. Dead. Day. Dead. Dad. Day.

Instead of fading with the passage of time, that hideous morning continues to haunt me – what in God's name was I thinking? With cold-blooded premeditation, I set out to murder my father and not only do I think I succeeded, but I also appear to have got away with it. By now, I should be banged up in a young offenders' institution with other killers and delinquents.

Although the Bible says 'an eye for an eye and a tooth for a tooth' *did I really have the right to do what I did?*

I keep thinking about walking into the nearest police station and handing myself in. Maybe that will bring me some peace because I don't know how much longer my conscience can take it. Of course, with hindsight, I should have reported him when it was all happening and not allowed myself to become his victim but then I'd probably have had to suffer some long-drawn-out court case and for sure, I'd have ended up in care.

At least this way, I have my freedom. But is this freedom or another kind of prison? I've been sentenced to live as sure as my father was sentenced to die. And I effectively murdered my mother as well, and as for poor Nanny Jean, the heart attack that killed her could well have been brought about by all those credit card bills!!!

It all plays in my head like a game of cat and mouse. I had wanted them dead and now they are dead. (NOT Nanny Jean, of course! Poor Nanny Jean...) My mother no longer nags me, my father's no longer a threat. I can rest easy in my bed, but do I? Do I? Hell.

I wish I didn't miss Lee so much. I really enjoyed our time together, why did he have to be such an arse? He treated me like a proper person, made me feel accepted and acceptable. And who am I now – some kind of child/woman living a fake life? I've told so many people that I'm 18 and my parents live in Spain, I almost believe it. Even the lies I tell aren't true! The only person who knows (most of) the truth is Mr Fairclough. I really miss him. I wonder what he's doing now.

Today is NOT a good day. I'm a 16-year-old orphan whose childhood was ransacked with all the finesse of a pirate rifling through a treasure chest. And it's Sunday again. The most depressing day of the week. Mrs R's back in Ireland and I've never felt more alone. No wonder they called it Bloody Sunday.

Macy let her diary slide to the floor and pulled the pillow over her head, trying to suffocate her thoughts. Eventually around lunchtime, she got up and faltered to the window. She eased the curtain aside: The sky sagged overhead, grey, and grumpy, spitting silvery skewers of rain onto the street below.

No point in showering, no point in getting dressed. Nothing to get up for, nowhere to go, nothing to look forward to. She went to the wardrobe and got out the golden bag. Smoothing her hand over the surface was like stroking a much-loved dog or cat. She hadn't used it in ages…last time was when she and Lee had gone out for that Italian – the last time she'd seen him. She didn't even wander the city anymore – hadn't done that since the day they'd met.

Macy got back into bed, Pandy under one arm, the bag under the other and there she remained for the rest of the day.

Next morning, when she arrived at the library, she was unaware of the hooded man in the doorway opposite focusing a telephoto lens in her direction.

22

Lee drove up to Leicester with the photos. Starting in the city centre, he began to circle in a half-mile radius, targeting all the schools in the area. Mostly he drew blanks, but late in the afternoon, a teacher chatting to a caretaker who was about to lock up for the day, took the photo from the good-looking young Metropolitan Police officer and exclaimed: "That's Macy!"

"Honour," said Lee. "Her name is Honour."

"No. It is Macy. Macy Lord. It's definitely her. Poor kid. She'd come up from London – her mum was in a coma or may have even died – and she transferred here to live with her father After the accident, no one really knew what happened to her. They…"

"What accident?"

"Her father."

"He lives in Spain, doesn't he?"

"Not that I know of." She looked at her watch. "I've got fifteen minutes. Come through to the staff room, officer. It's quite a story."

She reached into a filing cabinet and brought out a sheet of newsprint. She handed it to Lee who noted the date, scanned the headline then read the full article:

Local Man Has Lucky Escape

A local man escaped unhurt from an explosion caused by a gas cooker left on overnight at his house in Bridge Street.

Fire crews were called shortly before 8:35 BST following the report of a loud explosion. There was no fire but 50% of the rear of the terraced property was destroyed and there was 'significant structural damage' to the front of the house.

The man, in his mid-40s, was carried to safety by firefighters and transmitted to the hospital by ambulance.

Station manager Roger Davies said: "The man usually sleeps upstairs but had been drinking and was asleep on the ground floor at the time of the explosion. Had he been in his bedroom directly above the kitchen, it could have been a very different outcome. Fortunately, no one else was in the house."

The explosion not only caused major structural damage to the house but also to the dividing walls to the adjacent properties.

"Our crew was able to quickly assess the scene, help the man to safety and isolate the gas supply. This is a very stark reminder of the danger gas can cause. People should always check that all gas appliances and cylinders are fully turned off before they go to bed or leave their house."

Lee processed the information as he headed back down the M1.
- Mother comatose or deceased? Accident? Overdose?
- Girl living with father. Alcoholic?
- Gas explosion. Accident? Intention?
- Girl goes missing.
- Girl reappears in London.
- Girl evasive, blocked, unable to engage physically.

As far as Lee was concerned, it was a no-brainer: The story had child abuse smeared all over it.

*

When Neville 'The Devil' had come around in the ambulance, he did not know what had hit him. It had, in fact, been:

→ A chunk of plaster from the front room ceiling.
→ A three-branch chandelier from a sale at Argos.
→ A shard of broken glass from a framed poster of Leicester City Football Club.

Apart from an ominous swelling of the cerebral cortex, multiple cuts and contusions, loss of hearing in his left ear, loss of vision in his right eye, a dislocated shoulder, and a shattered femur from being flung off the sofa onto the tiled fireplace, Neville Lord was also diagnosed with cirrhosis of the liver, type two diabetes, kidney malfunction and prostate cancer. The four latter ailments had been present but undetected at the time of admission.

He drifted in and out of consciousness for the first twenty-four hours until they put him in an induced coma to stabilise the bleed on his brain.

The explosion had shot the gas stove high into the air, blowing its door off and landing it face down on the kitchen floor. Gas Board officials and accident inspectors, bogged down with admin and bureaucracy, tried to absolve the company from blame to maintain customer confidence, playing down details of the event to avoid them having to pay large amounts in compensation. Because of their negligence and inattention to detail in the aftermath:

"I thought you'd checked that!"

"No! I thought you were doing it!"

The status of the gas taps was never verified.

Explosions happened all too often on post-war Jerry-built housing estates and the verdict of 'Accident Due to Gas Leak' covered a multitude.

The driver of the bulldozer employed to raze the remains of the property prior to it being rebuilt, scooped up the mangled cooker and transported it to the metal salvage dump. He didn't notice anything unusual – but then he wasn't looking. His missus was giving him brain ache about their neighbour's dog pissing on her petunias, and it was all he could do to manoeuvre the excavator with one hand and hold his mobile to his ear with the other.

It was inconsistencies like these that caused an item which would otherwise have become Exhibit A in an attempted murder case to find its way into a crusher and be lost forever.

23

As the next fortnight ended, Macy reached a conclusion. She'd batted the idea back and forth like a ping pong ball, but every time it landed, it made a hollow sound. Like the story of her life, it had a hole in it. The fact was: She could not cope with the guilt any longer which, instead of diminishing, grew like a malignant beanstalk. If she did not act now, she may as well have stayed with him and taken the rough with the rougher.

She'd read somewhere that when suicides finalise their death plans, they feel a sense of relief almost a euphoria, knowing their despair is finite and the end is within their control. She was not about to go that route, but she did feel relieved at having made the decision. She'd committed the crime; she must do the time.

When Macy arrived home from the library that day, she called out a brighter than usual "Hello!" to Mrs Reilly. The latter crossed herself like the good Catholic she was and praised all the saints for lifting her little lodger out of the doldrums.

Macy declined a cup of tea and hurried upstairs. She knew Mrs R was watching *Neighbours* and would not come out of the living-room for at least half an hour. She washed her hands and face and changed into a pair of black trousers and a black top. In a rare moment of observance, she looked skywards and thanked her mother and Nanny Jean for guiding her to this decision. She considered throwing in a *Forgive him, Father, for he knew not what he did* but concluded that he knew very well what he was doing.

Macy packed all her belongings in her holdall, left Mrs Reilly her key, a week's money, and a note of apology. She looked around the rosy room with a deep sigh of regret, shouldered the bag and crept out of the house.

Had she decided to accept the offer of a cup of tea, and had Lee opted not to discuss his dilemma with a colleague, they may never have pitched up in the same place, at the same time, on the same day.

24

When the summer term ended on 14 July, the newly renamed AARON Fairclough walked away with no regrets. He had paid his dues to the field of education, tripped across its surface, and got his boots muddy. Handshakes and Good Lucks were all he carried with him as he left the staffroom and exited Saint Columba's for the last time.

His colleagues had been polite about his departure; his students less so. That relationship tended to be fit for purpose, with a deeper commitment on one side than the other. Emotions only escalated if one party wound the other party up sufficiently for a higher discipline to become involved. All the striving he had put into trying to make their shallow lives a little deeper had been about as much use as a Kleenex umbrella. Except for one pupil…but who knew where she was now?

He arrived home, dumped his stuff in the hall and went to graze at the fridge. There was little to tempt him except a packet of ham, a chunk of cheddar and a vintage bottle of Thomas Hardy's ale. He chose the latter, prised off the cap and took a long pull.

I hope I've done the right thing, he thought, as he untied his laces, removed his shoes, and stretched out on the sofa. A bit cavalier, isn't it, to leave one job before securing another? Yet wasn't there something thrillingly liberating about *not* having a plan? It was the first time in his life he had experienced such autonomy. The old Airey would never have taken such a leap: He'd never been out of 'the system', having progressed in an orderly fashion from playgroup to nursery to pre-school to junior school to senior school to university to teaching. Baby Airey's arrival had come as quite a surprise to his parents. His 47-year-old mother, Gwen, and 52-year-old father Egbert, had resigned themselves to a life of cats (hers) and tropical fish (his), relentlessly trying to keep the two apart. She had accepted her infertility with the same resignation that she accepted her husband's occasional request for 'bedroom unpleasantness'.

When her monthlies ceased abruptly, she expected hot flushes and mad moods, but instead she found herself 'with child'.

Fairclough Senior was even less prepared for the scrawny scrap who landed in his lap. He ignored him for the first four years, occasionally regaling him, if pressed, with passages from The Good Book or excerpts from *Noddy in Toyland* and *The Hobbit*. The BBC Home Service and a comprehensive collection of scratchy classical LPs were delivered to the infant's ears via a 1940s Marconi radiogram veneered in walnut, though he may have been more roundly educated had his father also enjoyed rugby and Formula One racing.

The Church had always been a focal point with all the festivals observed, if not with fervour – an emotion markedly absent at 17 Willoughby Avenue – but with a degree of quiet dedication. Young Airey managed to avoid the persecution suffered by many choir boys and it was not until That Curious Incident…that he realised his visceral awakening needed to be explored further.

Aaron muddled through his first free weekend in the usual way: He did a supermarket shop, organised his laundry, listened to his favourite programmes on Radio 4 including *The Archers* Omnibus and caught up on his reading. He was relieved not to have to waste valuable leisure time ploughing through the lamentable scribblings of his unlamented Year 11s.

He wished, not for the first time, that he had asked Macy for a copy of her famous essay: *The Goddess with the Thousand and One Vaginas*. Just thinking about it made him stir…Could he be nostalgic for that seminal morning? He had always acknowledged that the girl had bigger balls than he did.

He recalled again that complex night: First at the club and then in the car park and the sequence of events that followed: The hospital, the surreal and dramatic piece of live theatre unfolding before him, that culminated in her falling asleep on his shoulder. His heart quickened as he recalled the inner turmoil he had felt as he'd dared, not once, but twice, to hover his lips mere millimetres above her hair, close enough to inhale the *Very Berry* scent of her.

Going into the nearest branch of The Body Shop and sniffing all the products to rekindle that night could have been considered creepy, but he had become a man that night and a man had to do what a man had to do – even if he had to do it by himself.

When Macy had awoken in the early hours of that traumatic Saturday night/Sunday morning to find his shoulder underneath her tousled head, she'd shown neither surprise nor embarrassment. She had simply said: "Thanks for being here."

He may have imagined a lot of things, but he had not imagined that indefinable something that had passed between them.

When the doctor followed the ward sister into the family room and told her that, with regret and despite their best efforts, her mother had suffered severe brain damage from which she may not recover, she took the news with silent stoicism. When they asked if she would like to see her, she shook her head fearfully, afraid of what she might find.

"Are you sure, Macy?" Mr Fairclough.

She thought about it for a moment then took hold of his hand and said: "Come with me, please?"

And so, a different bond had been forged: An egalitarian grown-up bond broken only when she'd left the school abruptly and moved up to Leicester to live with her father leaving no forwarding address.

Although it was officially the summer holidays, Aaron's second day off opened its maw to him like a yawning shark. He woke up with no idea what to do with himself. 'Retire from Teaching' had not exactly been at the top of his 'To Do' list.

Lighten up! He told his reflection in the bathroom mirror as he flossed and brushed his teeth. *Why does everything have to be so regimented?* Although he hated the cliché; 'Today is the first day of the rest of your life', an unexpected frisson ran through him as he realised that:

A. He did not have a Plan B and
B. He did not even have a Plan A

The first thing he decided to do was to shave off his silly facial fuzz, originally intended to make him appear older, wiser, and more authoritarian. All it had done was turn him into a laughingstock as it never managed to attain the hirsute heights of a handle-barred pilot in the RAF, creeping instead along his top lip like a millipede stalking a caterpillar. And so, in the spirit of New Man, New Life, he shaved it down the drain.

Aaron was surprised at how different he looked and how green his eyes appeared with his face clean shaven. He stood back from the mirror dabbing himself dry and nodded approvingly.

With a face matching his age rather than his IQ, he opened his wardrobe for a sort-out. He discarded all the knitted ties, Fair Isle tank tops, checked waistcoats, twill jackets and paisley cravats, and folded them neatly into a black rubbish sack to drop back at the local charity shop. He then dressed in the mufti of beige chinos and a white shirt and walked into a hairdressing salon, where he had himself a modern haircut which the crimper assured him would "bring 'em flocking", whoever 'em were.

As Aaron continued down the high street, a flyer in the window of The Flight Centre caught his eye.

Kolkata – £359

Calcutta! Good grief! Probably the last place on earth anyone would want to go visit in July but how exotic!

It occurred to him that if he walked into this travel shop right now and put his money down, he could be on another continent, culture, and time zone quicker than you could say, "Where's the nearest Job Centre?"

And maybe, he thought, fifteen minutes later as he punched his pin number into the credit card machine, he might even come across Ling and his naughty Goddess made flesh!

25

Lee knew full well that he could have arranged to meet his mate Jordan anywhere other than just around the corner from where Honour – *tsk*, Macy – lived. Conscious of the emotion her proximity provoked, he walked towards the pub thinking – not of the girl who had played him like a harp – but of the imminent pleasure of a nice cold pint.

As it turned out, serendipity and circumstance played their parts in pointing the star-crossed 'lovers' in the same direction: The corner of Montrose Avenue and Salusbury Road just along the pavement from Queen's Park Tube.

When Lee saw Macy striding purposefully towards him with her holdall slung over her shoulder, his first instinct was to duck into a doorway.

Macy didn't notice him. She was a girl on a mission: To where she was going, why she was going there, and what she was going to do when she arrived. Had she lost track of this focus even for a second, she may have wavered and hurried home.

Just short of where Lee stood, she turned and hurried up the steps leading into the red brick building with the blue lantern above the door.

At that precise moment, something went off in Lee's head and he lunged forward, overtook her on the top step and grabbed her firmly by the shoulders.

Tuesday 2 October 1986

I didn't really mean to whack him so hard, but he scared the living daylights out of me, he really did. I thought I was being mugged, right there on the steps of the cop shop! I surprised myself the way my hand shot out as I never thought I could punch anyone as hard as that. Lee yelped and stumbled backwards down the steps. He tried to save himself, but his arms were flailing like a deranged windmill. If it hadn't been so awful, it might have been funny. A passer-by caught hold of him as he landed and twisted his arm behind his back to make a citizen's arrest. Lee was struggling to get free, clutching the eye I'd thumped while trying to get out of the arm lock. I just stood there not knowing what to do then I heard myself say: "It's OK. I know him. Let him go." I went back down the steps to see if he was alright. I was livid. It had taken months of soul-searching to do what I was about to do, and he'd gone and ruined it. Still, I suppose I owed him an apology.

"Lee! I'm so sorry! I didn't mean to...God! Are you OK?" He was finding it hard to blink let alone talk.

"Oh no...your eye!"

It was swelling up like an aubergine and tears were pouring down his cheek. "Don't worry. I'll...Ooh! That hurts! Remind me to teach you how to punch properly. You fight like a girl."

"I am a girl."

His mobile rang and he grappled in his pocket to find it, wincing as his wrist reacted to the pain.

"No problem, mate," he said through gritted teeth. "We'll do it some other time."

The confession Macy had so carefully rehearsed tumbled through her mind like an upturned Scrabble board. She wondered fleetingly whether to rush back up the steps and just get on with it, but her feet refused to move. Lee dropped his phone back in his pocket, his other hand still clamped over the injured eye.

"I need a steak and a stiff drink," he groaned theatrically. "But not necessarily in that order."

Macy stood there not knowing how to react.

"Come on," he said taking her by the elbow. "There's something I..."

"I can't," Macy answered shrugging him off. "I've got to..."

"No!" Lee said resolutely. "You haven't got to ANYTHING!"

"But you don't know..."

"I *do*," he insisted as he steered her towards The Salusbury. "Trust me, Macy!"

She stopped dead. He'd called her Macy. How in hell...?

"Come on. I'll explain over a..."

He'd been about to say 'glass of wine' but said 'orange juice' instead.

Macy felt like she'd been hijacked. All that lovelorn longing – what a load of rubbish! She didn't even fancy him with his short-cropped hair and puffy eye, yet she allowed herself to be led into the pub because she wanted to know what he knew and how he knew it. She sat down stiffly on a low stool while he went to the bar.

The barman whistled appreciatively.

"Blimey!" he said. "I'd hate to see the other bloke!"

"She's over there, mate!" and they both laughed.

Lee returned to the table with the drinks. Macy narrowed her eyes at him. He positioned the glasses carefully on two beer mats and sat down on the stool opposite.

Lee took a long slug of his lager and cleared his throat. Macy looked at her juice as if it was cat's piss. He'd been happy to buy her alcohol before. Why not now when she really needed it?

Neither of them spoke. If he was wondering *where* to begin, she was wondering *how*.

Lee eventually broke the ice.

"I'm a police officer," he announced.

"And I'm a murderer," she countered.

They eyeballed each other for a moment and Lee took another slug of his beer, buying time before he spoke again.

"You're *not* actually," he said, eventually. "He's not dead."

Macy shot to her feet knocking over the table and upturning the drinks.

When Lee replayed the scene later, all he could think of was her horrified face as she fled from the pub.

He'd bloody misjudged it again.

Instead of getting her back, he'd lost her for a second time.

26

He awoke from a broken sleep surrounded by people talking, sniffling, snoring. Babies wailed as they wriggled restlessly on their mothers' laps. Sitting forward in his seat, he peered out of the window: The horizon was on fire, a dazzling curve of flame sandwiched between the darkness and the dawn. Beneath him, spread out like an old, embroidered carpet, lay the Jewel in the Crown of the British Empire: India.

Aaron disembarked into the filthiest airport he had ever seen. The once-white marble was grey with grime, walls splattered and stained, floors filthy with food and drink spills. Flying insects buzzed about – moths the size of eagles! He ducked in terror beating his hands about his head, afraid to breathe. What other horrors lurked in the foul and fetid air? Cholera? Typhoid? Dengue fever? Anthrax? They could be invading his lungs at this very moment! He stood rigid at the luggage carousel, damning his keenness to come on this trip. He should have taken the tour operator's advice and gone to The Eden Project, or at least to the Travel Clinic for the recommended jabs!

Aaron eventually exited Immigration into a heaving horde of humanity. An onslaught of sweat and spices attacked his nostrils as meeters and greeters swelled forward in search of family and friends. They waved and called out in Hindi and Bengali, a symphony of strangely foreign sounds. Beyond the multitude, buses and taxis hooted impatiently as they tried to navigate the stragglers who had spilled into the road. Mocha-coloured goats grazed nonchalantly alongside grey-skinned bovines. Old men in white dhotis crouched Ghandi-style on their haunches chewing betel leaves and smoking bidis.

Dorothy, muttered Aaron, *we're not in Kansas anymore.*

The cab journey from the airport was a sphincter-clenching rite of passage to India. Aaron couldn't work out which side of the road they actually drove on: All the lanes were used at once. Knackered old buses with passengers hanging off the rooves, motorbikes weighed down with entire families and a goat – none wearing helmets! – cyclos, taxis, trams, trucks, tuk-tuks, rickshaws – all hurtled haphazardly towards each other – Destination: DEATH.

Road signs advised:
'Alert Today, Alive Tomorrow' or 'Take Your Time, Not Your Life' but when the cabbie went over his third red light, and Aaron asked tremulously: "Isn't that a bit dangerous?", the fellow laughed good-heartedly and said: "Oh no, Sir! Red light is only a suggestion."

As they approached the city centre, modern monoliths rose out of the gutters in which lay piles of rags. On closer inspection, the rags were people…not homeless, as they had never had homes, but street dwellers who lived there, come heatwave or monsoon. Beneath a half-finished flyover, a market had been set up selling cracked toilet cisterns, bits of old piping, scrap metal, rusty chains. A dead dog was splayed out nearby like a bloody buffet. Come Die with Me.

They turned a corner, and out of the mist loomed the Victoria Memorial, dominating a lush green garden. The driver pointed it out proudly, testament to the long-gone Days of the Raj and the supremacy of its ruler, Queen Victoria, Empress of India and all her dominions.

Eventually they arrived at The Palace Hotel. It may have been a palace once but as Aaron stepped out of the rattling death trap, he was glad to enter an enclave that would soon become his haven of calm and karma from the madness of the street.

He sat on a wicker throne on the hotel's sun porch leafing through a local guidebook. Calcutta! What sensuous imagery this name had once evoked: be-turbaned Maharajas defending stately forts; ex-pats taking tiffin on colonial club lawns; dark exotic beauties with jasmine in their hair.

Forget all that, he thought. It's called Kolkata now and it's a drab, decaying bag lady of a place, behind whose misty eyes glow the dying embers of a long-forgotten flame. He left the book at Reception and steeled himself to step outside and experience it for real – wasn't that what he was here for?

As he set off into the heat and dust, his first impression was of utter chaos: a hopeless confusion where everything seemed broken down, bashed up or busted. Great mountains of garbage littered the streets, picked over by dogs, cats, vermin and, pitifully, children, scavenging for scraps to sell or eat. Amidst this detritus, the pavement dwellers lived, apparently with dignity. They rose at dawn from their concrete mattresses to perform the holy ritual of cleanliness. A nappy-clad, cavern-bodied man, who could have been 45 or 90, rested some scraps of cloth, a piece of soap and a toothbrush on an old brick beside a standpipe. This was his ensuite bathroom, the brick his vanity unit. He scrubbed his rags with diligence, bashing and wringing them in the tainted waters that flowed freely through the channels than ran along the gutters. When the man was satisfied that his clothes were clean, he put them on again and settled back in residence on his little piece of hell. A woman nearby swept a pile of dirt from one place to another.

In the past, whenever he had thought of India, Aaron had seen himself atop an ornate elephant, swaying up a hillside in romantic Rajasthan. Now he was actually on this confusing sub-continent, the mean streets of Kolkata had wasted no time in shattering his dream.

Yet there was something seductive skulking in the squalor. Years before he had read a book called *The City of Joy* by Dominique Lapierre, documenting life in Calcutta's greatest slum. It was clear that the term 'joy' was an irony, though in the context of finding joy in freedom and small things, it didn't take a Professor of Anthropology and Humanities to work out where that 'joy' was found: a population of 1.27 billion stood testament to that.

The place was a maze of chaos and colour, like a Jackson Pollock on mescaline. Crossing the Howrah Bridge, Aaron was staggered by the amount of stuff a cyclist could carry on his back while peddling a wobbly bicycle: three carved wooden headboards, the severed fronds of several palm trees, enough cauliflowers for a thousand portions of Gobi Aloo. No Health and Safety here! – and no suing the council for tripping on a loose paving stone and spilling headfirst into a hole in the road. It was a good job they believed in the afterlife. It had to be better than this one.

On the other side of the Hooghly River, Aaron stopped to watch a young woman stringing heads of marigolds into sunny orange garlands. Her sari, a panoply of peacock, green and gold, reflected her life in its well-washed faded tones. She glanced up at him shyly from where she sat cross-legged on the ground, in expectation of a sale. He offered her a few rupees. She handed him a garland but not wanting it for himself, he bent down and looped it around *her* neck. She looked surprised, and an anxious frown distorted the blood red bindi between her kohl-ringed eyes. The parting in her hair was tinted red to indicate a marriage, but married or not, the dark-skinned girl gazed at the pale white man and gave him a dazzling smile. Aaron placed his hands in prayer position and bowed a 'Namaste'.

"Namaskar," the woman answered bowing her own head.

I bow to God in you, I love you and respect you as there is no one like you.

And there is the joy, thought Aaron, as he went on his way. There is the simple joy…

The more he wandered the streets, the more he realised that up till now he had lived a life of luxury and excess. A cocktail of emotions was shaken up within him: he felt blessed, ashamed, and guilty all at once. Eventually these feelings turned to anger at the politics of a country with Nuclear Power and a Space Programme who regarded their poor, if they regarded them at all, with all the compassion of dog poo on their shoe.

He remembered an arrogant Indian billionaire interviewed on TV who, when criticised for driving around Mumbai in a £100,000 Bentley while leprous beggars died in nearby gutters, justified himself by saying: "We all have many lives and that is their life now. Those beggars may come back as me; I may come back as a cockroach!"

I hope you do, thought Aaron. *I would crush you underfoot.*

27

Heart pumping from her panicked flight home, Macy realised she no longer had a key. She stuffed her holdall behind the bins – God! that brought back memories – and rang the bell. Mrs R opened the door, surprised to see her lodger standing there panting, hair awry.

"Sorry!" Macy burst in. "Went for a run. Forgot my key." And she took the stairs two at a time leaving Mrs R wondering why she was being lied to.

Back in the safety of her cabbage-rose room, Macy rushed to close the curtains. Peeping out through the crack, she half expected to see her father storming up the road after her.

The key, the note and the week's rent lay untouched on the quilt.

Fear impeded her from rationalising that she had been safe so far, that how could he know where she was and if he did know, why hadn't he found her sooner? Tears of anger and frustration welled up in her eyes but when the comforting call of: "Supper's ready, dear", came up from downstairs, she went by rote to the bathroom to wash her hands.

"You've had a hard day."

The statement was dished up with a healthy portion of shepherd's pie and peas.

"You could say that…" said Macy, and finally – like an overfilled sack – her seams split and out spilled all the beans.

"It started soon after I got there. Mum never told me why they'd broken up – well, she wouldn't, would she? I was just a kid, and I probably wouldn't have understood anyway. I loved my dad, and I really missed him when he left. He used to give me cuddles whereas Mum was always caught up in herself, though I do remember she would always push me behind her if he was going off on one. She worked nights, office cleaning, always the obsessive cleaning, maybe it was her way of trying to purge herself, cleaning for other people when all she really wanted to do was clean herself. She always said the bruises were 'from work'. It would have been better if she'd told me the truth, though. I knew he was a bit of a loose cannon, and it didn't take much to set him off. Things like his supper not being ready the minute he walked through the door. He pushed her over and stamped on her hand once when she'd bought the wrong brand of beer. But he was always affectionate with me, very touchy-feely, especially when he'd had a few. I didn't think much of it at the time, but the hugs were always a little too tight and went on for a bit too long..." Macy paused. Mrs Reilly sensed a shudder running through her.

"After Mum...well, after she...after we agreed for them to switch off the..."

Macy stopped talking and held her breath; the truth still shocked her. "When they told me – well, they told *us* 'cos Mr Fairclough was with me – when they told us there was no brain activity and there was nothing more they could do, I called Nanny Jean and she called my dad, and he came down from Leicester. They let us sit with Mum till he arrived..."

Mrs R was conscious of the supper going cold, but she hadn't the heart to interrupt. When Macy continued, her voice was barely above a whisper.

"It was so scary in that room, so quiet except for the machines making this *oosh-pouff* sound. It terrified me to see her lying there – I thought she'd sit up any minute like in a horror film. Then I got upset 'cos she didn't, and I wanted to grab her and shake her awake and tell her...tell her I was sorry. But it wasn't my mum anymore. It was this pale, beautiful waxwork, very peaceful and very...dead."

Macy wrapped her arms around herself and rocked back and forth like a mourner unable to accept the facts.

"Sorry to lay all this on you, Mrs R," she sniffed. "Truly, I am."

"It's better out than in, love." Mrs R handed her an Irish linen napkin embroidered with forget-me-nots. "You should have told me a long time ago. No child should have to carry such a burden around with them."

Macy nodded and blew her nose. "Oh, and now I've let our lovely dinner go cold."

"Don't you mind about that. It'll soon heat up. Best carry on with your story."

"Well, er...yes...well, when the machine went quiet, I couldn't believe that was it, that I'd never see my mother again."

Tears rolled silently down Macy's cheeks. "Mr Fairclough helped me up and eased me away from the bed. I felt so guilty. I'd been such a cow at home and now I'd lost her, I'd lost everything: my family, my home life…everything. It was like my childhood died that night and I was suddenly a grown-up. It' funny because when you're young all you want to be is grown-up, but when it happens, especially like that, you just want to be a kid again and have someone protecting you. I kept saying 'Sorry' to Mum in my head 'cos there were times when I'd wished her dead and now she was... It didn't feel much like a victory though…"

Another sob wracked Macy's body.

"Who was this Mr Fairclough, dear?" Mrs R asked.

"Oh, he was my RS teacher at school. I really liked him. He never judged me, he was just there, in a way no one else had ever been. Everyone else thought he was a pathetic loser, but he really took an interest in me. I was a bit of a loner, but he encouraged me, brought out the best. When Dad arrived at the hospital though, Mr Fairclough left. I was pleased to see my dad, but my God, he had got fat, and he didn't seem at all sorry about Mum and was quite rude to the hospital staff, like he was in charge of everything. When we eventually got home, some of the neighbours came around to offer condolences and bring food. The news had spread 'cos they'd all seen her being taken away in the ambulance, and they were being really kind, but Dad just told them we didn't need their charity and were perfectly capable of feeding ourselves. Even before the funeral, he was chucking Mum's things into rubbish sacks and I was so…so rattled by the whole thing, I just let him do it. He told me I'd be going to live with him, and I just stood there wondering how I was going to get to school every morning from Leicester." "*It'll be good, eh? Just the two of us? Me and my Mace. Be sweet, yeah?*" she mimicked. "Turned out to be sweet as poison. Do you know not one of my school friends contacted me after Mum died? Not even one – not a message, not a visit, no phone calls, nothing. Mr Fairclough and the Head, I think, came to the funeral – it's all a bit of a blur now. I remember getting a letter from the school about 'dealing with bereavement and going through a period of re-adjustment' but it seemed very detached considering. The day after the funeral, I was upstairs and I could hear Mr Fairclough's voice at the front door. I rushed down but Dad shouted: 'Go back to your room! I'm dealing with this!' in that threatening way he had. I listened from the landing, and I could hear Dad saying: 'No. She's fine. She's coming to live with me now.'"

"Then he slammed the front door in Mr Fairclough's face. I ran back down, and Dad was holding an envelope which he tore open and inside there was a cheque made out to me for £100! He asked me why the teacher was giving me money, and what I'd done for him to be paying me! His question was nuts, of course – I should have realised then he was a psychopath. He screwed the note up and threw it in the bin and pocketed the cheque. When I finally retrieved the note after he'd gone to bed, it said that I had come second in a writing competition – an essay I'd written from the point of view of a horse. I was really pleased and dying to discuss it with Mr Fairclough, but I never did, nor did I ever find out what happened to that cheque. I did have other money though…money I never told Dad about…The next day, the day we were leaving, there was a parcel for me, hand delivered. It was a book called *The Fountainhead* by Ayn Rand. I hadn't heard of it, but I found out later that it was considered visionary in its day, the story of an architect who'd always struggled to be individual, ignore criticism and follow his creative potential. Inside the front cover, the sender had written: *Never conform. You're better than that* and underneath, there was a phone number. I was pretty sure it was from Mr Fairclough – at least I hoped it was – but Dad had already called BT to cancel the phone, so I couldn't call."

"We drove up to Leicester in Dad's old banger with my entire life crammed in the back. Dad lived in a dirty little house and the following week, he stuck me in the local state school which was a bit of a culture shock. Nanny Jean phoned me once a week and she'd always let me speak about Mum. I suppose she didn't want me to forget her, but she kept insisting that Mum was in 'a better place'. Once I got over the novelty of being with Dad, which was pretty quickly, I realised I'd always had an idealised version of him. He ate, drank, and behaved like a pig. I did all the cooking though I barely knew how, plus I had to clean up after him, I mean, the way he left the bathroom…you cannot imagine Mrs R, it was disgusting."

Macy grimaced through her tears at another recollection.

"One teatime, I decided to give him something different. I was bored to death with his awful diet of chips with everything, and I wasn't feeling that healthy myself. He usually settled for doorstep cheese and pickle sandwiches washed down with six pints of Tennent's, but I wanted to liven things up, so I cooked us a chilli con carne. That livened things up alright! You'd have thought I'd fed him dog poo. He took one mouthful and spat it across the table then threw the dish at me. It cut me on the eyebrow – see? I still have the scar. I went back to serving him frozen pies and oven chips – really unhealthy food. Most evenings he'd go off to the pub after supper then pick something up on his way home, a burger or fried chicken or something. He got so fat he couldn't do his trousers up…" Macy pulled a face.

"My escape was always reading. I never appreciated private education until I compared it to the place he'd dumped me in. Dad insisted the money my grandad had put in trust for me was needed for my keep, so I never saw any of that until much later. I did go into a phone box once though and called the number inside that book, but there was no reply. I would have loved to have spoken to Mr Fairclough again but what would I have said? I s'pose I could have written to him at my old school…"

Macy took a drink of water, then looked down at the congealed food on her plate.

"Oh no. You must think…"

"I don't think anything, dear. Nothing bad at any rate. It's good for you to talk. I always knew you'd had a wicked time of it – I just didn't know why. I'd like you to finish your story and I'll heat the dinner up, no problem."

"Thank you," Macy said quietly. "It gets…it gets quite…"

The word 'ugly' was barely audible.

Mrs Reilly picked up the plates and put them in the oven, then she sat back down and said: "Now. Where were we?"

Macy seemed to perk up suddenly and said: "I had an exit plan, you see. To make a bit of money, I got the idea of selling my brain at school. I'd do people's Maths or English homework and they'd pay me for it. I started to build up my own nest egg like my mum used to have in her shoebox." She cocked her head to one side. "I wonder what ever happened to that. *He* probably stole it, like he stole everything else…Anyway, my form teacher complimented the class on their unexpected progress, and I became something of a silent hero. She never sussed that I was teaching them more than she was, but that didn't last long. Running away had become an obsession with me but I needed more money to fund my escape. Nanny Jean sent me the occasional tenner…plus the, er, the other money I had from her, but then she died quite suddenly from a massive heart attack. I felt guilty all over again, like that had also been my fault. Some of it may have been – I know I'd caused her stress – but losing her severed another link to my mum, the last one actually. The upside was she left me all her money. Dad was furious but he couldn't do anything about it."

Macy put her hand up to her head. The memories were butting the lids off their boxes. She was getting to the worst part, trying to go the long way around.

"I'll make us both a cup of tea," Mrs Reilly said. "Then if you feel it'll help, you can finish the story."

Macy swallowed hard and nodded.

"In your own time, love." Mrs Reilly slid the sugar bowl across the table. "Just be sure to let those devils go lest they possess you from the inside out."

28

Dear Mrs Reilly

I want to apologise for leaving you high and dry in more ways than one, especially as you've always been so kind to me. If I'd stayed, I'd never have been able to leave because you've been like a mother and a grandma to me, and it would be too hard to say goodbye. Because of something I learned earlier, I must move on quickly. Also, it's time I found out what the world holds beyond the safety of your four walls. As I find it easier to write than to speak, I'm going to finish my story here. What happened happened but I'm trying not to let it ruin the rest of my life. I can't stay broken; I have to glue myself back together. I've been reading lots of self-help books in the library which teach you how to accept what you cannot change and change the things you can. It's not easy but others have done it, so why not I?

Thank you, dear Mrs R, for looking after me these past few months; you are a sweet and lovely person and I've loved living with you. The rest of the story is not pretty, but you deserve to know.

Take care and thanks again for everything.
Love,
Macy x

Mrs Reilly sighed deeply and put the first page down on the bed. She embarked on Page Two dreading what it might contain.

I'd only been in Leicester for a few days, and I was just going off to sleep one night when I heard my father come home with someone – a woman by the sound of it. That really upset me. Mum had only just died, and I'd hoped he would have respected that somehow. I pulled the pillow over my head to block out the noise then the woman suddenly shouted: "F*ck you!" (Sorry Mrs R) and he yelled back: "NO! F*ck YOU, sweetheart!"

Then I heard someone stomping down the stairs and the front door slammed. I bet she didn't even know he had a daughter in the house.

Next thing I knew, he came into my room. I lay there rigid, my heart thumping so hard I thought it would burst out through my chest. He shuffled around the room a bit then left. I didn't sleep a wink that night.

After that he started coming in regularly, usually once I was in bed. He'd pick up my books and try to read out loud to me, but he wasn't the greatest interpreter of the written word...

The first time he laid down on my bed, he said he was tired and needed some company. I wriggled back against the wall to give us both more space, but he stretched his arm out and sort of gathered me underneath it. He didn't smell very nice – he stank actually – but I didn't know how to get rid of him.

He started stroking up and down my arm in a way that made me shiver. There was something not quite right about the way he touched me, and I obviously tensed because he stopped for a moment then started again. I could hear him panting in my ear. I thought he was about to fall asleep, and I'd be stuck with him there all night, so I shoved him and said, 'Go to your own bed now, Dad'. He kissed me really hard, a wet slimy kiss, full on the lips. Nothing had ever felt so wrong.

A few nights later, I was in bed with my pyjamas buttoned up to the neck and I'd kept my vest and pants on too. He burst in and hovered over me like some great menacing giant and then he reached down and started unbuttoning my top. I clutched it closed and shouted: 'What are you doing?' but he had this cloudy look on his face, like he was on drugs or something and his hands were strong.

He suddenly tore my top open and a few of the buttons shot off. I tried to grapple with him, but he reached down and cupped my boobs, one in each hand. I smacked him away and he made a weird gurgling sound deep in his throat. It was really frightening but thank God he left the room. I planned to get a padlock for my door but next night, really late, he came in again. I could smell the beer on his breath. I'd stayed dressed that time sitting at my desk to avoid a repetition of the night before. I told him I had homework to finish but he sat down on the bed and said he'd wait. I said: 'Wait for what?' but he didn't answer.

I carried on pretending to write and turning pages noisily and after a few minutes, he came up behind me, lifted my hair and started slobbering down my neck. I was so tense, and I tried to get up, to push him off me, but he had me trapped. Then he literally lifted me out of the chair and pushed me back on the bed. I was kicking and struggling and telling him to stop but he kept going 'Ssshh, ssshh, come on, make your old man happy'. He was so heavy, and I was locked underneath him with him shushing me with his smelly breath. Then he started fumbling and I just lost it, and I bit him on the cheek. He whacked me across the face, one way then the other. That's how it started, Mrs R, and it didn't stop till the day I ran away.

Mrs Reilly took a handkerchief out of her pinafore pocket and spat out the bile that had risen in her throat. That poor, poor girl – no wonder she acted like a frightened rabbit half the time. The letter ended with a renewed apology and a promise to keep in touch, but no forwarding address. Neither did it explain why she had left so suddenly, only those words about something she'd 'learned earlier'. She wished she knew where the girl had gone. Just to know she was safe, at least.

Mrs Reilly picked up the handset of her phone and scrolled through Calls Received. She didn't get many phone calls and she recognised all the numbers except two. One said Withheld but the other was a mobile number. She pressed Redial. It went straight to Voicemail.

This is Lee Watkins. Please leave a message after the tone.

"Lee Watkins? This is Mrs Reilly in Charteris Road. I wonder if you know where our young friend has gone. Please call me."

29

If the nuisance neighbour hadn't rung the bell wanting to discuss the new fence separating their gardens, Macy may have been able to unburden herself fully. By the time Mrs Reilly returned to the kitchen, the flow of recollection had been interrupted and Macy had gone to her room. Talking about him had dug up too many buried memories and she knew she had to disappear again before he found her. Her holdall was packed and hidden, but if she tried to leave now, Mrs R would surely stop her. She felt bad: her landlady had been nothing but kind to her, but she couldn't allow that to influence her decision.

Macy sat on the edge of her bed, frightened, and confused. She felt safe here but if he was alive…the repercussions were unthinkable.

When Mrs R knocked and asked if she'd like to come down and finish her dinner, she said she was sorry, but she'd lost her appetite and was going to have an early night.

She crept out before daybreak, leaving no body in her wake, just the letter, the key, the rent, and a promise to stay in touch. She walked the silent streets until a night bus passed going in the direction of Waterloo. She got on it knowing that the main line station would have a train going somewhere. Anywhere.

The terminus was quiet. Macy found a bench and settled down with her head on her bag. She didn't sleep, she was too wired. When the concourse came to life around 6 am, she got up and mingled with the early morning travellers.

The school trip could not have been more opportune. A tired troupe of untidy teenagers lugging bags and backpacks gathered beneath the Departures Board. Somewhere about their persons, they might have what Macy lacked.

She joined the edges of the group then blended in amongst them, checking the girls out one by one. When their train time and platform number clicked up, they turned in unison like a shoal of fish and made their way towards the barriers. Macy let herself be swept along, staying close behind the girl with the denim jacket slung across one shoulder. A gentle tug in the hubbub of the crowd brought the jacket to the ground. Without breaking stride, Macy swooped it up then let the crowd push past her before checking the contents. *Result!* One navy blue passport (United States of America) and one travel ticket to…Paris! Macy re-joined the horde, flowed through the barrier, and boarded the train. She didn't take a seat but camped between the carriages, merging back with the students at Dover as they made their way towards the Channel Ferry.

There was a queue up ahead. Stern-faced men in uniform were matching passengers to passports. When it was her turn to approach the desk, she feigned a coughing fit, covering her face with her hand and mumbling: "Ugh, sorry, very sore throat…"

The Immigration Officer had no wish to catch her germs with his own holiday imminent, so he stamped the passport, slammed it shut, handed it back and waved her through.

It only occurred to Macy, once she was safely ensconced on the ferry, to check and see who she'd become. On the photo page, plainer than her in many ways, a girl stared blankly back. She had long mouse-brown hair and a similarly oval face. Her name was:

Amber Lynne

I am now *officially* 18, Macy thought. Odd choice of names though. I'll have to be careful not to lose my head.

30

The *pension* on the rue Cortot was a tall, narrow, slightly crooked building with cracked floor tiles that hadn't seen a mop in years. The peeling paintwork was the colour of dirge. Spindles were missing on the staircase that wound upwards in ever-decreasing circles and was adorned by a filigree of cobwebs. To add authenticity, the smell of stale garlic hung heavy in the air.

The attic room had been allocated to her in exchange for a fistful of ten-pound notes. It was redolent of a nineteenth century garret. Every surface was thick with dust and fossilised insects. The Verdigris taps in the hand-basin dripped with the unforgiving tempo of Chinese torture, and the single mattress looked lumpy enough to house the long-dead corpses of failed authors and struggling Impressionists. She'd given the concierge enough money for a week, but she didn't think she'd last the night never mind seven. A wave of longing for Mrs Reilly's cosy kitchen washed over her but she sighed it away, dumped her bag on a bamboo chair missing its cane work seat and opened the window as far as it would go. Could she see the Eiffel Tower? No, she could not.

As soon as Macy hit the street, she started to feel better. The area around the station had a buzzy vibe with people coming and going. She stopped at a *bureau de change* to buy some French francs then walked over to a sidewalk café and ordered a Croque Monsieur and an Orangina. She wasn't sure what they were but they were easy to point at and she was starving. She sat down at a small round table flanked by two wicker chairs. She might find a crash course to attend, brush up on her school French.

Sharing her story with Mrs Reilly, both verbally then in writing, had provided a much-needed release. She wished she had done it sooner. Escaping London the way she had had boosted her confidence. She dared to feel a little excited, optimistic even. Although the thought of her father not being dead was alarming, he would not find her here. She was in Paris. The sun was shining. According to her passport she was 18. And she was free.

*

The busker set up right opposite the café where Macy was enjoying her snack. He opened his guitar case, removed the instrument, delved into his pocket, tossed a few coins into the case's lid, tuned up and began to sing.

He was terrible. His strumming was out of synch with his singing and his voice was raucous rather than refined. Notwithstanding this, Macy couldn't take her eyes off him. Despite having zero interest in the opposite sex, she did recognise that this was a jaw-droppingly handsome specimen – the best-looking man she'd ever seen. He was over six-foot tall, slim-hipped and broad-shouldered with a square-jaw, a straight nose, high cheekbones – arched eyebrows, and honey-coloured skin, all framed by a torrent of hair so black it looked like liquorice twists. She couldn't see his eyes because he was concentrating on his chords, but he wore low-slung faded blue jeans, a Che Guevara t-shirt and double-soled leopard-print creepers – the sort of guy a model agency would snap up soon as look at.

Macy was not aware that she was gawping until he raised his eyes. God, they were green, SO GREEN! – and as they locked with hers, he began to sing right at her. Flushed with embarrassment, she focused on the last bite of her toasted sandwich wishing she were doing something more productive than sitting there chewing. She could not, however, still the flutter in her chest. Dare she steal another look? He was still singing straight at her.

The passers-by ignored him. Not a single person slowed their pace, stopped to listen, nodded in appreciation (of his looks if not his music!) or threw him a single sou. After about fifteen minutes of off-key strumming and discordant warbling, he paused to attract the waiter's attention. The *garçon* went over, listened to his request, nodded, and went back inside the bar. He returned moments later with a demi-tasse which he placed on Macy's table.

She looked perplexed. She had not ordered this – she didn't drink tiny cups of coffee. She sent the busker a visual query and he made a 'pick-up-the-cup' motion and pointed at his own mouth. Was he actually asking her to feed him? Hold it for him while he drank?

He made a pleading-little-boy face which dispelled her reserve, and she picked up the cup and saucer and crossed the pavement to place it at his feet.

The brightness of his smile almost floored her. This was not a Down and Out in London or Paris – he had the most spectacular set of Hollywood teeth! She scuttled back to her seat to pay and leave when he started singing again, this time in broken English, something about 'a beautiful stranger who seduced him with espresso'. Macy couldn't help but grin.

The busker paused – which was a blessing – and bent down to lift the cup in salute. He downed the contents, wiped the back of his hand across his mouth, flashed her another killer smile and offered the cup back to her. She didn't budge. She'd done her bit. What did he think she was – a bloody waitress?

He laid his guitar carefully in its case and ambled over to her table with the empty cup. Holding her gaze tightly in his, he set it down and stood there scrutinising her. Some primeval gene kicked in and she unwittingly batted her eyelashes, a moment only broken by what she suddenly saw happening behind him.

She leapt to her feet shouting: "HEY! STOP!" and he whipped around to witness an opportunist on rollerblades slaloming away through the traffic with his precious guitar held aloft. He charged across the road in pursuit, and narrowly missed being run over by a honking tour bus.

"*Putain! Espèce de connard*!" he yelled, but the thief was gone.

Gesticulating and swearing loudly, he marched back to the café and plonked himself down at Macy's table.

"I'm so sorry…" she whispered. "*Je m'excuse…*"

"*Non! Tu ne t'excuses pas!*" he retorted. "*C'est moi qui t'excuse – ou non!*" She vaguely remembered, from some long-ago French lesson, about not being able to excuse yourself but having to ask to be excused.

"*Excusez-moi?*" She offered, correcting herself.

He looked at her derisively, clicked a finger for the waiter and ordered '*deux blondes*'. Macy picked up her bill from the steel saucer and reached into her gold bag for her purse.

"*Mais où vas-tu?*" He demanded. "Where do you going? I 'ave not to work now! You stay and drink with me!"

She sank back slowly into her seat, captured by his command and his charisma.

31

The Sundarbans region, as well as harbouring snakes and crocodiles, is famous for the Royal Bengal tiger, the only animal that drinks seawater. This fearsome creature is a merciless man-eater with a penchant for the cadavers that float along the Ganges, bodies only partially cremated for the simple reason that their families cannot afford enough wood for a decent funeral pyre.

Local farmers in the region wear masks on the backs of their heads because the tigers are alleged not to attack if you are looking at them. This is poor protection, however, when you consider the annual number of deaths.

The money to build a house (one room mud hut) and start a business selling pens and paper for the islands' schoolchildren would cost around US$300.

Additionally, the remote islanders are in dire need of all types of medical assistance. Cataract removal, cervical screening, malaria control, leprosy treatment. All donations are gratefully accepted.

Three hundred dollars! Aaron thought, as he closed the guidebook and put it back on the hotel's bookshelf. The price of a good lunch.

From having been afraid Day One to touch anyone or eat anything other than boiled rice and dahl, he was now tucking in to all the local delicacies and grasping any outstretched hand that reached for his. He smiled at scowling babies and stroked their silky hair: the charcoal bindis their mothers placed between their eyes would ward off evil spirits and keep the *bachchas* safe. On what should have been his final day, he visited the Kolkata slum immortalised in the book he had read, where the hero, a rickshaw puller – *ergo* human donkey – died of TB aged 32.

On an area the size of three football pitches, thousands of people lived, loved, were born, and died alongside open sewers, stinking latrines, and polluted wells. Empty coffee jars, the sort every Western household throws away, were used as storage containers, water vessels, grain pounders, rolling pins.

He watched an old man crouched beside a random pile of clothing marking each piece with a stick dipped in henna. Next to him was a plastic bowl filled with murky water into which he swirled each garment. This was the local laundry: the go-to man to get your washing done.

Aaron peered into an open window and watched a group of teenage boys sticking beads and sequins onto lengths of coloured cloth. The decorated fabric would later be wholesaled to a sari manufacturer who would trade it to a clothing merchant who would sell it to a customer who would take it to a dressmaker who would fashion it into an outfit. Further down the street a woman of indeterminate age was boiling up a massive vat of curry – some for her family, the rest to sell. Around the corner, a young man flattened empty oil cans to make metal suitcases. Along the alley, a tiny girl, no more than five or six, pumped water from a well to fill her neighbours' buckets. An ancient granny crouched nearby, hand eternally cupped and begging, her cataract-clouded eyes unseeing amid the scars of pain and poverty etched upon her face. All human life lived here in conditions unfit for dogs.

Aaron had heard said that India changes you. He had never believed it before.

He did now.

Either he left this place before it really got to him, or he dug himself in for the long haul.

32

Macy was partly flattered but mostly awe-struck that The God of Frogs considered her old enough – and good enough – to drink with him. In a period of some twelve hours, she'd abandoned her safe house, stolen a passport, crossed to France, rented a room, and become acquainted with a busker on a Parisian pavement. Living the dream, some might say. The last time she had drunk alcohol was the night her mother died, a memory that would haunt the rest of her life, while conveying the counter-intuitive need to have a drink.

Macy sipped the blond and bubbly lager and immediately understood. Although there was a faintly acrid aftertaste, it was cool and refreshing. She took another sip and then a longish gulp.

"*Comment t'appelles-tu?*" he asked suddenly.

"Macy…er *non*! Amber. *Je m'appelle* Amber."

"Really?" He arched one perfect eyebrow. "*Je préfère* Mais Si. It means 'But yes!' Amber is traffic light, *non*?"

She giggled then shrugged. "I can't argue with that!"

"Where you live in Paree?"

"Er…nowhere," she answered which was true. She certainly didn't want to live – or die – in the Horrible House of Horrors.

"Look," she said, taking another pull of lager. "It's my fault what happened. If I had taken the empty cup & saucer back like you'd asked me to, you wouldn't have put your guitar down and it wouldn't have been stolen. I really feel bad about that. Could I make it up to you? Buy you another drink or something?"

"Make it *up* to me? What does zis mean? You want to make *IT* up to me? Is not up to me. Is up to you!"

Macy frowned. There was clearly a language barrier.

"You offer me *l'amour*, yes?" He went on. "Oh! You English girls…"

"NO! That is *not* what I offer you!" Macy stood up to go. *Men! With their egotistical and ceaseless sense of entitlement.* "I was offering you another drink, but you know what? You can…"

"And you sink I take drink from a girl? I am not gigolo."

Uncertain that she understood, Macy finished her lager, picked up her bag and made to leave.

"*Où vas-tu?*" He pleaded, his hands in prayer position. "Please stay wiz me. Be my company?"

She looked at him and her stomach confirmed what her knees still thought. He certainly knew how to charm. And disarm. She sank slowly back into her chair, and he motioned to the waiter to bring two more *blondes*.

"So, Maissi…"

"What's your name?" she asked simultaneously, trying to smooth over the uneven ground between them.

"I am Franky wiz my friends. Jean-François Montdidier with…"

"Jean-François?"

"You are not my friend?"

"I don't know. Am I?"

Macy was surprised by how she felt at the thought of *not* being his friend. And 'Franky' was so similar to Francine, she thought…maybe Mum has forgiven me and sent him as a gift?

Franky looked pensive for a moment as he sipped his drink, then said: "You want 'elp me buy new *guitarre*? I 'ave idea. Finish your *bière*."

She did as she was told. He tossed a hundred franc note onto the saucer and stood up to go. Macy rose as well, uncertain of what might happen next. Franky walked to the kerb and hailed a cab. He opened the door to let Macy in then followed with his empty guitar case.

Busking one minute, flashing notes the next? she thought. Fate was dealing her a hand she had no idea how to play – plus she'd just got into a taxi with a strange man in a strange city and she was mildly tanked so *WHAT THE HELL WAS SHE THINKING*? She wished she could get out and go back to the grim safety of the wonky Pension.

They steered through the traffic for about fifteen minutes then stopped on a quiet residential street. Franky paid the driver and got out. Macy followed hesitantly as he walked towards a massive pair of ancient, studded doors. Halfway towards them, good sense prevailed, and she stopped.

"Look, Franky. Thanks for the drinks and all that, but…"

"Where you live tonight?" he queried.

He had a point. Did she even know her address? She had walked into the first place she'd seen when she'd come out of the station.

"I…er…"

He took her hand and said: "*Viens, ma petite,*" and against her better judgement, she followed.

They crossed a cobbled courtyard and walked towards the rear of the building. The ground floor ledges were all adorned with white window boxes planted with red geraniums. It looked very well-maintained, affluent even. They entered the building and as they passed a cubbyhole, an old lady's voice called out: "*Bonjour Monsieur Montdidier. Bonjour Mademoiselle.*"

"Bonjour Madame Lalande!" Franky shouted affectionately.

"*Madame la concierge,*" he confided to Macy. "Very useful but a little…'ow you say? Deaf!"

He slid open the concertina gates, she stepped in, he followed, and they rose in silence inside the gilded cage.

33

As Aaron made his way out of the labyrinth back into the chaos of Calcutta, he wondered how a god of love and compassion – be He Allah, Buddha, Christ or HaShem) could allow His children to suffer like this? He questioned his own faith, wondering again if he was truly a man of religion, or simply a man. The Hindus and Sikhs had their own beliefs so there was no converting to be done there. He had considered staying on here to do something useful, but as he was neither a philanthropist, a medical professional, or a missionary, rounding up random kids to teach them the ABC seemed something of a lost cause.

He wandered back to the hotel, his desire to remain weakening by the moment. By the time he reached the dubious comfort of his room, Aaron decided that he had not come on this trip to feel worse about his life than he'd felt before. He would travel west to explore another side of the culture: the origins and legends behind the Kama Sutra.

The next morning, he took the mail train to Satna, a journey of some seventeen hours. He slept part of the way, stared out of the window the rest, and marvelled – if that was the right word – at the sights, sounds, smells, and personal habits of his fellow passengers. This was no Maharaja Express-type palace on wheels. This was a people, goats and chickens train.

Aaron's fastidiousness, repression and British reserve had not prepared him for a journey this far removed from National Rail: exotic it may be, but smeary windows, filthy toilets, inedible food, and indelicately curious travelling companions made the journey an experience he would never forget. The ensuing bus ride to Khajuraho was the fly-infested icing on a rather poo-ey cake. Aaron arrived bone-rattled and road-weary. He staggered into the first hotel he came to, took a room, flung his bag down and slept for ten hours straight. When he awoke, he showered and changed, then set off to find the famous holy shrines.

A thousand years previously, Hindu warrior kings who, above all else, worshipped sensuality and eroticism, built their temples in Khajuraho setting their beliefs in stone. Out of an original eighty-five constructed, only twenty remained but the architectural skill and scale of the 'erections' widened Aaron's eyes and hastened his heart.

To these royal rebel rousers, devotion to the art of pleasure was a way of reaching spiritual enlightenment. Raging wars brought other satisfactions but none like the relentless practice of sex. Aaron, or Airey as he'd been then, had even taught this culture in class, and when he studied the positions and postures the carved characters had managed to twist themselves into, his brain boggled, and his head ached.

He heard a girlish giggle behind him and turned, hoping – inexplicably – to find Macy and a group of schoolkids studying the stones. Instead, he found two women – mother and daughter or maybe sisters? – both clad in khaki combats performing similar head rotations to his own.

"I'll bet the yoga helped!" commented the elder of the two. Aaron nodded and laughed. They moved on in unison, studying each carving. Surely here lay the inspiration for Macy's *Ling and Yoni* story?

The mother and daughter as they turned out, did not hesitate to introduce themselves as: "Beth and Bryony from Brisbane!" They were following the same route and by the end of the s-excursion, Aaron had agreed to meet them for dinner.

The pleasure of travel and more specifically travelling alone, is the freedom to do what you want, when you want, with whom you want. On previous trips, usually with a university chum or in childhood with his parents, Aaron had barely conversed with anyone except the people he was with. Now he found himself in the middle of India having dinner with two Antipodean ladies discussing everything from the excesses of Hindu kings and their concubines to the differences between an authentic mutton biryani and the Western version.

The Bs, as they called themselves, were so uninhibited one even told the story of how, on a previous trip, she'd suffered such a prolonged bout of Delhi belly, she would scrape the contents of her dinner plate straight into the toilet bowl: "Cut out the middleman!"

The night grew sultry. The sitar music became hypnotic as one lager followed another until they all lost count. When he eventually got up to leave, Aaron was swaying like a pendulum. Beth and Bryony caught him one on each side, linked their arms through his and walked him effortlessly back to their hotel.

The toxic mix of heat, alcohol, and enough soft porn to make a hooker blush, had furnished Aaron with a hard-on the size of an obelisk. Swept along the corridor, feet barely touching the ground, he was led to their room, stripped of his clothing, and jumped – or was he pushed? – under a torrent of tepid water.

The shower was welcome but what followed…well, let's just say he did not object. Without so much as a "Y 'aright, mate?", the determined duo joined him in the shower. Liberally lubricated with a bottle of bubbly body wash, they slithered up and down him, snaking their way between his legs like a pair of sex-crazed serpents. He stood rigid in every way, head thrown back, eyes closed, mouth gasping as Beth and Bryony wove their dirty magic. Not such a Lonely Planet after all, he marvelled, as he finally learned the true meaning of the words: International Relations.

The following morning Aaron cut and ran. Being sucked off was one thing. Being sucked in was another.

34

The gates of the brass and oak elevator opened onto an apartment that could have featured in a six-page spread of an urban chic interiors magazine. Franky stepped aside to let Macy enter. The marble floor spread before her like a polished black ice-rink. A pair of angular steel chairs covered in crocodile skin stood either side of a Mongolian sheepskin rug; in the centre of the rug the base of a sequoia tree, roots and all, served as a coffee table. A TV screen the size of an arthouse cinema took up most of one wall; a rose-tinted Art Deco mirror reflected the room from the other. Illuminated crystal drops of varying lengths hung suspended from the ceiling; in an ocean-sized aquarium swam, or rather posed, a mummified Galapagos turtle and a hammerhead shark. An exotic shoal of tropical fish swam amongst them flashing past like shards of rainbow. In the far corner, each on its dedicated stand, stood a Fender Stratocaster, a Gibson and a Les Paul guitar. The fourth stand, which had held the Martin, was now empty. Of course, Macy didn't know any of this until it was explained to her, but her first impression was to try and make sense of it, bearing in mind the apparent employment of the person who'd invited her in.

"I show you up the stairs," Franky said, like it was normal for buskers to own, let alone live in, a pad like this.

"Y-yes...but...?"

"*Viens!*" And he took her hand again and led her up the glass staircase to the upper floor. The studio was decked out like a film set for *The Private Life of Pablo Picasso*. Easels, canvases, and frames were propped against the walls; a Coromandel dining-table (inside which dwelled an unseen metropolis of woodworm) was daubed with streaks and splodges of every shade; palettes, oil paints, charcoals, acrylics, watercolours, rags, and brushes lay randomly discarded in a strewn artistic mess. A Majolica jardinière complete with giant aspidistra stood to the left of a chaise longue covered in faded burgundy velvet.

A silver-gilt three-fold screen draped with a Spanish shawl stood behind it, the perfect backdrop to the scene it set.

"You take off cloths. Lie zere."

Franky motioned in the general direction of the furniture as he leafed through a stack of stretched canvases looking for a blank one.

"I wh-a-t?" Macy stammered.

"I paint you."

"Oh, not that old chestnut! First, you're a musician, now you're a painter! What next? The architect who built that famous tower?"

She turned to go back down the spiral staircase, but he crossed the room in long strides and caught her arm. She whipped around and a flash of warning flared in her eyes. He let go as if she'd scorched him.

"Whoa! OK! *Ça va! Pas de problème.* Stay as you like but please…just stay?"

*

When Franky sketched her fully-dressed that first afternoon, Macy realised he had no idea what he was doing. His method, like his singing voice, was raw and unsophisticated. Although no expert, her tours of London's art galleries had taught her a little about genres and styles. She had formed the opinion that most of the modern art was a con designed to fleece the pockets of the impressionable rich. The way Franky had drawn her was sketchy and amateur, lacking structure, characterisation and technique. But it did show a certain flair and some talent. She felt she could help improve on that.

After his presumptuous request and her adamant refusal to strip off, she realised that historically all the best representational drawings and paintings of the female form had one thing in common: the women were all naked. If she could detach her hang-ups from that fact, she could pose for him properly, but she needed to know who she was dealing with – who was this man, and could she trust him? And so, she asked the question.

As they sat side by side on the chaise longue sipping tisane, he told her his life story. His father had been a diplomat, the French Ambassador to Egypt. One night, at a reception in his father's honour, an exquisite belly dancer, Safiya, arrived with her entourage to perform for the guests. His father fell madly in love with her, and despite her earlier resistance, she fell in love with him too. Against the advice of colleagues, family, and friends, they married.

After a few years, it was clear that this happy marriage was doomed to produce no issue. In a gesture of love and generosity, Safiya suggested that her twin sister may be more fertile than she was and allowed the couple to 'lie together'. The resulting child, Franky, was brought up in a loving household by his birth mother and his other mother, i.e., his father's wife. He was told this story once he was old enough to understand.

Returning to Paris from Cairo with his three parents, he'd been brought up in a grand apartment on the Avenue Foch. He was secure, well-educated, and well-travelled. His birth mother sadly passed away and his remaining parents were now retired and living on the island of St. Barth in the French West Indies. He lacked for nothing except direction.

Halfway through this fairy story, it occurred to Macy that it was so fantastical, he was probably making it up. If so, he had a vivid if not clichéd imagination. She decided to give him the benefit of the doubt however, especially as she had noticed family photographs in beautiful Art Deco frames and the faces fit. Franky posing with a pair of exotic-looking identical women flanked by a tall, handsome man.

After recounting this tale, Franky phoned down to the concierge, Madame Lalande, and asked her to kindly order some food from the local *traiteur*. Macy noted that he had lovely manners, and they shared a picnic of pâté de foie gras with a selection of cold meats and cheeses washed down with an excellent bottle of Bordeaux.

"Now your story," he said, breaking off a chunk of baguette, spreading it with runny Brie and aiming it at her mouth. Macy chewed slowly and appreciatively which gave her time to think.

"I had a bad experience, and I don't get on with men."

She may as well tell it like it was. She hadn't bargained on his candid curiosity. "You are *lesbienne*?"

"NO! I'm not anything. That's it!"

"But not *pour toujours*? For always? *Pas possible!* You waste yourself!"

She took a long sip of red wine, the superiority of which was completely lost on her.

"Let's talk about your art…"

"Iz bad. I need new model."

"What happened to the old one?"

A seductive smile creased the corners of his eyes. "You are more beautiful! And younger!"

"Jean-François! It's never going to happen. *Jamais!*"

"*Jamais*? Or maybe tomorrow? You will be *ma nouvelle muse*."

"I don't think so!"

Macy and Franky talked deep into the night. The wine softened her in many ways and when the sun rose and stretched its ribbon rays across Parisian skies, she allowed herself to be led, fully clothed, into the spare room where she lay down atop a puffy white eiderdown and fell into a dreamless asleep.

35

Aaron decided to take the scenic route home. No point in going travelling if you're going to scuttle back to safety the minute things got weird. The Aussie duo had opened his eyes wider than he thought possible. He would always remember his Intrepid Lady Travellers in a similar way to That Curious Incident…Away from the restrictions of homes and husbands, their morals had become as loose as their knicker elastic.

Aaron zipped up his backpack and checked himself in the hotel mirror. He needed a shave but frankly: why bother? He rather liked his new rugged look – it was certainly proving to be a hit with the 'laydeez'! He undid the top button of his pink linen shirt and rolled up the sleeves. His jeans were tightly buckled around his waist making them a little short at the ankle, the same way his father wore his Comfy-Fit Leisure Slax purchased from the pages of a Sunday supplement.

Aaron undid the belt a notch and dragged his jeans down to reveal the slightly perished waistband of his well-washed Y-fronts. *Maybe not,* he thought. When he reached civilization, he'd buy himself some of those designer boxers, but for now, he'd hitch these up again and bid a fond farewell to Khajuraho and its titillating temples, and head west along the dusty road through Rajasthan.

The rickety old bus lurched its passengers in and out of their seats as it circumnavigated cavernous potholes and holy cows sitting dumbly in the middle of the road. Aaron stared out of the grimy window as the landscape bounced by, mile upon mile of nothing much. This did not dull his buoyant mood, however. Could it only be a few weeks ago that he had been confined to a classroom? Macy Lord came to mind. Macy – bless her – where was she now? He hoped she was happy, getting on with her studies and settled down with her father, though the man had been quite unpleasant when Aaron had knocked on the door.

"Whaddyawant?" he had barked in Aaron's face. "Don't need no do-gooders 'ere!"

That was hardly the way to deal with people who had come to offer their condolences. Aaron had wanted to find out how Macy was coping with her loss and to give her the good news about her prize in the writing competition. Too bad he'd been sent away without being able to see her. He had not dared knock the next day when he'd dropped the book off, and it upset him to have lost touch – they had shared something special, something profound. He presumed she'd seen his number written on the fly leaf, but of course he wasn't reachable at that number anymore.

The bus's bumpy motion sent Aaron off to sleep, to dream of the jewelled cities up ahead, cities of sultans, lakes, and palaces: The Pink City of Jaipur, the Blue City of Jodhpur and what he would later recall as the Shitty City of Udaipur, which was where his bowels finally gave up.

After too many mind-numbing hours on the road, he was disappointed to find that all these cities had little to redeem them except A Fort or A Temple. Extraordinary as these structures were, their surroundings were not. Nothing, of course, could detract from the majesty of the Taj Mahal whose marble magnificence shimmered in the sunlight, changing colour like a chameleon as dawn turned to dusk. It appeared to float above the earth's surface, and the moment he turned away from it, he was compelled to turn back and gaze at it again.

He queued with other tourists for the elephant ride up to the Amber Fort but on arrival, the décor was being faked up, Bollywood-style, for some glamour model's birthday party. This rather detracted from its organic deterioration and decay.

Elsewhere, the streets reeked of rubbish and wretchedness. It was all very well for the rich and shameless to 'Do India' from the comfort of an air-conditioned limo being whisked in and out of the gates of 5-star hotels. They had come home cooing about how much they were *"totally into the culture, dahling"* when all they'd really brought back with them were posh pashminas and the memory of mock Maharajas serving sanitised cocktails around the pool.

*

The 52-hour ferry trip out of Bombay across the Arabian Sea gave Aaron the opportunity to consider where he'd been and where he might be headed. Once installed in his cabin, he went up on deck to look for a sun lounger and breathe the fresh salt air.

The deck was deserted except for a woman standing at the rail looking out to sea. She was tall and slim, wearing a long, cream linen dress and flat lace-up shoes. Her hair was alarming: orange, wild and wiry like *Der Struwwelpeter* in the German children's story. He watched her for a moment, contemplating with his new-found confidence, whether to amble over and start a conversation. He was on the verge of getting up when she moved along the deck away from him. He sank back onto the slatted steamer chair; his To-Do list had yet to include Active Pursuit.

On the lounger next to his lay a book which he presumed belonged to her since there was no one else around. He tilted his head to read the title then reached over and picked it up, marking the open page with his index finger.

MUSCAT AND OMAN, he read.

Long ago, there existed a biblical empire called Magan, where the air was fragrant with frankincense and the land rich with bountiful minerals.

Migrants from other cultures journeyed from afar to explore its craggy mountains, golden deserts, and azure shores. This was the Arabia of Aladdin, Sinbad, Ali Baba and Scheherazade who hailed from Babylon, Mesopotamia, Byzantium and Samarkand – magical, mystical kingdoms from *The Tales of the Thousand and One Nights.*

Aha! Aaron thought. *The Goddess with the Thousand and One*...but no. That was something else. Sounds fabulous, though. He read on:

With its rich and varied landscape of canyons and hot springs, caves like cathedrals lurk beneath the ground festooned with stalagmites and stalactites. Under the waters of the Gulf, a vibrant tapestry of flora and fauna sways where shark and barracuda swim. In the forests, 2000-year-old baobab trees grow up to 30 feet in diameter, and on the beaches, 100-year-old turtles return to their birthplace to lay their eggs.

This is the land that time forgot, where Marco Polo's footsteps traced the trail of the old Silk Route.

Throughout history, due to uprisings and rebellions, the country that is now Oman developed at a slow pace. Cultural differences flared between the seafaring Sultanate of Muscat and the interior Imamate of Oman. In the early 1820s, the Sultanate lost most of its territories and the divided country was governed by two rulers. This led to it being named 'Muscat and Oman'. The split continued until the discovery of oil, most of which lay within the Imamate, and the ruling Sultan granted licenses to European oil companies to help him re-establish pre-eminence over most of the country.

One Sultan followed another until 1970, when the current ruler, HM Sultan Qaboos bin Said acceded to the throne. As a young Prince, Qaboos spent his teenage years enclosed within the palace walls. At the suggestion of his father's British advisors, he was sent to England to complete his education at Bury St Edmunds then Sandhurst Royal Military Academy. He served with the British Forces in Germany absorbing Western culture with voracity, but on returning to Oman, he was again sequestered within the palace grounds.

At the age of 30, in a non-violent *coup,* he deposed his aging father, took over the throne, and the old Sultan retreated to a comfortable exile where he lived out his days at London's Dorchester Hotel.

The young leader's first declaration was to give the country a new flag and a new name: 'The Sultanate of Oman'. He then embarked on the painstaking task of eradicating disease, poverty, and illiteracy, encouraging his countrymen to help him build a modern nation. The vast natural wealth of oil helped him in this mammoth enterprise.

Sultan Qaboos's first major project was to establish a government with himself as Prime Minister, Foreign Minister, Defence Minister, and Finance Minister. This may sound a job too far, but his deference to democracy earned him global respect.

Famous for his inspirational one-liners like: *'Oman is rich in resources and its resources belong to its people',* he soon began to use the oil revenue to build the modern infrastructure that is Oman today...

"Finding it interesting, are we?"

The shadow looming over him, of which he had been unaware, had a gritty voice. He shielded his eyes to see the forbidding-looking woman, eyes narrowed, sharp as flint. Her tightly pursed lips were heavily laden, not with lipstick, but with reprimand.

Aaron leapt to his feet, not easy from a recliner. The awkward action caused him to inadvertently flip the book into the air and he grappled for it like an inept juggler, just managing to catch it before it hit the deck. The woman watched the gauche performance with a mix of exasperation and contempt. With the sun setting behind her, her mane of marmalade hair fanned out around her face like a burning bush.

"I'm so sorry – do forgive me!" Aaron blustered as he slammed the book firmly shut and pushed it towards her, quickly reneging on its return as he fumbled through the leaves to find the page on which she'd left it open.

"Give it to me!" she barked, like a schoolmarm to a child.

She snatched the book back and stomped off further down the deck. She plonked herself down and flipped impatiently through the pages trying to find her place.

"Muscat and Oman?" Aaron offered timidly, but his voice was borrowed by the breeze. "Fascinating place by all accounts…" he muttered to himself.

The woman ignored him. She'd found the page and had immersed herself in it. Aaron stood there feeling discomfited.

He had no precedent for what to do next. Slink away in shame? Offer her a drink? He began to sit down, changed his mind, stood up again and walked over to the rail. Out of the corner of his eye, the woman logged his every move.

Aaron gazed blindly towards the horizon. He had only borrowed a book for God's sake – she didn't have to be so rude. He didn't know much about women but if he'd coped with the Bonkers of Brisbane, he could surely cope with her.

He took a deep breath and turned around, but when he opened his mouth, a strangled seagull came out.

"Ergh…*arck*!…I didn't mean to…I was just…"

"Just what?" she snorted. "Feeling at liberty to help yourself to someone else's property?"

"I never intended to offend," he explained. "You were not around to ask! I didn't even know it was yours – and it's only a book, not the crown jewels. I was just curious…"

"It killed the cat!" she countered. "Where do you disembark?"

"I'm not sure, but having read that chapter, I might…"

"You will escort me. To Oman. Carry my bags, hail taxis – that sort of thing. It is not prudent for a woman to travel in Arabia by herself. India was bad enough! I'll see you when we reach port!"

And she returned to her reading, effectively dismissing him.

36

Macy awoke swathed in 1000 thread count Egyptian cotton sheets with the smell of freshly brewed coffee and oven-baked *pains au chocolat* wafting up her nostrils. After a nanosecond of *I've died and gone to breakfast heaven*, she realised where she was, leapt out of bed, got dressed and emerged from the room, ready to leave.

"*Bonjour*! You take sugar?"

Again, the disarming smile, the stature, the self-assurance, the good looks. If anything, he had improved during the night.

"Er…just one please…" He poured her coffee from a cafetière into a bone china Fornasetti mug.

"I'll…er…I'll just drink that and then I'll go."

"Why?"

To her surprise, Macy couldn't think of a suitable response, apart from the fact that he was a guy, and she was a girl, and her thought process didn't go beyond the fact that that was a bad thing.

She sipped her coffee and munched her croissant in pensive silence. Both were utterly delicious.

"You 'ave things?" Franky asked.

"What do you mean 'things'?"

"Clothes, books, toothbrush? You did not came to Paree *sans rien*?"

"No. I have things. Not much but…"

"Where they are?"

"In some pension near the Gare du Nord."

He wrinkled his nose in disgust. "So?"

"So what?"

"Pension near Gare du Nord is *charmant, non*? Clean? *Confortable*? Furnish like *Le Palais de Versailles*?"

Macy sniggered and stuck out her bottom lip.

"*Alors?*" he asked, raising his shoulder.

"I don't know, Franky. It's just that…we've only just met and I'm…I'm not…"

They took a cab to the station and retraced her steps to the rue Cortot. Franky even managed to get some of her money back by convincing the wizened old crone at Reception that she was his runaway sister and a minor *en plus* and that the law had been broken by charging her one week's lodging without checking her ID.

With the words *Are you out of your mind?* screaming unheard on her lips, Macy sat stiffly in the cab clutching her holdall on her lap. He looked across at her and smiled which set her pulse racing, but she focused on devising the conditions of her stay:

1. She would pay her own way and would only model fully dressed.
2. She would attempt to help him with his singing and his art.
3. She would be free to leave at any time without explanation or prior notice.

And most importantly:

1. The arrangement could only work if he put a lock on the door to the second bedroom and promised never to lay a finger on her.

Franky agreed. He agreed to everything, because his father had taught him that women – and even girls – no matter how pretty and clever they appeared to be, would inevitably change their minds once they'd fallen hopelessly in love.

*

As promised, Franky respected her space and privacy, and Macy began to feel reasonably safe. She appreciated the luxury of her surroundings and more importantly, she knew her father would never find her there.

They settled into some sort of polite domesticity, skirting around each other like birds of a different feather. Some mornings, after she'd cleared away the breakfast things – Madame Lalande always sent up fresh croissants or warm, crispy baguettes – Franky would sit strumming one of his guitars while Macy wrote random lyrics for him. He loved the fact that she sung in English – it would be good for attracting American tourists. She was adamant that she could not and would not sing, but they rehearsed together to improve his repertoire.

As she began to feel a little more secure, Macy let him draw her. It was summertime, a really sweltering summer in the city. She mostly wore shorts and vests, leaving her arms and legs bare. She knew that to improve, he needed to see form and contour, so she dragged him around the art galleries and museums: The Musée d'Orsay, the Louvre, the Luxembourg Gardens, Le Petit Palais. She pointed out the genres and variations of renowned artists who had made Paris their home – it pleased her that, although he was twenty-two, she seemed to know more about it than he did. He confessed to only having visited his city's museums on school trips where he and his mates would spend most of the time giggling at the 'tits and fannies', never appreciating how hard it was to paint them accurately.

Whenever they stood before a painting or a sculpture of a nude, he would wind Macy up.

"Where iz 'er dress? Why she az no trouser?" or "What she is 'iding behind 'er and? I need ze X-ray vision!"

She knew he had a point, but she stuck to her rules.

He never touched the money she left out for him always putting it back on her dressing-table. In return she kept the apartment spotless, and he fed and watered her, wined and dined her, and provided her with a home and security. She offered him her bare limbs and her company, nothing else.

One evening, after they had prepared a gourmet meal of lobster with white asparagus bought fresh from the market, washed down with a bottle of Domaine Ott Rosé, Macy found herself with an excess of deliciously Provençal Dutch courage. As he sat practising a song they'd written, she cleared away the supper things then went upstairs to the studio. The man in the moon observed her through the skylight, his eyebrows raised, his mouth an "Oh?"

Macy was keyed up, nervous and tipsy. The heat was oppressive. She opened the skylight to let in some air then stripped off and reclined on the chaise longue, draping the antique shawl across her thighs. She could hear Franky strumming downstairs, but she knew he'd come up soon enough – he always wanted to be where she was. The music and the wine had lulled and mellowed her and before long, her eyelids drooped, and she fell asleep.

Franky replaced the Gibson on its stand. He got up and stretched. The apartment was eerily quiet. The kitchen was clean and tidy. His *petite muse* was nowhere to be seen.

He climbed the staircase slowly, bare feet soundless on the crystal treads. He reached the top and halted, listening to the silence, broken only by a soft and regular purr. The skylight was open. Had a cat got in? He took a few steps forward and then stopped again. On the chaise longue lay a goddess blessed by moonlight, skin like polished ivory, exquisite in repose.

Torn between the urge to take her or to sketch her, he approached stealthily peering with awe at the gift laid out before him. Her body was shaped like a guitar: Oh! How he longed to play her. Her breasts – such perfect breasts! – the left relaxed towards her underarm, the right so pert, so alert, with nipples pink and rosy like a new-born baby's lips.

Her subtly parted legs invited him to worship at the very V of her, denied him by that promise he so much longed to break.

Franky reached for a pad and stick of charcoal. He sketched quickly, inflamed by what he saw, and she flowed out through the graphite and found life on the page. Her contours were clear, unambiguous: a soft, celestial creature just slightly out of reach.

Macy stirred and turned onto her side. The buttocks she now offered him were perfect marble orbs, the cleft a smile or a frown, depending how you looked at it. Barely able to breathe, he did a second sketch, then propped the picture up where she would see it when she woke. Covering Macy gently with the paint-stained woollen throw, he tiptoed back downstairs to his ever-lonelier bed.

Franky gave way to his desire, praying that when she saw the art she had inspired, she'd let him break his promise and see her nude again.

*

Through the open skylight, dawn's delicate breeze raised goosebumps on her skin. The sheet – where was her sheet? – felt scratchy and she grappled for her duvet but felt the throw instead. Her eyes shot open, and she realised where she was, recalling last night's weakness and her drunken little ruse.

With the shawl wrapped around her, Macy scuttled downstairs to her bed. She was shivering now and anxious in the early morning chill. Franky stirred across the hall, dreaming of a mermaid with oil paint in her hair.

When Macy finally emerged at 11 am that morning, Franky was on his third coffee, tapping an impatient rhythm on the countertop.

"*Bonjour.*" Her voice was a little higher than usual. She cleared her throat, hoping last night's insanity had passed unnoticed.

"*Bonjour toi,*" Franky answered, gutted that his magnum opus had not received its due acclaim.

They skirted around each other; the air was thick with unasked questions.

"What?" Macy asked.

"You see ze picture?"

"What picture?"

"Ze one I made last night!"

"When last night?"

"Zis last night! *Dans le studio.*"

They both bounded across the room; Franky's limber legs scaled the staircase just ahead of her. He grabbed the sketch and held it flat against his chest, afraid for her to see it, certain she would object, sorry it wasn't good enough in the cold light of day.

Macy jumped up like a terrier, trying to flip it over, seize it, see it. Franky dodged around her, holding it aloft.

"*Arrêtes!*" he shouted as she caught the corner with her hand. "*Tu vas l'abîmer*! You spoil it! I show you but you do not laugh. Zis piece: *C'est sérieux*!"

Macy held her hands up in submission and sat down on the chaise. "Go on then," she taunted, feeling anything but sure.

In slow and torturous motion, Franky turned the picture around. Macy craned forward to take a closer look.

Oh. My. God! she thought scanning every line, stroke, and nuance. He had captured her so honestly, turned her blatancy into virtue. The image was neither timid nor overt but showed the confidence of an artist who understood his muse.

"Franky!" Her eyes shone. "This is *good work.* Your best. The sketch is…luminous, it's beautiful…you've made me beautiful!"

"I know," he answered simply. "I only could do it because you are beautiful." And he leaned over and kissed her on the cheek.

*

Although at first uneasy in the unforgiving light, Macy modelled for him in the poses of her choice. She revelled in her muse-fulness, rearranging the studio to maximise its space, bringing pillows and cushions up from downstairs, moving his cluttered table to where he could reach it best, ensuring his creativity was fed with food and drink.

She raided a nearby record store and bought some second-hand LPs. By experimenting with different types of music, they found he worked best to Edith Piaf and Mahler, translating onto canvas the notes that pleased his ears.

Franky's productive energy crackled between them like an electric current. The more prolific he became, the more inventively she posed. Her nudity – her freedom now – the gift with strings attached, became his passion and his pain. He experienced every inch of her, and that made the 'Look, Don't Touch' rule more unsustainable. How could she lie there naked and expect him to abstain? Something had to give. And soon.

While Franky painted with the right side of his brain, the left side made a plan. His knew from his father: 'All women have a price', and he supposed his gorgeous girl was no exception. She obviously cherished that tacky gold bag of hers, but he hated it. It was garish and lacked class.

I will take her shopping, he thought. *That should do the trick.*

Franky stood in the kitchen in a pair of navy track suit bottoms; his chest was bare, his muscles well-defined. His skin was tawny, his feet long and slender like his hands. Macy appreciated his male beauty. How could she not?

"No work today," he stated, biting into his *pain aux raisins.*

"Why?" she asked. "Don't you want to finish that study? It's going well and if we're going to take the canvases to a dealer…You're on a deadline now – you know that!"

For someone so young with such a complex past, she had embraced this role as if she'd been born to it. Franky allowed her autonomy in most things, building her trust by sticking to his promise. And now she never questioned it – it was their way of life – her with her naked power, him tempering his frustration by painting it away.

"No work today." He repeated. "Better things to do. We work again tomorrow."

Macy felt a pang of jealousy. What did he mean 'better things to do'? What things? Things that didn't include her? She wondered momentarily how she would spend *her* day.

"You're not going busking, are you? That's OK, if you need a change. I'll come with if you like. We can practice the…"

"*Non*. No busking." And he flashed her a conspiratorial wink.

Macy's mind began to race. Did the wink signify he had something up his sleeve to do with *her*, or something down his trousers to do with *himself*? She wasn't stupid. As grateful as she was that he had kept his promise, she knew that a fit 22-year-old would need some hormonal outlet other than painting and singing.

"We go shopping," he announced, saving her from the slippery slope of her own imagination.

"Shopping? What for? We're not short of materials, and Madame Lalande always gets our…"

"*Non ma petite!* Shopping for you. Something to wear."

"Something to wear?" She joked. "I'm in the buff most of the time!" He had never wanted to grab her more than he did just then.

Maissi, Maissi – ma petite ingénue – so easy with me now you don't realise the effect. You offer me your beauty like a sacrifice, your skin so smooth, your body so nubile, your figure like God's own egg timer. Legs – folded or relaxed – one knee up, one knee down, arms above your head, hands coiled through your hair, breasts like fresh-picked peaches, your nipples erect when you get chilled…and your motte, *your* mons Veneris, *that tempting triangle of downy hair that conceals the highway to the stars, why will you not allow me one tiny, little peep? Whichever way you arrange yourself,* ma belle, *you always look to me like you are longing to be fucked!*

Franky felt himself harden as he struggled to control the complex mélange of emotion and desire. Angry with her, and himself, he crashed his cup down on the counter and stormed out of the room.

"Get ready!" he shouted and headed into his ensuite to relieve the tension once again.

The interior of 5 rue Cambon in the 1er arrondissement was a shrine at which only the super-rich were welcome to worship. Grungy tourists and skanky backpackers may have peered through the *vitrines* like little match girls and boys, but they were discouraged from entering the hallowed portals by a staff whose training included:

- *Haughty Sneering Unless Customer is Already Decked Out in Chanel*
- *Being Respectful to Russian Hookers, Arab Princesses and Chinese Diplomats' Wives and Mistresses*
- *Mental Assessment of Customer's Bank Balance to Verify Worthiness to Tread on Sacred Carpet*

If ever the expression: *If you must ask the price, you can't afford it* was well-suited to a retail establishment, this was it.

Macy tried not to feel intimidated by the effortless chic of her surroundings. If anyone had told her a year ago when she was effectively nicking a designer bag from Selfridges that she would be in Chanel's flagship store in Paris with a man who actually Wanted to Buy Her Something, she'd have told them to apply for a brain transplant.

The black, white, and cream interior, the fashion and accessory displays, the counters sparkling with jewellery, the strings of trademark pearls, the air infused with the heady scent of the boutique's actual street number, were all quite overwhelming. Strategic spotlights highlighted the mannequins that wore similar expressions to the shop girls, and the couture dotted around the boutique was probably what Venus would have worn had she been going on a date with Adonis. Macy had her own Adonis, but she didn't really see it like that. She felt unkempt, irrelevant, and totally out of place in this elite institution.

Franky folded his long, lean body onto a cream leather, black-piped sofa and waited for the *défilé* to begin. Fawning sales assistants hovered around him like bees around lavender, suspicion replaced by sycophancy. They brought him a glass of champagne but didn't offer her one. Perhaps they thought he was a rock star. They obviously hadn't heard him sing.

Choosing from the plethora of items being presented, Franky gestured for Macy to try them on and walk around for him. He had probably seen this in a film somewhere and now fancied himself as the protagonist.

Fighting her irritation – *what is the likelihood of this* ever *happening again?* – she allowed herself to be led into a subtly-lit changing room with floor to ceiling mirrors where a selection of couture was presented for her to try on: suits, dresses, skirts, blouses, tops, jackets, belts, shoes. For someone used to padding about barefoot in shorts and vest tops or lying still wearing nothing, this all seemed *de trop*.

The beauty of these items wasn't lost on her, but she wasn't sure any of them were actually her thing. She started to try the garments on and quickly realised the quality of the fabrics was akin to being kissed by angels. But it was all so rigidly structured and grown-up like she'd raided some *grande dame's* wardrobe and was playing dress-up.

She emerged from the *vestiaire* in a classic navy and white bouclé two-piece suit to find Franky holding court. He took one look at her and burst out laughing.

"*Maissi!*" he chortled, draining his flute of champagne, and taking another while munching on a pistachio *macaron* – coincidentally the exact colour of his eyes. "You look like my *Tante Mathilde*! I think Coco Chanel herself said: '*Before you leave the house, look in the mirror and take one thing off.*' I want you to take everything off!"

"No change there, then!" Macy muttered and marched back into the changing-room.

She stepped out of the suit and put her denim mini-skirt and black t-shirt back on. How drab she looked against the soignée salesgirls. She picked up her gold bag – even that looked cheap in this environment – and for the first time ever, it failed to up her cred. To think she actually preferred lying naked on a moth-eaten sofa than being taken shopping at Chanel came as a shock to her. She was used to having Franky to herself and seeing him with all these women really wound her up.

By the time she emerged, the angle of Franky's recline had deteriorated to horizontal. Some of the *vendeuses* had left to attend to other clients but three remained, encircling him like a vortex of vaginas. Macy was used to his astounding good looks and unpretentious charm, but he'd pulled his hair elastic off, and his luxuriant liquorice mane now tumbled around his shoulders. She suddenly got the whole Delilah thing. If there had been a pair of clippers handy, she'd have shorn him like a sheep.

Franky's self-esteem had grown by becoming a better artist, but his male ego had suffered through Macy's continued denial of him. He was having a wonderful time, so he ignored her visual plea to leave the boutique now and ambled over to the handbag counter where the most attractive shop girl stood waiting to assist.

"*Quelle est la nouvelle vague?*" he asked.

She reached for an ice-blue tweed *sac à main* with a bamboo top handle and placed it tenderly in front of him.

"And the most classic?"

A jumbo size cream quilted lambskin bag with a gold chain handle was set down on the counter.

"I'll take them both," he said.

What should have been *the* most exciting moment of Macy's life was ruined: as he swung the two enormous black carriers with the white lettering and the signature ribbon adorned with a camellia towards her, he kept his eyes firmly locked on those of the salesgirl.

It occurred to Macy afterwards that she should not have reached out her hand. She should have just let them drop to the floor. But honestly, what woman in her right mind would have done that? Even at 16¾, she was fully aware that the gift of two Chanel handbags was THE GIFT OF TWO CHANEL HANDBAGS.

They returned home in silence. She got out of the cab leaving him to bring the carriers in.

"Why you not 'appy?" he asked as they crossed the cobbled courtyard.

Macy shrugged. She was annoyed by her own reaction, confused because she always had him to herself. And she'd never experienced romantic jealousy before. Yet, how could she accuse him of flirting with other women when *she'd* made the ground rules which *he'd* been sticking to? She went into her bedroom feeling more maladjusted than ever before.

Franky marched over to the cocktail trolley and poured himself a large whisky. He downed it in one and poured another. His body language was tense, like a greyhound straining to leave the trap. He could still smell the shop girls' perfume, their female pheromones. He wanted them all, with their tight French pleats and their tight Parisian pussies. He looked at his wrist where one of them had branded him with her phone number.

"*Je termine à dix-huit heures,*" she'd whispered – I finish at 6 – but it was barely lunchtime now and he couldn't wait that long.

The carrier bags stood unopened on the black marble floor like a partition between them. Franky knocked back his second drink and picked the bags up. He crossed the living area and rapped on Macy's door.

"Just a moment," she called out, like he hadn't seen her naked before. She emerged in a short white towelling robe with nothing underneath. "Are you ready to work?" she asked.

"I'm ready for somezing..." Franky slurred.

He handed her the bags and after a moment's hesitation, she took them, unable to meet his eye.

"Are you sure?" she asked softly. "I don't know how to thank you..."

"You *do* know how to zank me!" And he grabbed her by the shoulders.

She let the carriers drop and winced as she heard the gold-tone hardware rattle like convicts' chains.

Franky's mass towered over her, his jaw clenching and releasing as his grip around her tightened. For the first time in his presence, she felt afraid.

She swallowed hard and placed her hands on his biceps to keep him at arm's length.

"Come upstairs, Franky," she urged quietly. "You need to redirect this...this energy into something more positive, onto the canvas."

He slapped her then, a swift, sharp slap which shocked them both. Macy rocked sideways and her palm shot to her cheek. Franky collapsed onto his knees, clutching her around the hips.

"*Pardonnes-moi, Maissi*...I'm so sorry...*je n'sais pas*..."

The power shift was tangible: she felt it and he knew it.

"Come on," she said, and pulled him to his feet. Franky shrugged free, poured another drink, and followed her upstairs.

She didn't recline on the chaise, and he did not ask her to. The intensity of his maleness was an elephant in the room: the morning had changed the whole dynamic between them. The trust and ease with which they lived together, their joint appreciation and respect, had been replaced by something edgy, toxic, filled with tension. Macy clutched her robe around her, unwilling to offer him the gift that kept on giving that she never truly gave.

Franky swore under his breath and tore off his shirt and trousers. He crossed the room and opened all the skylights. It was muggy in the studio, a low oppressive heat that softened all his paints.

He marched over to his easel to check his latest *oeuvre*, staring at it with a look of pure disdain. He grabbed a paintbrush, daubed it with Chromatic Black and smeared it everywhere, destroying the image, the background, everything.

"What are you doing?" Macy cried. "You've ruined it! That was...!"

She ran to see the damage but before she reached his side, he kicked the easel hard, sending it flying across the room. The canvas pirouetted in mid-air and landed at her feet. She lunged to retrieve it, but he caught her by the wrist, wresting her backwards towards the dining-table laden with materials. She stumbled and her robe fell open. His eyes ignited as he pushed her down; she felt the metal paint tubes dig into her skin.

He climbed onto the table and pinioned her, smothering her face with his.

Macy struggled...then stopped. Such savage memories assailed her that she gulped, a gulp that he mistook for something else. He slid down her torso, sniffing her armpits like a hungry dog.

"I must to love you," he panted. "I cannot wait no more."

"But we had a pact!"

"Fuck you and your *pacte*!" he snarled. "All great artists sleep wiz their models!"

"You are *not* a great artist!"

She wasn't sure what had offended him more – that insult or her continued negation of him, but she could feel his thickening hardness forcing at her groin.

"Franky! Please! I beg of you! Don't!"

She wriggled one hand free and tried to push him off.

"FRANKY!" she insisted, and using all her weight and might, she heaved him over, so he was underneath and she on top. She tried to clamber off the table, but he would not loosen his grip. Macy swept the surface with her free hand searching for something to use in self-defence; pots, paints, palettes, brushes, bowls, and jars went crashing to the floor.

A shift in stability made them both start, then the table creaked, quivered, sloped, and collapsed, spilling them onto the floor in a mass of jumbled limbs. Macy rolled away and got to her feet, closing her robe around her as she backed across the room.

"Aaooww!" she cried, hopping on one foot, lifting the other up to see what caused the pain. A stream of blood trickled down her sole onto the hardwood floor.

"Look what you've done now, *imbecile*, you've ruined everything! Get up! Or are you too drunk to move?"

Franky did not react.

"Franky!" she shouted angrily, hobbling towards him. "Get the fuck up!"

His head was lolling sideways, his eyes were open and staring straight ahead. Macy limped over to where he lay and kicked him in the ribs. His body rocked then settled slowly back. She was about to kick him again, harder, when she noticed a viscous ooze creeping out from underneath him. A punctured tube of Spanish Crimson? No. It couldn't be. The consistency was wrong.

Pupils dilating in terror, Macy backed away. Franky was lying in one of those shapes the police drew chalk around. Chunks of broken glass were scattered everywhere: one sharp and jagged shard upended like a monolith. It was one half of the chipped Lalique vase he'd kept his brushes in. Where was the rest of it?

"Franky?" she whimpered, rushing forward and falling to her knees. "Please wake up."

But all that moved was a slick-like pool of blood and linseed oil.

37

She stood on the deck ready to disembark, her ginger frizz stuffed beneath a wide-brimmed Panama hat. An oversized Louis Vuitton holdall squatted at her feet like a lion in repose. Aaron approached her with a new determination. He hadn't introduced himself properly and if they were going to be travelling together…He stuck out his hand.

"Aaron Fairclough. On leave from my job as Head of Religious Studies at…"

"Flame Maxwell-Arlington." Her handshake nearly broke his fingers.

"Come!" She ordered and stepped off the ferry leaving the 'lion' at his feet.

Aaron picked it up, muttered a minor blasphemy and let it drop again. He un-shouldered his own rucksack and tried to slip his arms through the Vuitton's handles to wear like a papoose.

"Not like that!" She commanded from fifty feet ahead of him. "It's a piece of vintage luggage, not a bloody baby carrier!"

Aaron considered kicking the thing overboard but gallantry prevailed. He would figure it out somehow. What else was he to do?

The Bedouin encampment was as unexpected as it was welcome. After leaving port, they had circumnavigated the city and made straight for the desert heading along an unmade road with high dunes on either side. Wahiba Sands – he later learned – was three agonising hours away. Hanging on to the jeep's grab rails, the unsecured canvas flapping in their faces, they bumped along like jumping beans. Grit blinded Aaron's eyes and chafed his throat – how in God's name had he got himself into this? He had not expected a fractured spine just for borrowing a book.

Flame Maxwell-Arlington managed to look aloof while also hanging on for grim death.

When he had questioned her as to where they were going, she'd ordered him to: "Just get in".

Now he studied her from behind his sunglasses and noticed that the hauteur was wilting. She seemed on edge, nervous. She looked younger than he'd originally thought – probably in her early forties – whereas during the book debacle, he'd pitched her at around fifty. Her face, although fiercely freckled, was unlined, with strong features, a shapely mouth and skin the colour of skimmed milk.

"Where were you in India?" he asked to relieve the tedium.

"Everywhere!" she answered, like a smack in the face.

The sand dunes rippled with laughter, mocking his discomfort and uptight British *politesse*. Eventually his brain, turned to scrambled eggs by the jolting of the jeep, managed to compose another simple question.

"Anywhere particularly appeal?"

She looked at him with such contempt you would have thought he'd questioned her preference for syphilis or gonorrhoea.

The jeep rumbled on and eventually veered left towards an oasis of palm trees. The driver performed a hockey-stop in a blinding cloud of dust and Aaron shot forward like a cannonball. He instinctively put his arm out and his hand landed flat on her breast. She huffed loudly and swatted him away with a: "How dare you!"

"I was only trying to…"

"Well don't!"

Flame sat ramrod straight staring towards the tents. He could no longer read her. He clambered down, stretched his sore back then offered her his hand. She dismissed it so he withdrew.

The driver got out, offloaded the bags, did a lap of honour to raise another sandstorm and drove away.

Thanks, thought Aaron. And how do I get out of here? Dial C for Camel?

Flame remained where she stood. Aaron went to lift the bags, but she hissed: "Leave them!" Which he obeyed without question. He'd got the measure of her now: regimental sergeant major.

Kohl-eyed children wandered out of the tents and stared inquisitively at the road-rattled pallid couple. Flame's aloofness seemed to soften.

To Aaron's surprise, she looked across at him and said: "Follow me and watch my back." Then she smoothed down her skirt, took a visibly deep breath and set off towards the tents.

That evening, Aaron logged their arrival in his travel journal:

I followed close behind, realising this was no holiday village pre-booked through Thomas Cook. Bedouins began to emerge, some carrying khanjars *(curved daggers), tucked into the sashes around their waists. They wore embroidered caps and long white* dishdasha *robes and they fiddled with the tassels that dangled from their necklines; I learned later these are impregnated with sweet-smelling frankincense to allay unpleasant smells.*

The women wore brightly coloured, multi-patterned salwars *with muslin cloths atop their heads; they whispered amongst themselves. Their faces, but for their eyes, were covered by* burqas *so it was impossible to tell whether they welcomed us or not. Then in unison they parted like the Red Sea and bowed as we walked through.*

Flame squared her shoulders and with slow and measured steps, approached the entrance to the largest tent. She hovered on the threshold, hands against her heart before ducking and entering through the slit in the canvas. I followed close behind. The palm fronds on either side brushed our arms like ghosts requesting recognition.

Because she stopped short on entering – either to delay or allow her eyes to adjust to the light – I stumbled right into her. She whipped around and tutted at me. I was just trying to look out for her, but yet again, I felt like the court jester.

*

"I thought you'd come alone."

The accent was a cocktail of Bombay Sapphire with a dash of bitters and a twist of lime.

"How are you, Baba?" Flame's voice was a strangled whisper, the lofty anger giving way to gentleness and respect. "Where is he?"

"Here. With me. Where he has always been."

She shielded her eyes and peered into the gloom trying to discern a shape, a silhouette, a clue. A minute passed, maybe two, then a younger white-clad figure emerged from the shadows and walked slowly towards her. Flame gasped and her hand went to her mouth.

"Edward? Is it really you? I've missed you so…"

"It is Amit now. Remember?"

Flame rushed forward and crushed him to her breast. He was taller than her, but she hugged her arms around him, for all the missing years. He remained impassive, neither returning the embrace nor denying it. Flame released him and stared into his eyes.

"Edward…"

"It is Amit, my flame. It was never really Edward." And then, barely discernible: "You live on in my heart."

He stepped away from her and turned. Flame's memory reached out to retrieve him, but he was gone, like a dream in the dawn.

"Too long has passed," the older man intoned. "Too much water. Too wide a bridge."

"I know…" Flame acquiesced. "…but thank you, Baba, at least for this." She went over to where he sat and bent down and hugged him.

"God bless you," she whispered, then she too turned to leave.

Aaron pre-empted her and lifted the canvas flap so she could exit first. She crossed the encampment and went straight to her tent – and he to his.

The logs rustled and crackled in their bed of stones then settled for the night. Aaron was unable to do the same. He had come outside with a rug to lay by the fire and stare at the stars. He didn't hear her approaching, barefoot through the sand, until she was towering above him like that first day on the boat.

He went to get up, like the gentleman he was, but she stayed him with her hand and sank cross-legged by the fire. They sat in silence for a while; she sifted her fingers through the sand, watching the grains run through them like time. She seemed more yielding now, like the meeting had removed her stiffness and her angst. Eventually, Aaron steeled himself to speak.

"Who was he?" he asked. "My brother…" she replied, lifting the words off her shoulders, and laying them on the ground. And then, the coup de grâce:

"…my lover too…"

She looked up for a reaction. There was no one to impress now: Elvis had left the building.

Human after all, thought Aaron, *and vulnerable too.*

"My father was posted here just after I was born," she began, and he knew the story would contain herbs and spice. "I was a small child, aged three or four…an only child then. Father was a high-ranking officer in the British Army, and we lived in a grand house with servants. I was Daddy's little girl: he would tease and tickle me and take me riding – he even bought me my own camel. Mother insisted I go to the local school rather than be sent home to England like the other ex-pats, so I made friends with the local children. The older man you saw today was my father's aide-de-camp, his adjutant and personal assistant. He spent a lot of time with us. I even called him Baba, which means 'father' in Arabic. Of course, I didn't know that he and Mother…" She searched among the stars for the right words. "I suppose they fell in love…I had an *amah* – a nanny – so Mother didn't look after me much, but when she told me there was going to be a 'new arrival' – a baby brother or sister – I was thrilled. Little did I know…Father didn't know either, well not until…" She sniffed. "Father was fair-haired, you see, and Mother was a raving redhead, so it was pretty obvious when Edward was born that she'd gone 'off piste'. My baby brother was a dark-skinned, black-haired crossbreed – tarnished with a touch of the tar brush. Father took one look at him and went for his horse whip. He whipped my mother till she bled, then rode out into the desert and shot himself."

Flame looked confused as if she were hearing a story she'd never heard before. Aaron reached out but she recoiled, so he withdrew.

"He couldn't bear the loss of face, you see, the shame…Could not bear to keep on living, not even for me…his only child…"

Aaron held his breath hoping she would go on.

"Mother became ill after the birth, both physically and mentally. The aide-de-camp had helped himself to more than he was due, and once Father was gone, he no longer fitted into the equation. He'd been responsible for his boss's suicide, so he lost his job, his mistress and his son. My mother lost her husband *and* her lover, but she was besotted with little Edward, as far as her health would allow. Nanny mostly cared for him, so I was pretty much left to my own dev…well, *vices* as it turned out."

Flame returned to raking her fingers through the sand, not sifting this time, but scratching as you would an itch.

"I adored my little brother. Oh, how I loved that boy with his treacly eyes and jet-black hair and skin as smooth and as brown as a conker. Once the Army deemed my mother sufficiently recovered, they demanded the house back. My father's job had been reassigned and Mother had no rights. She wasn't fit for anything really: demented by that time – literally – out of her mind. I caught her once marching around the compound in my father's dress uniform shouting for him to come in for tiffin. Baba wrote to her suggesting she and I return to England. I think that was the final straw. Edward, or Amit as Baba called him, would be taken in, and looked after by his tribe…And so, both of us distraught but unable to express or share our pain, we sailed home and Mother ended up in a mental institution near Tunbridge Wells where they medicated her so heavily that she died, though I think the cause of death should have read: Broken Heart. I was taken in by a stiff upper-lipped Army family who immediately sent me to boarding school to be educated 'in the manner to which I must become accustomed'. The day I turned 14, I ran away. I'd saved up my pocket money and I took a train to the nearest port which was Plymouth. I was sure there would be a ship sailing to Muscat – all I wanted to do was come home. Of course, there weren't any ships travelling that route, plus I'd been spotted, so I was returned to boarding school, and it wasn't until I was nearly seventeen, just after my 'O' levels, that I finally returned to Oman with a school friend whose parents had military links here.

I searched high and low for Edward, but I couldn't find him, then by complete chance, on the day before we were due to leave, I saw my old amah in the souk. Even in a *burqa*, I recognised her immediately – she always had this funny gait. Of course, she knew me by my red hair and freckles, and she also knew where Edward and his father were, so with much joy, we were re-united. I decided not to return to England…I never considered it my home anyway. Baba arranged for me to stay with family – I guess I brought him closer to my mother."

Flame shivered. It was getting chilly now. Aaron was loath to rebuild the fire in case he broke her train and after a moment, she continued.

"Edward was fourteen by then, one of the most striking young men I had ever seen. He was tall and muscular and held himself with the deportment of an Army Officer combined with the exoticism of a well-bred Omani. It was an intoxicating blend. I got a job teaching English to Omani children and he and I started spending time together. There was such a strong bond…we shared a mother, after all…"

Flame paused in her narrative and got to her feet. She started pacing like a caged animal desperate to be let out. Aaron sensed the next part would be more difficult.

"W-would you like a drink?" he asked, suddenly remembering the miniatures in his rucksack.

"A G & T would be ideal, but I don't think we've got much hope here!"

"I might have something in my bag. Purely medicinal, of course…"

Flame's eyes widened and she smiled, a different woman to the ogress he'd first met.

"Hold that thought," he said and hurried to his tent.

When he returned, she was sitting on the rug with her knees hugged against her chest. She had arranged a few more logs on the fire, sparked it up again.

"I forgot how cold the desert gets at night," she said, then: "Oh! Well done!" – as Aaron handed her a tiny bottle. He placed one of his fleeces around her shoulders and she shrugged her arms into it and zipped it up.

"Thank you," she said with sincerity. "I know I've been a cow. I get like that sometimes. Defence mechanism and all."

"Defence against what?"

"The world in general? My life in particular?"

Aaron didn't argue. He found her fascinating either way. "So, er, when you saw Edward today, how long had it been?"

"Too long…but what happened…neither of us could forget."

Aaron could relate to unforgettable incidents. They were becoming his stock in trade.

Flame knocked back the miniature Courvoisier and shuddered like a puppy emerging from a pond. Aaron handed her the second one.

"Are you sure?" she asked, cracking the lid, and doing the same. "Gosh! I needed that!"

"Thinking back, there had always been that pull between us, that inexplicable chemistry. I never realised how powerful it was until…that afternoon. He'd always been intrigued by my hair, you see. He loved touching it, even as a little boy, the texture, the colour, I suppose it reminded him of Mother. He would try to smooth it down, running his fingers through it…I enjoyed his touch, it induced…feelings in me…like a poodle being petted by a panther – two different species who should not really mix…"

Her voice trailed off, then she looked directly at him and shook the little empty bottle at him. "Any more of these, by any chance?"

"Sorry," Aaron answered. "I only had two and you've drunk them both!" Flame let out a girlish giggle that sounded like a fountain flowing with gold coins.

"It was a Sunday," she sighed after a long pause. "We'd been walking on the beach. It was getting late, and the sun was going down in such an explosion of fuchsia, purple, pink, violet, the sort of sunset you only get in the Gulf. We stood there watching it. 'Those colours reflect you, my flame,' Edward said. 'Majestic, exciting and full of fire.'

"His words touched every part of me. He'd often quote verses or poetry, but these were his words…and his voice that afternoon had a different edge, a kind of rasp. We walked on, keeping a respectable distance, then he suddenly said: 'Let's swim!'"

"OK!" I answered and he looked surprised.

"Omani women do not divest their clothing before a man who is not their husband," he said.

"So why ask me then?" I countered. "Anyway, we're family – and I'm not an Omani woman."

Impetuously, I lifted my dress over my head and said something stupid like: "Last one in's a rotten egg!"

"He pulled off his *dishdasha* and ran in after me. The water was a blessing, so cool and fresh and clear as glass. We dived like dolphins then he suddenly surfaced right in front on me and there we were…nose to nose, treading water. I remember marvelling at the droplets clinging to his eyelashes – I wanted to wear them like a string of pearls. His hair was long, as black as oil and as shiny as patent, and our lips were just a kiss apart…He suddenly spun around and went to swim away but I caught him by the ankle, and he towed me into shore. It was twilight by then and the beach was deserted. I never meant it as a come-on, but I took off my wet bra and dropped it on the sand. I was wringing the water out of my hair and when I looked up, Edward was staring at me like he'd never seen me before. I stared right back at him then my eyes dropped to the black streak that started at his navel and disappeared downwards in a fine straight line. I was mesmerised. We stood for a moment like a couple of statues, but the marble soon melted and turned to flesh. I do not know who made the first move…maybe we both did. We just fell into each other, and our mouths locked and the next thing I knew we were naked on the sand and when he…when he entered me, it felt like coming home. There was no shame…only joy, a burning, visceral, all-consuming joy…"

Aaron shifted across and put his arm around her as he'd been taught to do for a woman when she cried. She flinched at first but then relaxed, grateful of acceptance with no judgment or reproach. Without breaking contact, he eased them both down beneath the rug and gathered her closer to him, hoping the cold night air would not disturb her, hoping that in the morning, she would not withdraw again.

When the first Bedouin surfaced at sunrise, he found them fast asleep, cuddled up like children. He fetched another blanket and placed it over them, and they slept until the camp came to life. Aaron awoke first, amazed to have this woman in his arms, but when Flame stirred and sensed their proximity, she pulled away and hurried to her tent.

When she emerged later in the day, her eyes were concealed behind dark glasses. In deference to what had taken place, she sought Aaron out and without speaking, drew an X across his heart. He nodded, not really understanding, but promising, nonetheless.

38

She knew she ought to call an ambulance or the police or Madame Lalande at least, but they'd say it was her fault and cart her off to jail! She needed to rewind this nightmare déjà vu so she could act differently and change the ending. Oh, where was Mr Fairclough? He would know what to do! She had his number somewhere in the flyleaf of that book! She'd call him! She'd call him now and beg him for his help.

Scrabbling through her things, she searched for the book he'd dropped off a million lives ago. She would find it and she'd call him, and he'd come and sort this out. But the book wasn't there – what had she done with it! She yanked her holdall down from the top shelf and started ripping her clothes out of the wardrobe and stuffing them inside. She tore off her robe – it had blood and paint all over it! – and screwed it up at the bottom underneath the rest. She hadn't even realised her knees were gashed from crawling on the studio floor. She ran into the shower and let the water rain down on her head, hot then cold then hot then cold, but nothing – not all her scented soaps and body scrubs – could make her feel as clean as she now craved to be.

She had to get out of here, away from him, away from Paris, away from everything. Let whoever found him figure out the rape and murder scene.

And then clarity kicked in, and she had a job to do.

Upstairs.

Careful not to tread in the congealing mess, she covered his body with the throw. She could not look at him – how could she? If she didn't look at him, it meant he wasn't there.

Macy stood tight-jawed, ankle deep in chaos, trying to remain focused. The clutter was horrific. Could she burn it, start a bonfire in the middle of the room? Breathing in short puffs like a woman in labour, she thought: *Do not think, just do.*

Wrapping her right hand in discarded rags, she picked up a jagged shard of glass and set about slashing every painting he had ever done of her. She hacked the canvases into strips, jumbling them up like shredded paper and packing them randomly in different rubbish sacks. She wasn't sure what touched her most: his lifeless lump lying there or the destruction of his art, art that she had encouraged, nurtured, aided, and provoked. She longed to keep one, just one, but she knew she couldn't.

She tied the sacks up tightly and kicked them down the stairs; then she worked methodically around the flat, scrubbing every surface, scouring her bathroom and her bedroom to erase all trace, putting her towels and linens through a hot wash. She suddenly understood her mother: this obsessive-compulsive cleaning was cathartic because while you were doing it, you couldn't concentrate on anything else.

She went back upstairs and tried to view the studio from a stranger's point of view: the collapsed table, the materials strewn everywhere, the body on the floor. Did it look like a crime scene or an accident? A contrived setting for a play about a struggling artist who couldn't make the grade, so he impaled himself on a shard of broken glass?

She returned the easel to its upright position and placed one of his old works on the ledge. It was a badly-executed image of a busker – self-portrait, she presumed. God, they had come a long way…from him warbling at her then ordering that cup of coffee…

If only she'd been normal, they might have made it work.

Macy repeated her usual MO leaving the apartment late at night, creeping up and down the common stairs carrying the black sacks two by two. She knew the elevator made a grinding sound and she wasn't sure how light a sleeper or how hard of hearing Madame Lalande really was.

She carried the rubbish across the courtyard and out into the street wondering how the hell she was going to dispose of it all. The sacks weren't heavy but there were five of them as well as her own luggage, plus the Chanel carriers which she could not leave behind. If nothing else, they'd act as currency.

She contemplated going back upstairs for one last look, but she didn't dare. She'd gone down the crystal staircase backwards erasing every mark, wiping every tread clean for fear of her own footprints.

The street was empty save for a tabby cat. It slowed its late-night prowl to stop and stare at her. She whispered: *"Fou le camp!"* – which it did, walking haughtily away while letting out a long *miaow*. *I know you're up to no good but then so am I,* it seemed to say.

Just as she was about to step into the road with two of the rubbish sacks, a scooter come puttering past. She dropped them on the spot and plastered herself back inside the portal, heart thumping, sweat moistening her armpits.

The driver tutted beneath his helmet at *les salauds* who left their garbage on the street. He considered turning back to ring on all the bells, but he'd just come off a late shift at *La Brasserie du Coin* and wanted to get home.

The street settled back into silence. Macy stayed against the building wondering what to do. She needed to dispose of all this stuff and would have to make several journeys. She knew the *éboueurs* in their gnashing dustcarts would come by at 5 am but she couldn't very well say: "Help me out here, boys. There's been a little murder, so if you wouldn't mind?"

Leaving her own belongings against the street door, Macy picked up two sacks in each hand and hurried down the road. She dropped one into the first bin she came to, then turned a corner, smack into two men snogging. They scuttled off arm in arm tittering like teenagers. Macy turned back the way she'd come hoping they hadn't clocked her.

She threw two bags into the next recycling bin then dashed across the road into a small garden square. She tore the last bag open and began stuffing hands full of canvas strips into the waste baskets dotted around the green. She knew instinctively this was dangerous, so with increasing mania, she darted back around the square again snatching up all the strips and ramming them back in the torn sack.

Along the street, she spotted another wheelie bin. She ran towards it and threw open the lid. Clambering up, she pulled a bag out from inside, ripped it open and fumbled through the filth of household waste and crappy nappies to bury her own stuff underneath. Something slimy touched her hand and she whipped it out: her middle finger sported a condom like a fingerstall.

She shook it off in disgust then tied the refuse sack up as best she could and chucked it back into the bin. She ran for home, dragging her mucky hand down the leg of her jeans. Her holdall, Chanel carriers and the one remaining rubbish sack stood where she had left them. She scooped them up and headed in the opposite direction to before, away from the scene, away from the comfort, away from Franky and everything he stood for, but more significantly, away from all the memories of her most contented self.

When the clouds burst an hour later, Macy was in unfamiliar territory. She didn't know the neighbourhood and she was hot, sweaty, and strung out with murder, blood and garbage on her hands. The short, sharp shower was not unwelcomed and she dropped her stuff to the ground and raised her face and palms to the sky. Maybe the rainfall would wash away the filth.

A dark mass up ahead beckoned and Macy entered the Bois de Boulogne at Porte Dauphine. She threw the last sack into the first bin she came to. Relieved at finally lightening her load, she walked along a path until she found a bench. She dropped her holdall on the seat and made a headrest of the damp carriers. Exhausted by the effort of it all, she fell into the chasm of a twitched, tormented sleep.

*

Footfall from joggers and dog-walkers woke her up. As the nightmare flooded back, she got up quickly then staggered sideways with a head rush. She let out a sob of terror and desperation, longing for the habitual comfort of a warm croissant and a freshly brewed coffee. She felt sick, sorry, depressed, frightened. She'd experienced these emotions before but not with this intensity. Maybe she should head back to the apartment and face the music. Maybe she shouldn't.

She waited until the coast was clear then gathered all her stuff and walked deeper into the woods. Behind a stately oak tree, she changed her clothes, screwing up the dirty ones and stuffing them into her bag.

Where now? she thought. I can hardly hide in the forest forever – go feral. It may take a day or so for Franky to be found, but I'll need to be far away by then. She checked the side flap of her bag. Amber Lynne still snuggled safely there.

She exited the park onto the main road and kept going till she came to a bus stop which connected to the airport.

*

Her image in the Ladies' Room mirror at Charles de Gaulle was not much improved from the one in the filling station on her escape from Leicester. She was a little taller and had filled out physically, but her skin was pallid, her hair wild and straggly, her hands and face filthy, her expression frenzied and dispossessed. The Chanel carriers were split and creased and looked incongruous with the rest of her. She decided to ditch them – the carriers – not the contents. She went into a toilet stall and repacked her holdall, a sudden déjà vu of Selfridges flooding back. *What is it with my life? Is my Destruct button on permanent repeat?*

She changed her clothes again before exiting the stall and had a good wash, brushed her hair, put some make-up on and left the toilets in search of…What? Macy had never been in an airport before, let alone got on a plane. *A flight on a flight,* she thought ironically. Crowds were milling underneath the Departures Board. Looking at the names and timings, she saw that Bahrain, Alicante and Prague were leaving in around forty minutes. She didn't think she'd make any of those, neither did she want to. There was a flight to Gatwick – I don't think so! – followed by one to Prestwick then Ibiza.

The next departure was to a place Macy had never heard of. This had to be a good thing, right? If she hadn't heard of it, nor would other people. She needed to buy a ticket though. She looked around until she saw a Ticket Desk and joined the queue.

"Muskrat please," she said, reaching for her wallet. The desk clerk looked confused.

"Muskrat!" Macy repeated. "It's up there on the board!" The clerk gazed at his screen and shook his head.

"*C'est Moosca, mademoiselle. En Oman.* Whatever!"

"Via Amsterdam or Dubai?"

"Whichever leaves first."

"Aller-retour or one way?"

Just get me the fuck out of here.

Macy snapped Franky's credit card smartly on the counter. A few minutes later, pin number accepted, she left the desk boarding pass in hand, and passed smoothly through security in search of food.

39

Aaron had not recognised the sexual chemistry until she'd drawn the X on his chest. He'd dreamed of her that night beneath the stars as she lay sleeping in his arms, dreamed of them together, drifting out to sea like the owl and the pussycat. He had never invested emotion in a woman before, and it felt…different.

Later that afternoon, she'd gone back to the big tent with her game face on. Her manner was closed not exposed, as she'd been with him once the brandy had taken hold. It obviously didn't go to plan as she exited swiftly and barked: "We're leaving!" in her old commanding voice.

He gathered his things quickly and carried both their bags to the jeep which reappeared eventually in its customary cloud of dust.

Flame said nothing on the way back to the city. Three hours of long uncomfortable silence. He couldn't read her behind her Aviators, and he didn't dare invade her thoughts. The shared intimacy had dissipated; he would struggle to get it back.

"Where do we go from here?" he asked ambiguously, as the high rises appeared in the distance. She looked at him over the top of her glasses the way a princess might look at an unappealing frog.

"We?" she asked with her old hauteur. "What makes you think there is a 'we'?"

"Well, someone's got to carry Louis the Lion," he joked. "I mean, isn't that what I'm here for…that, and to keep you warm at night?"

Flame lowered her eyeshades and glared at him. If he was trying to seduce her, he was making a pretty good mess of it.

They shared a meal of *mashuai*, spit-roast kingfish served with lemon rice, then returned to the hotel where they'd checked in earlier. She had booked two rooms, each on different floors, but in a surge of bravura, Aaron exited the lift when she did.

"Where do you think *you're* going?" she asked.

"J-just to see you safely to your door?"

As she inserted her key in the lock, he touched her arm and gave voice to the proposal he'd been rehearsing all day.

"L-let me erase those p-painful memories. I would like to r-replace them with b-better ones…if you'll let me?"

Flame narrowed her eyes.

"You'll have to marry me first," she said.

"W-will I?" he croaked and was silenced by her kiss.

40

The black-robed women waiting to go through Customs flocked around each other like a murder of crows. Macy noted that they shared an individual invisibility. She followed the lead of other Western travellers and proceeded to the 'Visa on Arrival' desk. As requested, she withdrew some Rials at the ATM and handed them to the officer who scrutinised her passport more closely than anyone before. She did her cough-and-cover-face number and was relieved when he waved her through.

"Nice hotel, please? Central?" The cab driver nodded, and they drove off.

She showered and changed and unwrapped the beige Chanel handbag. The thought of Franky tore her heart. How could she have left him there? She would regret that for the rest of her life.

She left the hotel in search of a particular shop. She found this easily but the floor length *abaya* and *niqab* was more problematic. She bought it anyway but felt blinkered, with her boundaries distorted, and she almost tripped over once or twice. She grabbed at the skirt to steady herself but didn't want to lift it too high for fear of revealing her jeans and trainers underneath.

Groups of pretty girls with their faces on display sat chatting on the benches along the promenade. The act of wearing a face veil was 'for God alone' in Oman, not for government or culture. In social circumstances, some chose not to cover their beauty, enabling the male occupants of passing cars to toot appreciatively. Some of them tittered into their hands, others pretended not to have heard.

Macy was starving. She walked along the corniche that bordered the shoreline and to her great surprise, she spotted a pair of golden arches up ahead: the ubiquitous familiarity of a McDonald's! She hurried in, pointed to the pictures, sat down in a corner, removed her face gear, and gobbled up a Big Mac, fries and a strawberry milkshake. It was the best meal she'd ever had:

sometimes nothing else would do. Re-energised by the sugar rush, she returned to the hotel to seek tourism advice.

The receptionist raised an eyebrow when the fair young girl she had checked in earlier arrived back in full Muslim dress. When she commented this to a colleague, he said: "She'll be safer that way."

The flat-bottomed dhow sailed from Marina Bandar Al Rowdha at sunset. Macy chose to sit on the far edge of the carpet covering the base of the shallow boat; as they set off, she leaned out and trailed her fingers through the clear waters of the Arabian Gulf.

The guide's voice droned around the edges of her consciousness: *"...Fort al Jalili built in the sixteenth century AD before the arrival of the Portuguese..."* Macy spoke to no one, and no one spoke to her. She wasn't wearing her disguise, reasoning that a 'local' would not go on such a tour. She had opted instead for a plain top and a pair of baggy harem pants from Camden Market, which could, in effect, have originated here.

Her long hair was scrunched up under a peaked cap and her eyes were concealed behind dark glasses. She doubted that Scotland Yard or the Préfecture de Police would be on this particular outing, but one never knew.

The gentle lapping of the waves against the sides of the dhow as it sailed serenely through the tranquil waters was both calming and soporific. Macy's mood relaxed to a more manageable level. How pleasant it would be to share this trip with someone you cared about and hadn't killed.

She sneaked a peak at the other passengers, mostly couples united in peaceful harmony, gazing out to sea or towards the rugged shoreline.

It'll end badly, mark my words, she scorned. What you're feeling now won't last. He'll say or do something, and you'll just want to stab him.

She turned back to watch the sunset and a song lyric she couldn't put a title to flowered in her mind:

Where do we go from here?
This isn't where we intended to be.
We had it all, you believed in me.
I believed in you too...

Despite the picturesque surroundings and the option of company, Macy felt bitterly alone. She wondered what she was doing in this strange land all by herself. Her time with Franky had been perfect, in retrospect. She had believed in him, and they'd made a good couple, but who did she believe in now? And who would ever believe in her?

As usual, Mr Fairclough came to mind. She'd believed in him as a humanitarian, civilised person and a good teacher, and she'd believed in Lee Watkins before he'd turned into a tosser. And Franky had been her world while he was painting her or strumming up a storm…

She let her thoughts find their own level then tried to focus on the coastline, trying to find some deeper meaning in the forts hewn out of prehistoric rock.

"…of strategic and historical importance protecting the coastal areas from invasion by the Persians…"

The forts looked as abandoned as she felt.

Bottled water and fresh dates were passed around by the crew. Some of the passengers had started chatting to each other, comparing travel notes, sharing suggestions. One man said he wanted to go wadi-bashing – was the Wadi a tribe? Did tourists hunt them down and beat them? One woman said she and her husband had gone on a camel safari and she couldn't walk for days afterwards. Everyone laughed. They all seemed so carefree, but Macy couldn't engage with them, so they didn't engage with her.

When the cruise ended and the dhow docked, Macy hung back. She'd have willingly stayed on board forever, unplugged her brain and dropped it overboard.

The other passengers disembarked: elderly twosomes helped each other ashore; a pair of loved-up honeymooners stepped off hand in hand, and a man whose face she couldn't see beneath his desert hat and sunglasses, allowed his mum? – to step onto the quay unaided. He had tried to proffer his hand, but she'd waved it away. As she removed her Panama hat, a striking mass of carrot-coloured curls sprang out, encircling her head like a forest fire. Macy stared then turned away to watch the crimson crescent sink into the sea.

*

The following day she donned her disguise again and visited the Grand Mosque and the National Museum. She wandered through the Souk, avoiding the vendors of 'pure silk' scarves and fake Aladdin's lamps. She went for another Big Mac with a Coke this time, then returned to her hotel to think about her next move.

Macy had only come to Muscat because it was the first plane out of Paris to an uncommon destination. She'd enjoyed the sail and thought she might like to join the crew, but they were all men, and what if she got seasick? She wasn't qualified for anything except lying, cheating, stealing, and killing – Oh! And posing naked of course. Not much to put on a CV.

She re-packed her holdall, threw in the *abaya* and *niqab* as an afterthought, checked out of the hotel and headed for the airport. Time to move on.

*

The departure screens offered up an eclectic list of destinations none of which appealed at all. Zanzibar and Chittagong sounded exotic but remote, and what would she do in Istanbul except get forced into a life of slavery and belly dancing. It occurred to her that withdrawing cash on Franky's credit card would leave a paper trail, so she was going to have to use her own money carefully. At least what Nanny had left her gave her the freedom to go anywhere. She stood staring up at the bank of screens feeling like a gambler with a race card in one hand and a pin in the other.

A multitude of purposeful passengers hurried past wheeling their carry-ons towards security. Macy caught sight of a red-haired woman like the one on the cruise, and she almost ran forward to say hello.

The screens flashed up a new list of destinations. New York leapt out at her. She checked the departure time, made a quick calculation then marched resolutely up to the British Airways desk to book a flight.

41

"We are going to meet again, aren't we?" he pleaded as he carried her bags into the terminal. "You're not going to fly off into the wide blue yonder never to be seen again?"

Aaron's efforts to re-ignite her interest were about as subtle as a sardine trying to woo a shark. As soon as Flame told him she was going back to England, he had insisted on going with.

"I thought you wanted to carry on travelling!" she protested. "Anyway, I have things to do, people to see, business to attend to. I must come to terms with a certain situation…" She held up her hand to stop him. "Not *our* situation, *my* situation."

His ego receded like a lost erection. He'd shared her bed last night; she'd slept in his the night before. OK, nothing had happened – but it *could* have, if only he'd had more confidence. She was obviously still hung up on the whole Edward/Amit affair and how could he compete with that? Thirty years of her life spent wishing, hoping, and dreaming.

"I *will* marry you!" he whispered into her hair. "We've got something – you know we have – a connection I've never felt before."

"Yes, but that's all about you, isn't it?" Flame waved her hand as if swatting a fly.

"Anyway, it's all nonsense, I'm old enough to be…"

"I don't *care* about that! Age is just a number. And you weren't counting numbers last night when I wrapped you in my arms."

Flame smiled. She'd made the proposal as a joke, but maybe it was worth considering. It would certainly give the old vixens back home something to gossip about.

"Local Academic Marries Travelling Toyboy

Flame Maxwell-Arlington, spinster of this parish, looked radiant in écru silk..."

A marriage could raise her reputation. Or ruin it. Who knew? Who cared? Perhaps she and Aaron *could* make a go of it. He was certainly devoted and had been nothing if not obedient since they'd first met. As for the other issue...once he'd conquered his nerves, he'd make an energetic and willing lover which was more than she'd known in far too long a time.

"We'll talk about it when we meet again," she said appeasingly. "And when might that be?"

"When you've finished your journey and I've finished mine. Remember, we've only known each other for five days!"

He tried to hug her, but she held him at arm's length as an aunt might a nephew, then relented briefly and pecked him on the cheek. Tears of frustration welled in Aaron's eyes as he wandered blindly towards the exit straight past Macy buying her onward ticket.

*

The red-haired woman got up from the aisle to let Macy into the window seat. She seemed mildly irritated to be disturbed, but at least the seat between them remained empty so they weren't on top of each other. As the plane taxied towards the runway, the woman unexpectedly offered Macy a twist of barley sugar, the exact colour of her hair. Her mouth watered nostalgically at the sight of something Nanny Jean might have dug out of her black patent handbag, so she took it and said: "Thanks."

Half an hour into the flight, the woman spoke: "Do you live in London or are you in transit?"

Macy could have answered: "I'm on the run" but didn't.

"Can't bear the place," the woman went on, ordering a gin and tonic as the steward stopped at their row. "One big shopping mall and grossly overbuilt!" Macy wondered what was wrong with that.

"Were you on that boat trip?" she asked suddenly, desperate for human contact. "The dhow? Along the Gulf?"

"Yes!" And she stuck her hand in Macy's direction. "Flame Maxwell-Arlington." Then as an afterthought, "...soon to be Fairclough!"
And the woman threw her eyes skywards and giggled.

Macy wasn't sure what the 'soon-to-be' signified and was about to say, "I knew a Mister Fairclough once…" when the food trolley arrived and trays were set in front of them. They ate in silence. The woman drank two small bottles of wine, one white, one red, after which she fell asleep.

Macy thought about Mr Fairclough again as the plane droned on. He had once said: "You have two eyes, two ears and one mouth, so look and listen more than you speak."

She hadn't had any female company since Mrs Reilly, if you didn't count the odd "Bonjour" or "Bonsoir" to Madame Lalande. Since the past two years of her life had been spent developing her skills as a teenage serial killer, girlie chit-chat was not one of her fortes. She remained pensive until the plane landed at Heathrow, and they went their separate ways. As they disembarked, Flame Maxwell-Arlington-soon-to-be-Fairclough offered the girl her business card which Macy stuffed into the inside pocket of her travel bag and promptly forgot.

*

She lay low during the stopover, but once the plane began to arrow its way over the Atlantic, she fell asleep. It wasn't until the captain announced that they were coming into land at JFK that she awoke with a start wondering, yet again, what lay ahead.

42

Seven months later.

"Meet me at the Russian Tea Room on West 57th."

His reply was not so much a sigh as a silence.

"My treat?" I endeared.

"What time?"

"Six?"

Many of New York's most defining cultural moments had taken place at The Russian Tea Room. They were often documented by a prolific piece of prose in the popular press aggrandising a great or a good. I hoped however that our rendezvous would *not* be noted, as neither of us was a member of the literati, the intellectual elite, neither were we actors, politicians, business executives or acquaintances of a cousin of a descendant of The Russian Imperial Ballet.

We were not about to perform a magnum opus at Carnegie Hall or be propelled to the top of the New York Times' best seller list. We were not tourists, intent on revolving through the antique doors to glimpse the booth in which Dustin Hoffman sat while filming *Tootsie*, nor were we likely to be in awe of the cloakroom in which a heavy-browed Miss Ciccone worked as a hat-check girl before hurling herself, Christian name first, onto an unsuspecting public.

We weren't even bent on sucking inspiration from the fabric of the red plush seats on which Woody Allen had placed his skinny posterior, so why, of all the gin joints in all the towns in all the world, had I suggested that one? The answer was simple.

I liked the way: *Meet me at the Russian Tea Room on West 57th* rolled off my tongue and I had never said it before.

To feed her growing obsession with committing murder and getting away with it, and her curiosity about the pleasure/pain of sex, Macy wrote short stories when it was too cold to go out. She'd done her walking tours in the first few weeks, learning Manhattan from Battery Park to Harlem, but when the North Wind began to blow down the Eastern Seaboard freezing the very bones of the city, she stayed in her room reading and writing, hoping to create the happy ending she so craved. She studied books on Native Americans, slavery and the Deep South and got so tuned into Tennessee Williams, she began thinking in his accent.

The firstborn twin often carries with them a sense of duty towards their younger sibling. A hierarchy evolves in which the one who saw daylight first assumes responsibility for the other, should the parents go AWOL or become irresponsible in any way.

Arthur and Martha (our actual Mom and Dad) had nothing if not a sense of humour when they named us Martie and Artie. My protective gene kicked in the first time the sherry bottle in Ma's store showed noticeable signs of depletion. Artie pointed an accusatory finger in my direction and with no sense of fair play stated: "It was her!"

Having emerged some forty seconds ahead of my baby bro, I took the rap, a burden I carried with me through childhood and beyond. The blame for thieving dimes from the Dimple Haig bottle? Mine. The stolen smokes from Pa's chrome cigarette case? Mine. The dent on the nearside wing of the precious family Oldsmobile? Mine. All mine.

I could not however account for the soupçon of semen splashed across the bottom sheet of our parents' unmade bed the same weekend the Olds was hit by a truck on the way home from a music festival in Indiana thus reducing Ma and Pa to a pair of autopsies. All I could do was remove the metaphorical mantle from my late mother's shoulders and wrap little Artie in it – at least until he broke free at age 15 and disappeared.

The fourth-floor hideaway above the Dumbo Bistro in Brooklyn was Macy's first home alone in autonomous anonymity. She had been puzzled why you would name a restaurant after a Disney elephant until she found out that the neighbourhood was an acronym of Down Under the Manhattan Bridge Overpass. With retro furniture and remnants picked up from the Brooklyn Flea, she made the attic room her own and felt safe within its bare brick walls.

Working in the restaurant was role play, much like working in Kilburn Library had been. Although the **KITCHEN HELP WANTED** ad and enticing aromas wafting up through the vents had drawn her in like Mrs R's ROOM FOR RENT sign, she still had trouble with human interaction. Stuffing her fears into her apron pocket, she put a brave face on and faked it as she had so many times before.

Macy worked a ten hour shift, first as a *plongeuse* and then preparing vegetables. After a six month stint, she graduated to waiting tables:

"*Ya'll get moah tips if ya loine how ta smile, honey!*" a local had told her, and she tried, by God, she tried, using her 'Briddish' accent to its full advantage.

The trust-fund cool-hunters who slummed it south across the Brooklyn Bridge rewarded her with more than just good tips: she eavesdropped all their secrets as she topped up their troughs.

As a churchgoing, childless spinster, Ma's sister, Miz Esmée, was hardly equipped to deal with a pair of pubescent orphans. We cantered through our teens like unicorns, cavalier in matters of mortality. We stumbled over stones, broke hearts, fractured bones, and embraced each new experience as if it were our last.

It was obvious from Day One that Artie would go bad. The only job he could find was butcher's assistant in an abattoir or wiping windscreens in a carwash neither of which stimulated his overactive intellect. Instead, he directed his energies into more lucrative pursuits like shoplifting, petty larceny and trading stolen goods. Barefaced cheek kept him out of jail until the day his antenna picked up a different kind of vibe.

Missouri matrons, withering under the weight of widening hips and 'prostate problem' spouses, had begun fluttering their fans at him. With his James Dean looks and slow burning sensuality, Artie tuned in to these flirtations like a radio ham who'd discovered a new network.

For a bottle of Jack and a fistful of dollars he would service the old doyennes then help himself to the family silver on the way out. He only came a cropper when he gave the doctor's wife the clap which she selflessly passed on to her unsuspecting husband. Discomfited by the suspicious itch in his nether regions, Doc Clancey came home early one afternoon to find his lady wife, *not* sweating over a hard bridge hand, but sweating over the hard-on in her own hand. Artie grabbed his pants and boots and didn't stop running till he crossed the county line, somewhere south of Lexington. He hoboed his way down to Memphis keeping his spirits high and his Stetson low. Chancing into a saloon one night, he downed a couple of Buds, zipped the empty bottles along the counter, and jumped on stage. Grabbing the mic from a second-rate crooner, he spewed out a stream of lyrics one syllable off beat, but the fruity richness of his voice made the manager stop serving and take notice. The come-on in his eyes and the bulge in his jeans did the rest, and next thing Artie knew, he'd been renamed Tommy Tornado front man for The Tennessee Tornadoes, travelling across country in the front seat for a change.

My bro took to this life like shit to a shovel until a hip swiveller from Tupelo he nicknamed Evils Lepresy knocked him off the top spot.

Artie bought himself a two-tone Cadillac Coupe de Ville and packed it full of pussy. He held the door open whispering: "Slip 'em off, sweetheart!" as his fans climbed aboard. First, they'd giggle, then they'd wriggle out of their panties and throw them to the wind. Highway Patrol always knew when *'them Tornadoes'* was in town: the tarmac was strewn with scanties like a travelling salesman's suitcase had burst open and laced its contents all over the freeway.

Artie had the ability to unite Southern women in a kind of sexual sisterhood: they were bored with being good and it felt good to be bad. Pressing themselves into the front seat, they would reach across to stroke his thigh, blow in his ear or rake their nails through his hair. Those who sat in the back leaned forward and slid their fingers inside his shirt, tickling his smooth, tanned chest, moaning: "Tommy! Oh Tommy…"

If Easy Ellie couldn't sit up front, she would grab his attention from behind, spreading her long bare legs and resting her feet on his shoulders. In Artie's rear view mirror, that was the sweetest sight of all.

One afternoon, with the Caddy well loaded, 'Tommy' and his groupies headed out of town. Parking up amongst the dogwood trees, he cranked up the radio, popped the trunk and handed around the Jack. The girls swigged from the bottle egging each other on, daring whoever got high first to take her clothes off and dance. It wasn't long before they were all cavorting naked like wayward wood nymphs.

Slowed by heat and alcohol, the girls billowed their hair about as they swayed to and fro. Artie's blood was pumping but for now, he just observed. Propped up against a tree plucking his Gibson Flying V, he watched each girl as she slid into the creek. Caressed by the cool water, they swished around like mermaids, sun sparkling off the droplets on their wet and silky skin.

Artie put his guitar down, stripped off and dived beneath the surface. Above him there were gasps, and heads thrown back in ecstasy, kisses grazed on parted lips and breasts brushed against breasts. One by one they waded out and folded to the ground.

Artie followed and rode them each in turn.

He may not have believed in God before, but he sure as hell did now.

"Where's Ellie?"

The panic in her voice woke him from his sex-crazed stupor. Some of the girls were standing on the bank, shielding their eyes, calling her name.

"Ellie? ELLIE! Where are you? Come out! We're leaving soon!"

It wasn't until one of them screamed like a banshee that Artie realised he was up shit creek.

Four of them simply grabbed their clothes and ran. Another, passed out from booze and orgasms, came to, sensed a drama, and also fled the scene. Artie was left with just one girl: Donna. Dopey Donna.

Ellie was floating face down, arms splayed out like a sky diver. Donna splashed manically through the water and dragged her to the shore. She turned her onto her back, took one look, and threw up. The body was limp, already turning a chilling shade of grey.

"Ellie? Oh My GOD! ELLIE!" Donna screamed, trying to shake her friend back to life. "What're we gonna do now? Tommy! Tommy!!! It's Ellie!!! WHAT'RE WE GONNA DO?"

"Just shut up a minute and let me think!"

He dropped to his knees and began to prod the corpse, slapping it around the face, trying to make it wake. He flipped it onto its stomach and thumped it on the back, but it just lay there like a fucking broken doll.

"Wake up, you stupid bitch!" He yelled. "Wake up for Chrissakes. WAKE THE FUCK UP!"

"You'll fry for this!" Donna cried, her voice rising in hysteria. "You will FRY, you crazy bastard! I swear to God you'll fry in Hell!"

"So will you, honey!" Artie menaced. "So you'd better shape up and help me bury the bones!"

Donna gagged and a thick stream of whisky-coloured bile spurted from her lips.

"She may still be alive," she whimpered. "Tommy! Bring her around! SHE COULD STILL BE ALIVE!!!"

Artie knelt down to give her mouth to mouth then quickly stood up again. Ellie's bowels had opened creating an unholy stench.

"It was an accident!" Donna choked. "We can't just...we need to get help, tell someone what happened. I'm going to get my Daddy..." she was grappling for her clothes. "I'm gonna...I'm gonna..."

"You gonna *what*, sweetheart? 'fess up to what you been doing here all afternoon? How old are you? Fifteen? Isn't that grossly underage in the State of Tennessee? If I remember rightly, you were pretty keen..." and he made a vulgar movement with his hips. "Your Daddy gonna wanna know all about that, ain't he?"

Donna sank down on her haunches and began to sob. Artie caught her by the wrist and yanked her up to standing.

"Now listen up!" he said, pointing a finger in her face. "You're gonna help me drag her over there and cover her up. Then we're going back into town like nothing ever happened. I got a gig tonight. You *be* there and you act *normal* and when I'm done, we'll come back here do like I said. *Capiche*?"

Donna rocked from side to side, gasping for air, unable to catch her breath. Artie slapped her.

"CAPICHE?" he yelled.

"Yes," she whispered. "But Tommy..."

"My name's not Tommy," he spat. "It's Artie! And don't you forget it!"

Trouble was she didn't.

Later that night, laden with tools he'd picked up from the store, Artie drove Donna, white-faced and quaking, back into the woods. His brief stint in the abattoir held him in good stead, though hacking up the body proved harder than he'd thought. Donna's job of refilling the bucket to wash away the blood silenced her as deeply as if she'd been hacked up too.

He wrapped the bits in separate garbage bags and tied them around with tape, then he buried them in random holes he'd dug around the wood. Donna cowered behind the trees sobbing silently, urine drizzling down her legs like Mother Mary's tears.

Artie tossed the wrapped-up head and hands into the trunk of his car, and they headed back downtown.

My Best Friend Ran Off With a Rock Star was the story he fed into Dozey Donna's brain. Different bands were always passing through: Ellie could have run off with any of them.

"Only tell the story if you're asked," he warned. "And tell the others to do the same."

He need not have worried. Bonded as they were through underage sex and homicide, they bore the badge of *omertà* throughout their ruined lives.

Before dropping her home that night, Artie got the dead girl's address from Donna. Once The Tornadoes were on the road again, he set about forwarding little notes and postcards to the missing girl's family.

Sorry not to write this myself, Ma & Pa, but I got a hand infection from a thorn.

He introduced himself on the card as her 'boyfriend' and apologised for having absconded with their daughter but they were 'crazy in love'. He told her folks not to worry, that he was taking good care of her, that they were in good shape, and she would keep in touch.

He signed the cards RT. Artie always did like sailing close to the wind.

Macy reluctantly stopped writing for the day. It was time to get ready for her shift. As she put on her uniform, she wondered why her stories, which aspired to be full of light and love, always got so dark and difficult. Later that night, once the restaurant had closed, she went back to her attic and sat down at her desk.

Although Ellie's family were disconcerted by her departure and bemused by this sudden improvement in her communication skills, they were also quite relieved. There were five younger siblings in the household, and she had always been the problem one. Her fits and tantrums influenced the other kids, and her parents spent half their time trying to undo the bad she'd done.

As soon as she'd hit teen age, Ellie had started wearing make-up, strutting around in skimpy clothes, and staying out late. She did not respond to being punished, was lippy, argumentative, and sluttish, so maybe some time away would do her good. The young man she'd run off with sounded reasonable enough.

To save face with the neighbours, they explained that she'd gone to Hollywood to try her hand at acting. The postcards continued, on and off, then stopped, but by that time they'd got used to not having her around, certain she'd be back once fame or infamy had caught up with her.

By the time her head bobbed up downriver a few weeks later, it was too far gone for the coroner to assess to whom it belonged and from whence it had come, so it was sent to Forensics for long-term storage pending further investigation.

Artie had an innate ability to blank out stuff he didn't like. He'd consigned the events of that fatal day to a lock-up in his mind labelled Dog Day Afternoon. He knew all about the dog days: the hottest, most sultry days of summer: *an evil time when the sea boiled, the wine turned sour, dogs grew mad, and men developed fevers, hysterics, and frenzies*. He wondered if that myth would be enough to save him should he ever meet the judge.

The Tornadoes continued to tour with Artie travelling solo in his coffin Cadillac. The severed hands had been trying to claw their way out ever since he had stashed them there. Intent on getting rid of them far away from Ellie's head, he pulled over one afternoon and got out of the car.

The road was narrow. There was a sheer drop on one side, a wall of rock on the other. He opened the trunk, retrieved the bag then heard a police siren close by.

Artie panicked, took a step backwards, almost lost his footing, grabbed a handful of air, stumbled forward, and lost the package off the cliff. He was lucky he didn't fall with it. It thumped and bumped its way down the embankment till it landed on the river shore where it lay undiscovered till an autumn tide picked it up and carried it downstream. It got hooked onto a tree branch but when heavy rains swelled the river, off it went again.

An unsuspecting fisherman, angling quietly on the banks of the Morgan, caught something suspect on his line and the bag was finally reeled in, opened and handed hurriedly to the South Carolina PD. The angler was so traumatised that it ruined the pleasure of his lifelong hobby, increasing the time he had to spend with his wife which soon led to their break-up and divorce.

Bearing no rings or scars, the fingerprints matching nothing on their files, the gruesome twosome was consigned to the Unidentified Body Parts section of the local morgue, also pending further investigation.

The Case of the Empty Head, as the press called it, monopolised the front pages until some politician got himself killed in a plane crash. The story intrigued me: it was one of the most macabre unsolved crimes I could remember, certainly since I had qualified as a Criminal Defence Lawyer. They called the head 'empty' because the ravages of time, silt, brine, driftwood, rocks, weeds, tides, and river creatures had not left much for forensics to go on. The hair was long, and the teeth were sound so presumably the owner was young and female but without a body to attach it to, the head had been sealed in a plastic bag labelled 'Jane Doe' until such time as they could establish an identity.

Poor Ellie. She was certainly in bits, but you couldn't say she was 'beside herself'.

I read about the discovery of the hands in a four-line article in The Boston Herald. Although some time had passed, I put two and one together. The Empty Head had been simmering away on my back burner ever since I'd first become aware of it. I wondered if the hands had any connection. I was far too busy to pursue it further and it wasn't until they began to dig up the woods near the creek for a new housing project that the remaining body parts were unearthed. This provoked another outburst of media attention. Miz Esmée who had raised us was getting on in years, but I decided to pay her a visit in a lightly veiled excuse to get closer to the scene.

Our old aunty/legal guardian hugged me tightly as I got out of the cab. That one embrace held more affection than she'd given us in all the years we had been in her care. I guess I was more manageable now: a grown-up woman with children of my own. She ushered me into the house which hadn't changed an inch, and she sat down on the creaky rocking chair to chat as I unpacked. Memories of Artie swirled around like dust mites in the old familiar comfort of Miz Esmée's sitting room. Some of those memories were good and some were bad, but they brought me back to Artie with some fondness just the same.

"Do you ever hear from him?" I asked.

"Never!" she answered crossly. "Little tyke! How about you?"

"No," I replied wistfully. "We...we just lost touch. I do feel guilty though, being the older one. I often wish I could just pick up the phone, but I wouldn't know where to start..."

I'd never been much into pop music, always preferring classical. And when I moved up to Boston to study and then get married, I was too focused on becoming a lawyer to listen to the charts. For that reason, Tommy Tornado's rising star had never shone on me.

Over a dinner of fried chicken, cornmeal hushpuppies and grits, Miz Esmée and I talked about the old days. Eventually with a cup of sweet tea cradled in my hands, I turned the conversation to the reason I was there.

"Horror story!" Miz Esmée shook her in dismay. "They say those remains have been there for years. Young girl by all accounts...Who would *do* such a thing?"

It did occur to me that someone in the locality must know something. After all, why would a family not report a missing child unless they'd murdered her themselves?

I stayed with Miz Esmée one more day then drove west towards Edgewood. The offices of the local newspaper granted me a desk and access to their back catalogue. They had had a flurry of 'investigative journalists' taking up the story but never one from Boston. I was treated with respect, something to do with my having gone to 'Hahvahd' I expect.

What struck me as strange as I scanned the columns devoted to Cattle Auctions, Beauty Pageants and County Fairs was that in what seemed like a neat and tidy place, there had been one ghoulish murder, two suicides and the scandal of a stillborn baby born out of wedlock with the father never named. All these events happened in a similar time frame and involved young local women.

I made a note of some relevant names and addresses, thanked the guy at the News Desk and set off to continue my sleuthing.

Call it instinct or what you will, but my first port of call was a modest clapboard bungalow with an unkempt front yard. An old jalopy stood abandoned on the weed-ridden drive. I lifted the door knocker and rapped twice. The curtains were closed so I couldn't see in but eventually someone shuffled to the door and opened it a crack.

The wild-haired shadowy figure took a long drag on a cigarette and blew the smoke out through her nostrils like a dragoness defending her den.

"I'm...er...I'm trying to find my long-lost brother," I pleaded, as I slid my foot across the threshold. "I...er...I wondered if I might..."

Something in my vulnerability must have piqued her loneliness; she opened the door just wide enough for me to slip through which was fortunate as I had no idea how I planned to finish that sentence.

The smelled of nicotine and disappointment. The woman crushed her cigarette into a dish brim full of butts and lit another. In the brief flare from the match's glow, I saw the footprint of wretchedness branded on her face. Her hand shook as she topped up a streaky tumbler with a slug of amber liquid. Despite it being barely noon, this was not the morning's first.

The woman sank into a chair even saggier than she was and motioned for me to do the same. She gathered her faded bathrobe around her knees; it would have been a shade of pink once upon a time. I dropped my gaze to her cracked and veiny feet, partially encased in a pair of dog-eared slippers. As my eyes grew accustomed to the gloom, I looked around. A framed photo of a pretty young blonde smiled out at me from the window ledge. I squinted at it. A daughter? A niece? Not her, surely?

I kept the promise I had made to myself and stayed off the toxic topic. Instead, I skirted around it, asking innocuous questions about where she'd grown up, had the neighbourhood changed much, was she in touch with any of her old school friends? I had no idea where I was headed. I described my brother like he was till eighteen: handsome, mischievous, charismatic, extreme. I wanted to connect with her, anchor her to something in her past that would blow wind into her sails. While I talked, her eyes circled the room like cannibals around a cooking pot. And when I eventually said his name, she flinched. A purple cloud scudded across her face, the portent of a storm. She stood up, wobbled slightly, then barked in her 60-a-day voice: "You better go now!"

I thanked her for her time then drove to the nearest liquor store and bought six bottles of Jim Beam. As an afterthought, I picked up a stack of groceries then went back and left them on her porch with a note that read: *Thank you. May I come back tomorrow?*

Whatever that woman knew, I needed to know too.

It was 01:43 by the time Macy closed the lid for the night. She was surprised at how involved she had become, like she actually knew these people and was manipulating their actions. She wondered what she was going to do with the story once it was finished. She spent the next afternoon and evening only half concentrating on her shift dying to get back upstairs and carry on. As soon as she got back to her room, she put her tips in her tip tin, re-read last night's work, and waited to see where her characters would go next.

By the mid-1960s, The Tornadoes were going out of style. Although they continued playing small gigs in and around Memphis, they had all got married, got fat, got lazy, then disbanded. Artie continued singing solo in bars and clubs until the bookings dried up. Country music was no longer the sound *du jour*. Soul divas were climbing the charts with Bob Dylan and Joan Baez plugging their revolutionary causes.

The old Cadillac was limping. It needed a lot of coaxing to get started but he couldn't bear to get rid of it; although it linked him to a time best forgot, it also epitomised his glory days. He couldn't afford another car, so he'd spend hours tinkering underneath the hood just to keep it on the road. Despite his best efforts to blank it out, his nights were increasingly tormented by that Dog

Day Afternoon. It returned like an old ghost, rattling in his head, trying to find peace.

All alone and lonesome, Artie slept in cheap motels with even cheaper women, petty pilfering to stay alive, flirting with the fates to provoke them to decide his.

He awoke one Monday morning with a blank week ahead of him. He packed his few belongings, fired up the Caddy and began to drive. The radio had long since gone silent, so he didn't hear the latest news. Like a homing pigeon returning to its roost, he crossed the county line somewhere south of Lexington and kept going till he found himself on the outskirts of his hometown.

Coincidentally, it was the same week I'd gone back. I shouldn't have been surprised. We were twins, after all, and twins — no matter how long they've been parted — retain a special ESP.

The woman opened her front door to take out the garbage and found the boxes I'd left on the porch. Watching from a distance, I awaited my opportunity, I saw her glance from left to right. She even looked upwards as if to thank a Guardian Angel for the welcome late-night call.

I was just about to step out to greet her when she saw something behind me that made her jerk back in alarm. She slammed the front door, then opened it again, barely a smidge.

I turned my head slowly. An old Caddy was crawling up the road like a snail on vacation. Although the paintwork had lost its sheen and the chrome no longer lustred, its distinctive two-tone turquoise spoke of fancy days gone by.

I looked from the car back to the woman still squinting through the crack in the door. Then she opened it just wide enough for me to see the terror in her eyes, her jaw dropped on her chest. She stood there like a waxwork: deathly pale, transfixed in time.

The car crept past her house a way then stopped. The chrome wings were still in view, wings that had flown her and others to Hell and back — though I did not know that then.

With a sober sense of purpose, the woman suddenly flung the door wide open and stepped towards to the phone on a table in the hall. She picked up the receiver and dialled.

"I'd like to report a murder," she said into the mouthpiece.

"What is your name please, ma'am?" asked the operator.

"My name is Culvert," the woman replied. "*Donna* Culvert."

It all moved pretty quickly after that.

The police found him sitting at the wheel drumming his fingers to some soundless tune. They approached with caution.

"Get out of your vehicle please sir and place your hands above your head."

Artie continued drumming for a moment, weighing up his options.

- *If I fire her up, she might not start first time*
- *If I take a powder, they'll outrun me for sure*
- *If I slam the door open against this donut's legs, he'll draw his piece and use it*

He eased the car door open and stepped his well-worn boots onto the sidewalk in a breezy affectation of unhurriedness.

"What's up, dude?" he asked in a low, slow drawl tipping his Stetson back on his head.

And that was when the bomb went off in mine.

I cupped my hands around my mouth and shouted: "Do as the officer says, Artie!"

He looked towards me, squinting in the noonday sun.

"What's going on here, officer?" I asked authoritatively, marching towards them with as much officiousness as I could muster. "I hope you're not trying to apprehend this man. I can vouch for his good character. In fact, I am his lawyer and whatever you may want to question him about, I am certain there's a simple explanation. If you're taking him in, I'll accompany you to the station. I'm sure we can clarify the matter."

For once in his life, Artie kept his mouth shut. I don't know if he recognised me or not, but either way, he kept his counsel.

As for me, all our yesterdays came flooding back as my professional brain kicked in and tried to figure out how I was going to save my brother's sorry ass this time.

I never got to defend Artie in court, but I did manage to plead on his behalf. Mutilation was not deemed a first-degree crime if the deceased was the victim of accidental death or dead by other means.

For Donna, the liberation of finally being able to offload her story helped clarify the truth. She attested to the fact that Ellie had definitely been dead when she'd dragged her from the creek and a posthumous verdict of Death by Drowning was pronounced. She agreed that she had been an accessory because she had not reported the accident but had colluded in the disposal of the mortal remains, albeit under duress. She got off with a suspended sentence on the grounds of diminished responsibility and the fact that she was underage at the time.

Artie was convicted of the felony of not reporting (and absconding from) the scene of an accident then returning to conceal the evidence in an indefensible way. He chose not to ask for several thousand other crimes to be taken into consideration and was sentenced to a three-year jail term commuted to eighteen months. The female judge may have been influenced by recollections of a teenage crush she had had on a certain 'Tommy Tornado' which should *not* have but probably *did* help when she was deliberating the sentence.

The head, hands and bagged body parts were reunited and given a decent burial. Ellie's family put on a show for the cameras despite never having bothered to report their daughter missing. They subsequently made a killing with the gutter press by inventing ever more colourful stories about Ellie and her short and tragic life.

I visited Artie in jail once a month. He seemed quite at home there. As a 'local hero', he kept the other inmates and the 'screws' entertained, sang his hit songs and was generally unthreatening and well-behaved. Apart from the few short years we'd spent at Miz Esmée's, Dwayne County Jail was the closest he'd ever come to having a secure home.

The experience seemed to ground him. During my visits, we would talk about the past but also of the future. He wanted to get back into music and I suggested he pen some lyrics to while away the time. He certainly had enough material.

In the age-old tradition of creativity being born out of captivity, *The Ballad of Edgewood Creek* was written as a cathartic confession. It became a massive hit, replenishing Artie's coffers and spawning a whole new generation of jail and travelling songs culminating in Johnny Cash's *Folsom Prison Blues*.

And so, I arrived at The Russian Tea Room fifteen minutes early expecting my twin bro to be fifteen minutes late. To my surprise, he turned up ontime.

"What'll you have?" I asked once we'd got settled at a table. "No, sis," he answered confidently. "What'll *you* have?"

Despite, or maybe because of the spell behind bars, Artie looked fit, well and tanned from running circuits around the yard. We ordered drinks and clinked classes then I whispered: "How does it feel to be free?"

"I've always been free," he answered in that cocksure way of his.

"Have you?"

I peered at him over the top of my spectacles.

"Truly, Artie? Have you?"

"Let's order," he replied.

Later, after the butter-poached langoustines and pomegranate braised lamb shank with celery root purée washed down with a bottle of 1995 Krug (his CD was doing well!) his tie and tongue were sufficiently loosened for him to make a confession. "I guess you're right," he said, draining his glass.

"I'll never truly be free because I..."

"Be careful, Artie." I warned. "You swore in court to tell the whole truth and nothing but the truth. I'm not sure I want to hear this..."

"I'd better keep it bottled then," he sniggered, but of course he couldn't because the genie was out.

Artie ordered a brandy and sipped it slowly in a blare of silence. I watched him, my buttocks on the edge of my seat, heart beating like a jungle drum. I didn't want to hear some big revelation, but natural curiosity beat protocol everytime.

Diners came and went and soon the evening grew tired. Artie was systematically drinking his way through a whole bottle of Remy Martin. The restaurant emptied out, and although they do not stack chairs and swab floors around patrons in The Russian Tea Room, if they did, they'd have been doing it by now.

"Artie?" I said, after the silence had become unmaintainable. "Are you OK?"

"Yup," he answered, then he grinned that victorious grin of his and scrawled *Check please!* in the air.

We exited into the chill of a big apple-flavoured New York fall and stood for a moment face to face. I cupped his cheeks in both my hands and stared straight at him.

"I love you, kid," I said. "Whatever it is, I'll always love you."

He hugged me briefly then turned and walked away.

Although not a man generally bothered by conscience, it did occur to Artie, as it had in the throb of so many moonless nights, that maybe he shouldn't have held Ellie's head down quite so firmly when she took that final dive to perform what he had asked.

End

43

Often at night before she fell asleep, Macy would huddle Pandy in her arms and transport herself back to the time before her life went bad. The event that resonated most strongly in her mind was reading her 'outré' essay out loud in class, and how, for one brief shining moment, she felt her star begin to rise. Of course, it crashed and burned just as quickly, but if any good had come out of that whole episode, it was the care and kindness Mr Fairclough had shown her: she would never forget the way he'd been there the night her mother died.

And as with so many things that fit the lyric: *You don't know what you've got till it's gone*, she thought back to the classroom, a place she'd always trivialised until it had been denied her. Weren't parents meant to encourage their children's education, not destroy it by taking overdoses and behaving like filth?

She thought about the people lost and found, too many losses in her short life: her mother, her father, Nanny Jean, Mrs Reilly, her colleagues at the library, that awful Lee, Mr Fairclough, and of course Franky – gone…all gone. Weighed against the people she had found like that ginger woman on the plane and the staff at the Bistro, it was hardly an even balance. She was not what you could call 'surrounded by family and friends' and it occurred to her that if she ever had to fill in her Next of Kin's name on a form, who on earth's name would she put there?

Allowing Artie's dark side to triumph went some way towards expunging the demons which still lap-danced in her head. The Ten Commandments seemed easy enough to break, especially if you lived outside the box. Lying, stealing, coveting, blaspheming, idolising, working on Sundays, dumping someone else in it – all these acts came easily to many others too, she suspected.

Killing was out there on its own, of course, and she'd probably never do the adultery one. Shame really, she thought. Like starting a collection and not quite completing the set.

Tempered by a more stable lifestyle, Macy joined the local library. She borrowed the classics she had been force fed at school, and devoured the contents voraciously, enjoying them out of choice rather than obligation. It didn't take an English Lit graduate to work out that Jane Austen, Charles Dickens, and Victor Hugo had suffered deep emotional issues, otherwise how could they have penned such multi-layered narratives? She longed to experience the kind of love that locked people together rather than ripped them apart. How could she write with passion and conviction if she had never known those emotions? She did, however, suspect that torment and adversity made for a better read.

The library also offered writing classes which Macy's thought she might try; it would be another step towards social integration. She'd been in New York a few months now and had actually managed not to kill anyone, so things *were* looking up; and apart from that, hiding and lying all the time was exhausting.

Every Monday evening, on her night off, she'd walk down the wide oak staircase into the basement of the Brooklyn Library to join an eclectic mix of aspirant authors: a shaggy-haired poet, a freethinking philosopher, an aspiring autobiographer who reckoned he'd had a worthy life.

"Hey, you girl!" The class director snapped his fingers when it was Macy's turn to read. "Rabbit in the headlights?"

The group sniggered at her. You've got no idea what you're dealing with, she thought, then, channelling memories of the famous essay, she stood up and rustled her papers for attention.

In the event, it was not that different to reading out loud in class. Her story certainly held their attention far better than their *'Crunch of leaves in Central Park, walking, lonely, after dark'* or *'finding my inner child in the foothills of the Andes'* had held hers. Maybe she would recycle *The Goddess with the 1001 Vaginas*, shake this bunch of bogus bohemians up a bit.

Only the man skulking on the staircase did not applaud her efforts. He was far too busy planning his next move.

44

Since Mrs Reilly's kitchen had been the last place where Macy had felt relatively safe, she honoured her promise to stay in touch. Lee had his own reasons for popping round, and his tenacity paid off when he called on Mrs R one day to see if there was 'any news?' And there it was – on the mantelpiece: a postcard depicting the iconic Manhattan skyline.

With barely a: "May I?" – he snatched it up and delved deeply between the lines. It was dense with writing but *waiting tables in Dumbo* and *joined a writing group* were building blocks. Tiny little Lego-sized blocks, but building blocks, nonetheless.

Lee never really questioned his motives in wanting to hunt Macy down as robustly as he did. Apart from his justification of it being 'detective work', she had lied to and then rejected him. This did not sit well with a macho guy like him, a man puffed up by a rank and a uniform. Certain behavioural patterns could not be overlooked. He needed to redress the balance: crime and punishment, trial and retribution, subservience and power – these were the mottos by which he lived.

And so, he saved up his wages and his days off to make the trip to the place on the postcard, to track her down and make her right the wrong she'd done him.

*

Despite the puffer coat, gloves, scarf, hat, and boots, it was the coldest winter she had ever known. As the wind slashed her cheeks like rusty razor blades, Macy scurried from the library, head down, face drawn back into her fake fur hood. She felt encouraged though. The course director had allowed her to read for longer than the others and her story had been well received. But now she was freezing and longing to get home.

She unlocked the street door next to the Bistro and glanced behind her as she always did – force of habit. Not many people braved these unforgiving nights: a couple arm-in-arm scuttled towards the subway; a man with a turned-up collar glanced her way then headed off towards Met Avenue. Macy closed the door, began to climb to her attic room then stopped. She hadn't eaten since lunchtime, and she was starving. She exited again and turned towards the restaurant.

The man with the turned-up collar was now standing opposite, staring up at her building. As soon as he saw her, he took off again, away from Met Avenue this time. Odd?

Macy walked along the staff passageway that led through to the kitchens. The evening rush was over. Chefs and waiters were winding down, scrubbing pots and pans and polishing stainless steel ovens, hobs, and worktops ready for the next day. The clammy mix of steam and sweat felt warmly welcoming.

"Any soup left?" Macy asked. "It's like Siberia out there."

The head chef, Artem, who was an actual native of Siberia, snorted derisively then lifted the lid on an oversized pot. He peered inside and ladled out a bowlful of thick Halloween-coloured broth which he garnished with a flurry of quickly chopped chives. Macy took it gratefully, grabbed a spoon and stood supping at the counter.

"You wan' a bread?"

A lump of sourdough rye with cardamom seeds came sliding towards her from Mario, the man she'd nicknamed Flour Fingers, the Italian in-house baker. "Mario?" Macy asked him, biting into it and mmm-ing with approval. "Would you defend me if I was being attacked?"

Mario stopped kneading dough for the next day's loaves and brushed his hands down the front of his apron. He stepped behind her and hugged his arms tightly around her waist leaving floury handprints just below her breasts.

"Oy!" she shouted, smacking him away. "Who said you could...?"

"I defend de ice princess from de fire-breathing dragon!" he exclaimed.

"You do nothing of the sort!" She objected. "That was just an excuse to touch me up!"

"Toucha me up, toucha me down! Just toucha me, *bella*!"

Macy shot him a withering glance. Could men *not* think with their dicks for just five seconds of their entire lives?

Mario went back to kneading his dough with an extra dollop of suggestiveness. Macy threw her eyes skywards, turned away and loaded the empty bowl and spoon into a dishwasher.

"The soup was delicious thanks, Artem – but as for the baker, he's more of a butcher if you ask me. G'night everyone!" And she went to leave.

"I come with you." Mario stepped forward.

"You do nothing of the sort!" Macy protested. "I'm right next door and I'm hardly…"

"*Ti accompagno*!" he said firmly and took his apron off.

Macy shrugged and he followed her outside, winking at Artem as he passed. She sensed the interaction and turned to scowl at him.

Outside the restaurant, Macy looked left and right. No one in sight. "It's fine, Mario, thanks. No fire-breathing dragons. Now off you go."

"I not be gentleman if I not see up you…er…see you up?"

He did that helpless shrug he'd perfected for when his English failed him, then he followed her up the narrow staircase ogling her buttocks as she rounded the flight that led to the top.

On the final tread, Macy stopped and turned.

"I'll take it from here, thanks" she said, at which point Mario made the fatal error of lunging in for a kiss.

It wasn't exactly a shove. It was more of a push with a little added thrust. Mario rocked back on his heels, eyes wide with shock. Fearing she'd pushed too hard, Macy grabbed his shirt front and pulled him back to safety on the tiny landing. Thinking she had changed her mind, he lunged again. She instinctively landed him a karate chop on the bridge of his nose.

Mario's right hand shot up to his face and he cried out in pain. With nothing to clutch on to, he lost his balance and toppled backwards, arms flailing, left hand grasping randomly for the banister. A flashback to Lee on the steps of the Police Station zipped through Macy's mind.

Like a macabre slo-mo circus act, Mario tumbled slowly at first then faster, thwacking his head alternately on the pilasters then the wall. A stream of Sicilian curses sprang from his mouth like a Commedia dell'arte performer – without the comedy or the artistry. He turned the corner and disappeared, ending his descent with a conclusive clunk.

Macy took one step forward and two steps back, whipped around, unlocked her bedroom door, and spilled inside. A song lyric assailed her, and she flattened her hands against her ears to stop it. The action was futile. Freddie Mercury repeated the riff on a continuous loop:

And another one gone and another one gone, another one bites the dust…

*

To an obsessive, there's little difference between a stakeout and stalking. The former is a period of secret surveillance to observe someone's activities; the latter: to pursue or approach stealthily, watch, or harass without necessarily revealing one's identity.

It hadn't been difficult to join the dots. The first clue was rather too broad, but after checking several schools and drawing blanks, he was told to try the local library.

He'd enjoyed her reading from his vantage point halfway up the wide oak staircase. When they all got up to leave, he exited the building ahead of them and stood in a doorway until she passed. He followed at a safe distance, his hand buried deep in his pocket, fingering the little glass bottle of trichloromethane. Nobody actually reads your name when you flash your badge: they just stand to attention and ask how they can help. The story about 'researching Victorian crime for an analytical thesis' loosened the pharmacist's lips sufficiently to give him the information he needed. Actually buying the stuff proved a little more problematic, but again the badge was a door opener.

The use of a handkerchief soaked in chloroform had become a somewhat clichéd way of rendering victims unconscious, but if it was good enough for Agatha Christie and her ilk, it was good enough for him. The modern alternative, Rohypnol, had to be ingested one way or the other and took too long to work. He hoped she'd hurry up and go to sleep. It was bloody freezing out here.

45

Oman, which had sounded so *roman*tic on the way in, looked pretty tricky on the way out. Flame had suggested he continue his travels overland but whichever way he turned the map, a war zone got in the way. Bahrain, Baghdad, Basrah and Beirut may alliterate quite nicely but they were hardly Majorca, Marbella, Mauritius, or Mykonos. Jumping on a plane and heading home seemed lame: he had realised, in the short time that he'd known her, that his fiancée's suggestions were non-negotiable. She'd told him to finish his journey, so finish his journey he must.

As he studied the least hazardous route, Aaron's feelings veered between clarity and confusion. Flame now held him in her thrall: her cool superiority, her knowledge of so much that eluded him, her all-of-life experience, her actual interest in him. Her erudition had been reached with age, but her age was the least of his concern: she could be ninety for all he cared; he was besotted and to him she was A Queen.

The journey back would be challenging but it would be worth it if his fiery Flame awaited at his journey's end.

*

A union born of serendipity and circumstance has equal chances of survival or failure. In their case, 'doomed from the start' had been tailored to fit.

When the Registrar delivered his taciturn: "I now pronounce you man and wife" He accompanied the words with a subtly raised eyebrow in Flame's direction. Her mute response said it all: *I have no idea either.*

Aaron failed to witness this exchange but stood as pleased as Punch would have been had Judy thrown her arms around his neck and snogged him. However, as he leaned forward to kiss his new wife, she leaned away, leaving him suspended mid-pucker in mid-air.

The honeymoon in Boston, Massachusetts, produced less honey than a barren bee's abandoned beehive; the moon cowered beneath a thick covering of cloud, reducing the whole thing to little more than a cheap song lyric.

For Flame, returning to Muscat to rekindle her past had been brutally non-productive. Amid despair over Edward's lack of interest, Aaron's attentions had been welcome. But marry him? As good a salve for a broken heart as Vaseline for an amputation.

And yet it had felt right that night in the desert, with her head on his shoulder and his breath in her hair. She had been deprived of tenderness for so long, and Aaron had been there where Edward hadn't. Not really a good enough reason to lead him up the aisle, for had a camel shown her affection that night, she might have married him instead.

You can never go back, she mused as they exited the Register Office, a couple of coupled strangers. The world moves on, time evolves, people change. The passion she'd enjoyed with Edward had been at the right time in the right place, but when those memories intruded on her and Aaron's wedding night, she'd mumbled an apology, got dressed and gone down to Reception to request a second room. She never considered how damaging that would be; she only considered how invasive it felt to have another man beset her private parts.

The next morning, as Flame pulled on her regulation calf-length linen skirt in readiness for sightseeing around the city non-Bostonians called Beantown, she couldn't help but feel sorry for her new husband. A lioness, even with a gold band on its claw, could not become a pussycat. And so, to save them both from further heartache as they waited for their pancakes and crispy bacon with maple syrup to arrive, Flame took both of Aaron's hands in hers and requested an annulment.

Affrayed and affronted, Aaron flung his napkin down and stormed off to his room. This so-called 'honeymoon' – the visit to the world-famous university, the trolley bus tour, the harbour cruise to see where the Sons of Liberty had dumped their tea in 1773 were all worthless, pointless, tourist nonsense! What a sham! She'd dragged him across the Atlantic because she had 'other people to catch up with'.

Flame sighed, abandoned the breakfast, and followed him upstairs. She tapped on his door with cajolement on her lips. Aaron let her in but continued throwing his belongings into his suitcase. Flame folded her arms across her chest.

"Let's talk about…"

"What?" He countered. "Your dislike of me anywhere near you? My idiotic naivety in thinking we could *make* something of this. You have an innate ability to make a fool of me time and time again! *'Don't touch me here, don't touch me there!'* OK. You've got your way. I won't touch you anywhere. I'm leaving."

He zipped up the case and threw a fistful of dollars onto the bed. "Pay for the rooms! BOTH of them!"

Then he wrenched open the door and marched out, luggage veering crazily on one wheel as he rounded the corner that led to the lifts.

"Airport, please," he said gruffly, slumping into the back of a cab.

Halfway there, he tapped his top pocket and his heart stopped. His passport, unlike himself, was lying snugly on top of Flame's inside the hotel safe.

FUCK!

"Sorry, driver." He shook his head in despair. "Could you please take me back to the hotel? No! Actually, forget that – forget the airport and the hotel. Take me to a train station please."

Fuck the passport! Fuck Boston and fuck Flame Fairclough! – Because if she didn't want to fuck *him,* she could fucking well go and fuck herself!

The train thundered in and ground to halt with an agonised screech. Aaron disembarked and looked around. The skeletal structure towered above him like a burnt-out cathedral. He had never intended to end up here, especially *sans* passport, but he took a deep breath, squared his shoulders like his father and grandfather before him, and put one foot in front of the other towards the exit.

46

During her term as *plongeuse*, Macy had appropriated a paring knife from a sink full of soapsuds. 'Accidentally' dropping it on the floor, she'd fed it up her trouser leg handle first and wiggled the tip into the top of her sock, all without severing an artery.

The knife's loss had gone unnoticed for an hour or two until voices were raised and staff members questioned. Chefs were particularly precious about their paring knives, and this was indeed a precious paring knife: a gift to Mario when he graduated from college. It had a polished rosewood handle with his initials carved into it and a stainless-steel blade specific to an Italian manufacturer. Macy went through the motions of helping them search for it until everyone finally agreed it must have been thrown out with the garbage. Mario went on about it for days. He'd been extremely upset but short of going through the process of pretending to find it then having to nick another one, Macy remained silent.

Owning the weapon made her feel safe, especially at night. She couldn't carry it with her all the time, but it lay steely and sharp beneath her pillow awaiting to be used – or not.

Torn between calling 911 or going down to see if Mario was dead or alive, Macy did neither. She stayed on the edge of her bed, her legs jigging, the knife clenched tightly in her white-knuckled fist.

Twenty-eight minutes passed: one thousand six hundred and eighty interminable seconds during which nothing happened.

Macy went over to the window and peeped out. The street was deserted...No! Hang on! Turned-Up-Collar was back! Why was he staring up at her building in the middle of the night? She blinked hard and strained forward to get a better look. There was no one there. She was getting paranoid. Macy got undressed and climbed into bed, keeping a firm hold on the knife. She tried to breathe normally, calm her mind, rationalise her thinking. Nobody was staring up at her building and Mario had brought this on himself. If he was alive, he would have limped off by now. If he was dead, there wasn't much she could do about it.

*

He was fuming when he saw her go inside followed by a man: the anger even warmed him up a little. A spread of satisfaction took over when he saw the guy emerge minutes later holding his scalp with one hand and his nose with the other then stumble back into the restaurant and disappear.

Lee cupped his hands against his mouth and exhaled hard onto his fingers. It barely helped. He stomped his feet and drew his collar up, trying to stay focused, remain engaged. This climate was a killer: how could anyone actually live here? Eventually, after another half an hour during which he grew colder yet more determined than ever, the light in the fourth-floor window went out. Checking that the coast was clear, he crossed the pavement. He hoped the street door wouldn't pose a problem, but as he approached, he noticed it had been left open! What luck!

He entered, closed it quietly behind him and climbed the narrow staircase that led to the top floor. Outside her door, he stopped to listen. Silence. He unscrewed the top of the little glass bottle and doused the chloroform liberally onto his bunched-up handkerchief. The fumes made him reel – this would do the trick. He got out his credit card, slid it into the gap parallel with the knob and slipped the catch. He pushed the door open and stepped stealthily inside.

Holding his breath, he squinted around the room. The bed was in a corner; nearby stood a wardrobe with other furniture dotted around. He could see her shape beneath the covers. She was lying with her back to him. *It was now or never,* he thought.

He tiptoed over and in one swift move, smothered her nose and mouth with the toxic hanky. Her arm shot out with some violence, and she jerked once or twice and then went limp.

*

Mario sat in the empty kitchen nursing his throbbing nose with an entrecôte steak. He would stick it in the fridge and eat it tomorrow but for now it felt soothing. He'd totally misjudged her. Pretty girl, got on with the job, didn't mix much, then wham! Well, good luck to her. She hadn't invited the kiss, but he was Italian – what did she expect? He should probably apologise.

He looked at his watch. She wouldn't be asleep yet. He would go back up and say 'Sorry'. Show her some respect. Maybe he could talk her round.

Mario went to the key box in the staffroom and took the spare keys to the attic off their hook. Then he washed his hands and face, splashed on some aftershave, and went back next door.

He heard muted groaning as he climbed the stairs. That couldn't be her, surely? Mario took the last flight two at a time. Her bedroom door was open. He ran in and saw a man kneeling beside the bed!

"*Cosa fai qui?*" he shouted. "What you do here?"

He gave the man a hard kick in the kidneys, and he fell forward against the bed then slumped to the floor. Mario clambered over him to get to Macy. She was lying on her back as limp as a rag doll. He leapt astride her chest and started giving her heart compressions. She bounced up and down but failed to respond. He doubled forward, pinched her nostrils, forced her lips apart and gave her mouth to mouth. Not quite the kiss he'd envisioned, but still…He could smell *cloroformio* – the same stuff the vet had used to put his pet rabbit to sleep! She didn't seem dead, but she'd be out for hours.

Mario jumped off the bed and dropped to his knees. The man was lying there, eyes wide in surprise. Mario slapped him around the face, this way, then that. No reaction. He bent down to listen for the sound of breathing, heard none, then tore the man's coat and jacket open to look for signs of injury. Still *niente*. He rolled him onto his side – and then he saw it – a knife handle sticking out! A polished rosewood knife handle with his own initials carved into it! His missing knife! Madonna Santa! How on earth…? But where was all the blood?

Mario was about to extract his precious implement when he recalled something he'd learned during a First Aid course – stuff you had to know when working with knives. There are a few places on the body where a stab wound causes death without bleeding: the sides of the chest or the back.

The lung can leak air into the chest cavity and if the air can't escape out of the stab wound then pressure builds up in the cavity causing something called a 'tension pneumothorax' which eventually prevents the heart from filling, and you die.

Buon Dio! He never thought he'd have to draw on that!

The problem was there was now a dead man in Macy's room with Mario's distinctive knife stuck in his side. How in the name of his godfather was he going to get out of that?

47

Macy forced herself to open one eye; it felt like trying to raise a drawbridge with chains made of plasticine. She turned her head – Aaow! – and glanced at her bedside clock. 08:28? Her shift began at 9!

She tried to get up, but the room turned a somersault. She fell back, head pounding, thinking blurred, memory fuzzy. She reached for her temples but wasn't sure where they were. Her chest hurt, like someone had sat on it. She sniffed. What was that weird smell? An indistinctive mash-up of chemicals, aftershave and sweat. Had something happened in the night? Had she killed Mario? Or someone else? She glanced down at her bed: it looked wrecked, the sheets all stained and crumpled. Her pink blanket was missing! What the hell was going on?

Macy staggered out of bed, and, clasping the walls and furniture, made it to the window. She heaved it open and leaned out for some air. Her blanket was lying on the sidewalk three floors below! Shakespeare entered the fray:

Oh, cover of corruption, oh murderous mantle, Away! Ye stinking shroud!

Macy forced herself over to the sink. She splashed cold water on her face then threw on a tracksuit and took the stairs like her feet were made of jelly. She barely registered *not* stumbling over Mario as she lolloped onto the pavement and scooped the blanket in her arms. It stank! For no logical reason, she hared off down the street, across the square, around the corner and through the alley until she was so breathless, she had to fold forward, panting and gulping. She noticed she was barefoot. It must be -5°. A déjà vu of Paris made her want to gag.

An empty carrier bag from Bed, Bath and Beyond rustled in the gutter. She grabbed it and stuffed the blanket inside, thought to leave it there, changed her mind and set off again.

Rounding the next corner, she crashed into…MARIO! – out for his morning run, sporting two shiners he later referred to as 'The Flatten in Manhattan'.

Mario's face went through a catalogue of expressions like he was auditioning for a drama where he had to play conflicting roles. He was about to say something then changed his mind.

"Eh! Muhammad Ali!" He joked, ducking and diving with his fists beside his face. "I not know you punch so good! You OK, yea? You good? We keepa da secret, you an' me?"

"Yes! No! I…What do you mean?"

"Shoppy-shoppy?" He motioned at the carrier. "Fresh a-sheet for tonight?" Then he went white and raced away.

Macy limped home. Outside her front door, she scanned the paving stones. They were stained with a menu of spillages, but no obvious brains or guts.

Back upstairs, she surveyed her room. It looked…different. She'd be late for work, but she had to clean it. She moved the rug and furniture and swabbed the floor with bleach. She remade her bed with clean linen, shoved the mucky stuff into the carrier bag with the blanket, then showered, dressed, and sprayed herself with the last remaining drops of Elizabeth Arden's *Blue Grass*.

The aroma of nostalgia hung heavy in the air: Saturday afternoons in the changing rooms at C&A Marble Arch.

Macy yearned for home.

*

Waiting tables was mindless and her overactive brain kept trying to fathom out how her blanket had ended up on the pavement and what Mario had meant by 'keeping a secret'. And where was her – his – knife? She knew she'd gone to bed with it so it must be jumbled up with the dirty sheets.

Or had she stabbed someone in the night, wrapped them in the blanket and heaved them out the window? How could she have done that without knowing? She could murder in her sleep now? Stories started forming in her head:

- *As the body hit the pavement, a sinkhole opened and swallowed it up.*
- *A gang of drunken youths, brawling their way through Dumbo, saw the body fall. Assuming it was a suicide, they picked him up and threw him*

in a skip. The skip was collected, taken to a landfill, and buried under tons of waste.
- *A Canadian bald eagle with a ten-foot wingspan was flying high over Manhattan when it smelt carrion. It swooped down and snatched the dead meat in its talons returning to its mountain eyrie to feed its family for a month.*
- *The fall to earth woke the man from his coma and he staggered to a nearby hospital where he was treated for his wounds. Although he recovered, he suffered terminal amnesia and never remembered who he was or what had happened to him that night.*
- *A group of medical students about to fail their autopsy finals were on their way to the cemetery to rob a grave when the ideal solution fell at their feet.*

"Mario!" she whispered, the minute she got the chance. "I need to speak to you!"

"*Si, bella*! Me too. We go for drink tonight?"

"Alright…" she answered reluctantly – *if only to find out what happened and atone for your black eyes.*

*

She allowed Mario to take her hand for the purpose of protection. It made a change for her to be out, instead of serving others who were out. The Bridge Club, just beneath the Brooklyn Bridge, was busy but they found a table and sat down. People were dancing in the disco, separated, thank God, by a thick wall of soundproof glass. They looked like characters in the Hieronymus Bosch painting *Party in Hell*. All that was missing was the Devil himself, suspended in a cage, pitchfork in hand, twerking.

"What you drink, *cara*?" Mario asked. He seemed nervous, not his usual flirty self.

Macy did not tend to drink because it always ended badly but she said:

"Something with a tiny drop of vodka but not too strong, please?" He nodded and went to the bar.

Mario and the barman obviously knew each other. They brushed palms, made a fist, bumped knuckles, and interlocked thumbs.

Cocktails the size of fruit bowls were brought to the table, smoking with liquid nitrogen or something. Macy took a sip and then another. She was underage in the US, but who was checking?

"So, er…?" She began. "Last night? Something about a secret? I'm not sure what…"

Mario moved closer and leaned in towards her face. Her default reaction was to stiffen, but she went with it. She needed to find out what had happened and what she did not know.

48

Organising a new passport in The United States of America without the proper documentation was like trying to swim vertically up Niagara Falls.

After an interminable queue, Aaron reached the front of the line. "I need to apply for a new passport, please."

"Ya got photo ID, sah?"

The desk clerk was chewing gum.

"Photo ID?" Aaron repeated.

"Yea, photo ID? Like a passport?"

If I had a passport, you cretin, I wouldn't be applying for one, would I?

"Er, no, I don't, that's why I…"

"Driver's Licence?"

"N-no."

"Citizen Card?"

"No. I'm not a…"

"Common Access Card as issued to Active Military Personnel?"

"I am not Active in your Military."

"Credentials?"

"Like er…?"

"Proof of residency?"

"I don't live here. I do NOT have any official documentation. I am not in the Military. I am a citizen of The United Kingdom of Great Britain and Northern Ireland. I have mislaid my…"

"You Irish? Ma gran pappy was Irish!"

This must be how people develop high blood pressure and die of a heart attack, thought Aaron.

"I am not Irish, I am British, and I require…"

"You got mugged?"

"No, I did not get mugged."

"You lost your passport, buddy?"

"No. I did not *lose* my passport (*and I am not your bloody buddy!*) I know where it is but…"

Aaron was not about to explain that his wife of five minutes had dumped him and, in his hurry, to escape, he'd stupidly left his CURRENT VALID BRITISH PASSPORT in the hotel safe in Boston.

"If you know where it is, then why don' cha…?"

"It's in Boston. We're in New York. I cannot go back to Boston."

"*Bahston* Massachusetts?"

YES, YOU FUCKWIT.

The official – well, his shirt bore epaulettes – didn't have room to type Aaron's explanation in the space provided and it soon became clear that it would have been better if Aaron had been mugged because he would not have had to go through this rigmarole and humiliation on top of everything else he'd just suffered.

Eventually, after more questioning, form-filling, queuing, further questioning, repeated queuing and the absurdity of having to put exactly the right amount of money into a clunky old photo machine which involved him having to leave the building to find a Walmart's in which to buy something in order to get change, Aaron was told he would be issued with a Temporary Travel Document which would enable him to leave the country.

He couldn't wait.

He exited the Immigration Office feeling drained, deflated, and discombobulated.

49

Mario told the story as if it he was reciting the synopsis to a highly unlikely crime drama. Macy struggled to follow. There'd been a man in her room who was dead when he'd got there. How could that be? Why was he there in the first place? Why were either of them there and how had she not known about it? Mario had wrapped the body in her blanket and carried him away?

"So where is he now?" she screamed in a whisper.

"Is takin' care of," Mario answered, tapping the side of his nose. "Is better you not know…"

"But I *need* to know! I have a right to know!"

"Is to protect you, *bella*."

Well not many people had offered to protect her, so maybe she should just accept that and let it go, but she wasn't buying it. Not for one moment. And how come Mario was taking the blame? Why would anyone do that? He would obviously want something in return. There were too many questions and not enough answers. As usual.

Headlines whirled into view like an old-time movie sequence:

**BRITISH GIRL MURDERS INTRUDER IN BROOKLYN ATTIC!
ILLEGAL IMMIGRANT GOES ON STABBING RAMPAGE!!
INNOCENT VICTIM SLAIN BY TEENAGE SERIAL KILLER!!!**

It was self-defence, your Honour. It was always *self-defence.*

Mario was stroking his hand up and down her arm now, telling her everything would be alright: "…*tutto bene, cara, tutto bene*". You did not grow up in Sicily without knowing how to dispose of a body, *jajaja*!

Maybe he had a cousin in New Jersey who was a gravedigger, Macy devised, and they'd dug down deeper than was needed and filled in the hole halfway so it didn't look suspicious for the next funeral?

Mario took her hand and drew it towards his heart so she could feel what was in his inside pocket. It was the famous knife! She failed to feel the Metropolitan Police badge that he'd kept as a trophy.

Christ! Macy thought. He's hacked the body up like Artie in my story! Art(ie) imitating life! He's shoved the limbs down the garbage chute so whoever finds them won't be able to figure out which floor they've come from, and they won't be found till Friday when the trash men come, but where's all the blood and how had he squeezed the head into the opening when she struggled to cram in an empty box of Cheerios?

"You must tell me what you've done with him! I need to know who he was and what he was doing in my room! And if he was a random stranger or someone that I knew? It may have been my father…*it may have been my bastard of a father*!"

Aha. Mario thought. Her past was coming out. So maybe he'd done her a favour? They'd say no more about it, and she'd be grateful and sworn to silence like a true Mafiosa, part of a family that observed the rightful meaning of the pledge of Omertà.

*

Macy lay in bed trying to force her mind back as far as it would go to replay the events of the previous night and try to make some sense them. She had definitely blacked out at some point, but how? She had no sign of injury. Someone must have drugged her and that could only have been Mario. But if, as he said, he had come to her room to apologise for what happened on the stairs, then who was the man whose body he says he found and how come he'd been in her room in the first place and ended up dead? It was all too confusing.

By focusing very intently on every step she'd taken between coming home from the library, starting up the stairs, changing her mind, going back into the bistro for the soup, Mario insisting on taking her home then trying to kiss her and her punching him, the only bit that didn't fit was Turned-Up-Collar man. Who the hell was he? Her last conscious memory was of trying to get to sleep with the knife clutched in her hand and someone or something smothering her face and her knee-jerk reaction of lashing out. After that, it all went black.

Maybe she would never find out what really happened, but one thing was certain: it was time to move on. There was nothing left for her here. She was as vulnerable as ever, in mortal again, and sooner or later they would catch up with her. She didn't really want to leave New York, but what choice did she have?

The next morning, Macy got her holdall out and retrieved the stolen passport. She took it to the mirror and held it up beside her face. It was less of a match now than before, but people changed their hair colour and style all the time. She could probably get away with it if she did that coughing thing. And then she took a closer look. The passport had expired.

50

The eight major planets of the Solar System can never come into perfect alignment due to the orientation and tilt of their orbits. The last time they appeared even in the same part of the sky was well over a thousand years ago in AD 949 and they would not manage to do this again until the year 2492. Sometimes, however, on the rarest of occasions, the stars align sufficiently to create an event so unlikely that had it happened a millisecond earlier or a nanosecond later, it would never have happened at all...

This was one of those times.

It was the accent plus the strident sound that caused her to panic: a couple of passing Brits, loudly extolling the virtues of a TV series called *Make Mine MURDER* coincided, orchestrally, with a traffic cop doing what traffic cops do. The combination of word and whistle caused Macy – always on red alert between fight and flight – to shoot forward like a greyhound from a trap, across the road, through the traffic, and around the first available corner.

Aaron, marching purposefully en route to collect his travel document, was considering his current status. He had written 'Single' on the forms, but he was not really single. Nor was he properly Married, Divorced, Widowed, or Separated and he did not recall a box marked Dumped like a Dog.

As he turned the corner, his progress was broken by a missile hurtling towards him at full speed. He tried to do that left-right-left-right hip hop thing but was instead knocked sideways into a lamppost that caused him to lose his footing and topple over like a skittle.

Sprawled out on a New York sidewalk was the icing on a particularly tasteless cake. Damn This City and All Who Sail in Her! – he cursed. He tried to get up but there was a weight on top of him, pinioning him where he lay.

Too close to determine who or what it was, he eased his head to one side to see a forest of legs closing in. From high above came the muted mumble of insults.

"Dude's loaded f'sure!"

"Leave him, Su' Ellen! He's just a junkie!"

"Call the cops! I saw everything! He brought that girl down!"

These injustices were accompanied by the cacophony of tooting horns. The logo I HATE NEW YORK embroidered itself across Aaron's mind, but he couldn't see that catching on.

He tried to raise himself up but whatever felled him was still there, half on and half off his chest and legs. He tried to speak but no words came, then the weight lifted, and his lungs inflated as he took in air.

"I'm fine," a female voice said. "No damage done. Thank you. I'm sure he'll be OK." And the legs began to recede.

Aaron propped himself up on one elbow and gave his head a shake; he felt giddy as if he was hearing voices from the past. Well, one voice in particular…He lay back down and closed his eyes.

When he reopened them only one pair of legs remained, bare and youthful legs, with light blonde down on pale pink skin. He could hear giggling, gurgling, happy gasps of disbelief.

"Oh, thank you God! You *do* exist!" Then: "Up you get, sir!"

He reached out for the proffered hand that pulled him to his feet.

51

"Over there?" Aaron suggested. "On the corner? There's a Starbucks."

"I wouldn't set foot in the place!" Macy was gabbling like a spin cycle on overdrive. "Capitalist pigs! Brainwashed the public into believing that in order to maintain their visibility, they need to sport a cardboard container full of brown water with some noncy Italian name – what happened to a simple cup of coffee? – that costs them half their wages and makes them think it's a fashion statement to walk along the street clutching a piece of advertising material in order to fit society's model of what success should look like, plus you have to drink the stuff through a slit in the plastic which burns your lip and that can't be healthy, can it! I didn't have the best relationship with my gran – apart from nicking her credit card and using it till it snapped! – but at least she taught me that tea and coffee taste better from a china cup. Frankly, I would rather…"

"OK! OK! Slow down!" Aaron laughed. "You've made your point! And you've certainly honed your ability to articulate, Miss Lord. You win. We won't go to the evil capitalist coffee shop."

They walked towards a small independent café and sat down outside.

"I cannot believe this!"

"It's so totally random!"

Aaron proffered Macy the podium as he had that time in class.

"You go first," he said. "Start from when you left for Leicester."

*

A Cole Porter song that Macy used to listen to on Mrs Reilly's radio begins:

"My story is much too sad to be told,
But practically everything leaves me totally cold…"

It was a riff she had repeated often, but she'd never 'got a kick' out of anyone, not in a good way at least.

Reminding him how his faith in her had set her on the road to writing stories based on the *Thou Shalt Nots* of his original competition, she could not help but confess:

"I've broken every one of them…"

"I can't believe that!" Aaron said. "Let's see if you're right."

He raised one thumb and asked: "Lied?"

"Every day."

"Stolen?"

"Enough."

"Taken the Lord's name in vain?"

"Christ, yes!"

"Had strange gods before Him?"

"All gods are strange…"

"Worshipped a golden idol?"

"Er? The *handbag*?"

"Dishonoured your father and your mother?"

"You know about that…"

"Remembered the Sabbath and kept it holy?"

"I work Saturdays and some Sundays."

"Coveted your neighbour's ass?"

"Who hasn't?"

"Borne false witness?"

"I don't know what that means."

"It means telling tales on someone."

"That's called '*saving* your ass' not coveting the neighbour's!"

"Committed adultery?"

That question was greeted with a stony silence.

"Macy," Aaron asked. "I'm asking you if you're married but have slept with someone else?"

"Mr Fairclough! No! Of course I haven't! How could I have!"

"Killed?" He went on slowly. "You surely can't have killed?"

*

"I think it's time you called me Aaron," he said as they walked back together towards the Passport Agency.

"I thought it was Airey?" She blinked her puffy eyes.

"It was. But now it's Aaron."

The twitch of a smile cracked the corners of her mouth.

"What?" Aaron asked.

"Nothing…" Macy answered.

"No secrets!" he said. "After what you've just told me, I think we start this…this…new phase with *no* secrets."

"It's just that…well…you know at school, they – *we* – used to call you."

"I know exactly what you lot used to call me! Why do you think I changed it? Anyway, I am neither!"

"Neither what?"

"Neither Airey nor a fairy! I've been married, for goodness' sake! I *am* married."

Macy stopped dead in her tracks. What did he mean he was *married*? He was Mr Fairclough, *her* Mr Fairclough, the only constant in her entire life – how could he be married?

"W-when…w-who…?" She stammered, distraught by how upset she felt.

"Long story," he said curtly. "Anyway, it didn't last."

Macy exhaled a lifetime of relief.

"Oh, Mr F-f…! Er…Aaron. Do you have any idea how much I've thought about you, *needed* you, how cathartic it is to finally re-find you? You cannot imagine how grateful I feel right now!"

He took her hand in his.

"Are you planning to stay on in New York? We could…go home together."

Once again Macy stopped walking. He'd said the words 'we' and 'home' and 'together' in the same sentence, words that fitted like the final pieces of a very complex jigsaw.

Aaron watched her expression change and he hugged his arm around her. For the first time in forever, Macy's pull back instinct did not occur. She accepted his warmth and hugged him back, inhaling the old familiar Fairclough comfort.

Aaron's emotions swelled like a successful soufflé. How enriching to be genuinely needed. He held her reassuringly, willing her to feel secure. He had listened without judgement, passed no comment, and was ready to take on whatever lay ahead.

"Come," he said at last. "You're feeling chilly, and we need to get our passports."

So absorbed were they with having re-found each other, that neither of them noticed the poster outside an Art Gallery advertising an exhibition of nudes by wheelchair-bound French artist Jean-François 'Franky' Montdidier, who, according to his press release, had recently undergone rehabilitation following a freak accident.

"Mr F…Aaron…" Macy said. "Do you realise I'm actually walking down a street without looking over my shoulder expecting to get arrested!"

"You're not going to get arrested." He answered. "Not on my watch."

*

"I don't suppose you've got your birth certificate?" Aaron asked as they sat together waiting to be called.

"No. It was probably in the house in Leicester I…er…blew up."

"And no previous passport either?"

"Only Anne Boleyn's."

Aaron looked confused.

"The girl I stole it from. Am-ber Lynne?"

"Inspired name!" He laughed. "So how old are you now if I may be so bold?"

"Eighteen!" Macy answered proudly. "But I haven't celebrated a birthday in years."

"We'll have to do something about that!"

"And how old are you 'sir', if *I* may be so bold?" Macy asked.

"Just twenty-eight!" he answered. "Only ten years your senior."

"Only ten years!" She teased. "I always thought you were *so* much older."

"In many ways I guess I was, but I know who I am now."

"I'm still learning," Macy said. "Maybe you'll help teach me?"

They sat down side by side and she began to fill out the form.

"Wait a moment," he said as she was about to write L O R D in the 'Last Name' section. "It might be easier, in case there's an issue in the future and since you have no actual proof of identity, if you put another name in there."

"Like what?" she asked.

He paused and cleared his throat.

"Like Fairclough?" he suggested.

"But that's *your* name."

"It is," he confirmed.

"So how would that work then?" she queried.

"I'm not sure…" he answered. "But I *am* sure we could find a way."

Macy nodded, shrugged, smiled, and wrote F A I R C L O U G H in the boxes.

*

It occurred to Aaron, as they walked back hand in hand through Battery Park, that if their re-acquaintance reached what he hoped would be its rightful conclusion, and if and when that occurred, he was, in fact, still married, then *he* could break The Seventh Commandment and gift it to her to complete the set.

The End